Murder on the Eightfold Path

Diana Killian

BERKLEY PRIME CRIME, NEW YORK

THE BERKLEY PUBLISHING GROUP
Published by the Penguin Group
Penguin Group (USA) Inc.
375 Hudson Street, New York, New York 10014, USA
Penguin Group (Canada), 90 Eglinton Avenue East, Suite 700, Toronto, Ontario M4P 2Y3, Canada
(a division of Pearson Penguin Canada Inc.)
Penguin Books Ltd., 80 Strand, London WC2R 0RL, England
Penguin Group Ireland, 25 St. Stephen's Green, Dublin 2, Ireland (a division of Penguin Books Ltd.)
Penguin Group (Australia), 250 Camberwell Road, Camberwell, Victoria 3124, Australia
(a division of Pearson Australia Group Pty. Ltd.)
Penguin Books India Pvt. Ltd., 11 Community Centre, Panchsheel Park, New Delhi—110 017, India
Penguin Group (NZ), 67 Apollo Drive, Rosedale, North Shore 0632, New Zealand
(a division of Pearson New Zealand Ltd.)
Penguin Books (South Africa) (Pty.) Ltd., 24 Sturdee Avenue, Rosebank, Johannesburg 2196,
South Africa

Penguin Books Ltd., Registered Offices: 80 Strand, London WC2R 0RL, England

This is a work of fiction. Names, characters, places, and incidents either are the product of the author's imagination or are used fictitiously, and any resemblance to actual persons, living or dead, business establishments, events, or locales is entirely coincidental. The publisher does not have any control over and does not assume any responsibility for author or third-party websites or their content.

PUBLISHER'S NOTE: The recipes contained in this book are to be followed exactly as written. The publisher is not responsible for your specific health or allergy needs that may require medical supervision. The publisher is not responsible for any adverse reactions to the recipes contained in this book.

MURDER ON THE EIGHTFOLD PATH

A Berkley Prime Crime Book / published by arrangement with the author

PRINTING HISTORY
Berkley Prime Crime mass-market edition / April 2010

Copyright © 2010 by Diane Browne.
Cover illustration by Swan Park.
Cover design by Lesley Worrell.
Interior text design by Laura K. Corless.

ISBN: 978-0-425-23391-7

BERKLEY® PRIME CRIME
Berkley Prime Crime Books are published by The Berkley Publishing Group,
a division of Penguin Group (USA) Inc.,
375 Hudson Street, New York, New York 10014.
BERKLEY® PRIME CRIME and the PRIME CRIME logo are trademarks of Penguin Group (USA) Inc.

PRINTED IN THE UNITED STATES OF AMERICA

10 9 8 7 6 5 4 3 2 1

F

To the loyal fans of
the Browne Sisters and George Cavanaugh.
Thank you for listening—and reading—along.

Acknowledgments

The author would like to thank the following yoga students who offered their own stories and experiences: Alyssa Zulueta, Annette Tanner, Becky Hutchison, Claudia Horner, Debra MacDonald, D. P. Donavin, Jane Squires, Kris Markham, Lesa Smith, Lynn Salisbury, Michele L., Shelia Connolly, and Tara Stoutenborough.

One

⌐◦

The man in the mohair coat lay facedown on the cobblestone path, one arm outstretched, fingers grazing the
handle of the pink woven basket that had fallen on its side.
Scattered on the grass, little foil-wrapped eggs glinted in
the morning sun.

It was a very nice mohair coat. Camel-colored cashmere, probably Armani—but the bloody bullet hole in the
center of it did nothing for the tailoring.

It did nothing for A.J. Alexander's nerves either—as
though family holidays weren't trying enough. Nothing
says *Happy Easter!* like murder. For a moment she stood
perfectly still in her mother's front garden with the scent
of roses and death wafting gently on the spring breeze,
and tried to convince herself that she was hallucinating.
Too much cream cheese on her bagel, too much Irish in
her coffee. There could *not* be a dead body in her mother's
garden on Easter morning. It just wasn't . . .

Monster, A.J.'s golden Lab, waddled forward to sniff the utterly motionless form, nudging the still hand with his wet nose, and then—before a horrified A.J. could stop him—picking up a pastel-colored hard-boiled egg in his mouth and crunching it, shell and all.

"*Monster!*" A.J. shrieked.

Ears flattening, he gave her a guilty look—and continued crunching.

A.J. jumped forward. Her foot slid on wet grass and yet another hard-boiled egg, and she slipped, twisting her back as she hit the ground. The pain was shocking. For an instant she lay there stunned, blinking up at the azure sky. Birds were singing cheerfully, flowers bobbed overhead—and Monster loomed into view with little bits of colored eggshell on his muzzle.

As A.J. opened her mouth to yell for help, Monster slopped her face with his rough, wet tongue. She waved him away, biting back a cry at the bolt of fire blazing down her spine. It had been over a year since she'd had any back trouble thanks to her new fitness regime, which included yoga morning and night. But even before her aborted attempt to push up, she knew it was going to be a while before she was doing anything more strenuous than Corpse Pose. Speaking of which—A.J. shuddered and turned her gaze away from the thing lying a few feet away.

She groped for her bag, shoving Monster away as he anxiously snuffled her face and hair. Finding her cell phone in her fallen bag, she dialed, her gaze returning to the body on the path. She could see now that blood was pooled on the stones beneath the man's body. She swallowed hard.

Inside the house the phone began to shrill. A.J. could

hear it ringing and ringing. No one picked up. A.J.'s tautly strung nerves ratcheted up a notch. Her mother was occasionally oblivious to those around her, but no one could be oblivious to gunshots outside the front door.

So where was she? She had a house full of people coming and . . . going. This sudden absence made no sense.

Unless the killer had used a silencer? A.J. instinctively rejected this notion as too James Bondian, but . . . was it any harder to believe than the fact that a man had been killed in Elysia Alexander's garden?

A.J. disconnected and dialed Jake. Detective Jake Oberlin of the Stillbrook Police Department was A.J.'s current beau—in fact they had just said good-bye forty-five minutes earlier. He was scheduled to work that day, although no one was anticipating holiday homicide—and certainly not homicide hitting this close to home.

Jake answered his phone on the second ring.

"Hey," he said. And despite the terseness of it, A.J. could hear a certain warmth that, probably due to her current predicament, closed her throat with emotion.

"It's me," she got out. "Something terrible has happened. There's a dead body in mother's front yard."

The silence was filled with a windy blankness that indicated Jake was on the road, driving. "You're not kidding, are you?" he said finally.

"No. I'm not kidding. Mother's not here. I slipped and fell—" *I've fallen and I can't get up!* Suddenly those corny old commercials weren't so funny.

Jake said grimly, "Are you sure your mother's not there?"

She wasn't—and the realization terrified her. "She didn't answer her phone. Jake, it looks like this guy was shot."

"Are you in a secure location?"

"I'm lying in the middle of the path to the front door. I can't get up!"

"All right. Stay calm. I'm sending help." She heard him speaking away from the phone, his faraway voice crisp as he gave orders over his radio. Then he was back on the phone with her. "This guy, this body—do you recognize him?"

A.J. painfully lifted her head. Monster had scooped up yet another colored egg and was chomping away with that guilty but determined expression. She groaned. "Monster, *no*. Bad dog!"

"What is it?" Jake's tinny voice demanded from her cell.

"Monster is eating the evidence!"

"What?"

Perhaps that sounded a little more dire than she intended. "He—the victim—was carrying an Easter basket. Monster is eating the goodies."

Jake swore and then said, "All right. Do you recognize the victim?"

A.J. studied the man who lay a few feet from her. Gucci shoes, Rolex watch, no rings. Although she couldn't see his face, she had the impression of youth. His skin—what she could see of it—was brown and supple. His hair was black and shiny.

"I don't know. I don't think so."

Something about the shape of his head . . .

Surely not. Although . . . what on earth was a young, expensively dressed man doing delivering Easter baskets to Elysia?

"Okay," Jake said. "Take it easy. Everything will be okay. We'll be there before you know it."

He disconnected. A.J. eased back into the grass and tried to relax the muscles in her back. Pain was partly mental. So if she could control the mental part . . . mind over matter. . . .

She drew a long, slow breath and exhaled slowly, evenly. She took another deep breath.

Inhale. Exhale.

If there were ever a test for the calming powers of yoga's deep breathing exercises . . . well, this probably counted toward the final exam.

Inhale. Exhale.

She paused and tried to decide if she felt better or not. Not.

This called for more serious measures. She felt around in the grass and found one of the tiny foil-wrapped chocolate eggs.

It felt like forever, but in fact it was probably not more than thirteen minutes before A.J. heard sirens. Cautiously, she tried to turn, but any movement sent pain shooting down her spine and legs. Tears—not least due to frustration—stung her eyes. She heard the bite of tires on gravel, shortly followed by the swing of the garden gate, and then footsteps approaching. Monster, who had been sitting beside her—gently drooling—rose from his haunches, tail wagging.

"How bad is it?" Jake asked, kneeling beside A.J. He brushed his knuckles against her cheek.

She wiped her eyes. "Oh, it's ridiculous. I just turned wrong. It's happened before . . ." She pointed. "There he is."

Jake studied the waiting corpse, then turned back to

her, anxiety sitting oddly on his hard features. "Try to relax. There's an ambulance on its way. I passed it on the road."

He must have been flying. That was sort of . . . nice.

"Can you make sure my mother's not inside? Her key is in my bag. I've called the house and I've called her cell phone and she's not answering. I can't understand it, because we're having dinner in less than an hour."

More sirens floated in the distance.

"Stay put."

"Very funny."

Jake was already rising, striding quickly up the cobblestone path.

A.J. closed her eyes. The sirens drew closer. She didn't have to look to know that emergency vehicles were filling the drive. Sirens were cut but the rumble of engines and the crackle of radios filled the spring morning. In moments uniformed personnel were flooding the crime scene.

By the time Jake returned, A.J. was answering questions for an EMT who looked young enough to still be in high school. "My blood pressure is fine," she said as the kid wrapped the cuff around her arm. "I mean, all things considered . . ."

All things being the crime scene investigation going on about three feet away.

"She's not inside," Jake said, and some of A.J.'s tension drained away—to be replaced by bewilderment. To the EMT Jake said, "How is she?"

"We're going to take her to County to get checked. She seems to think it's a preexisting injury." His tone implied A.J. would probably say anything to avoid going to the hospital.

"There are dog's footprints in the blood," one of the uniformed officers called over.

Monster yawned uneasily as a battery of eyes turned his way.

"Great," Jake muttered.

A.J. guiltily met his gaze. "I couldn't exactly drag him away."

"I know." Wow. Jake *must* be worried; he was actually reassuring her.

Voices—one voice in particular—caught A.J.'s attention, and she turned her head.

"Bloody hell!" exclaimed the silken tones that had delighted a generation of men who thought bare chests and gold medallions were the height of sophistication. Other voices raised in protest, but the garden gate banged open and heels came swiftly down the walk.

The trim ankles of the British model and sometimes-actress formerly known as Easy Mason—but these days mostly known as *Mother!*—appeared in A.J.'s line of view. She looked up. Elysia, as Easy had been christened, was carrying a small, brown grocery bag.

Checking mid-step, she seemed to take in the tableau before her: the uniformed officers surrounding the body on the garden path, and A.J., waving off help, in the process of moving very carefully onto the collapsible gurney.

"Pumpkin!" Elysia cried, rushing forward only to stop short as A.J. braced for the onslaught.

"I'm okay," A.J. said quickly. "My back went out again." Biting her lip, she sank on the gurney. "Mother, where've you *been*?"

Elysia held up the small, brown bag.

"You went grocery shopping? On Easter morning?"

That was Jake, sounding skeptical, and A.J. winced inwardly at his tone.

Elysia pinned him with an inimical eye. "Why yes, Inspector. I needed evaporated milk."

"Evaporated *milk*?"

"For the potatoes."

"It didn't occur to you before this morning that you might need evaporated milk?"

"Oh, God," A.J. said watching her lover and mother square off against each other.

"What's wrong?" Jake asked, seeming to remember her presence.

"Are you in pain, pumpkin?"

"Of course I'm in pain, Mother. And being called *pumpkin* doesn't help. I thought something terrible had happened to you."

Elysia stared at her. A.J. could practically see recollection dawn. Her mother turned slowly and stared at the grisly scene just a few feet away.

Elysia's jaw dropped—a most un-Elysia-like expression.

"Do you know him?" A.J. asked uneasily.

At the same time, Jake said, "Can you identify the victim?"

Elysia stepped forward. The crime scene personnel automatically gave her room to view the man on the ground.

There was a funny silence.

"*Do* you recognize him?" Jake demanded.

"Blimey," Elysia said mildly. "That's my blackmailer."

TWO

❦

"Why, *why* did you have to call him your blackmailer?"

A.J., in bed at Deer Hollow, the farm she had inherited a year earlier from her Aunt Diantha, gazed reproachfully up at her mother as Elysia set a glass of water and two pain pills on the nightstand.

A trip to the doctor had resulted in the unsurprising news that A.J. had a herniated disk in her lower back. Basically, that meant the soft, gel-like substance inside one of the disks was creating pressure against the spine and nerves. It was not her first experience with back trouble, not by a long shot, but it was the first recurrence she'd had since she began practicing yoga regularly. As soon as the inflammation went down, her doctor was recommending a series of cortisone shots. For now she was on bed rest. Despite the pain, it seemed like the least of her troubles.

"Because he *was*, pump-poppet."

Pump-poppet. That was even worse than straight old *pumpkin*. Hopefully it wouldn't last, but her mother had called her pump-poppet three times in the last hour, and it was beginning to get old. "You're being blackmailed?"

"I am."

"Don't preen, Mother. It's not something to be proud of."

Elysia opened her mouth but before she could respond further, the doorbell rang. She went to answer it. A.J. stared at the ceiling and groaned. Monster, ensconced at the foot of the bed, thumped his tail.

A.J. had missed most of the excitement—and that, she was certain, was no accident. Jake had insisted that she be taken to the local hospital to get checked out, and during the interim of that lengthy process he had questioned Elysia. Though A.J. had yet to hear the details of this informal interrogation, she was pretty sure the only reason her mother was not currently decorating a jail cell was due to it being a holiday.

"Sure, and doesn't something smell delicious?" As the voices in the hallway approached, A.J. recognized Bradley Meagher's Irish accent—disconcertingly reminiscent of the Lucky Charms leprechaun. Mr. Meagher was A.J.'s lawyer. He was Elysia's lawyer, too, in addition to being one of her oldest friends.

"That will be the ham," Elysia was saying airily.

The other *ham*, thought A.J. darkly.

Elysia breezed on, "I'm afraid we were a little late getting it in the oven thanks to the earlier unpleasantness."

Earlier unpleasantness. Yes. Quite. A.J. closed her eyes and then opened them, pasting on a smile as her mother and Mr. Meagher entered her bedroom.

Mr. Meagher was short, slim, and dapper. He was as

tanned as a movie star and his hair was thick and silver and elaborately coiffed. But despite these little vanities he was a shrewd and tough lawyer and a good friend.

"A.J., me wee darlin'," Mr. Meagher said, dragging up a chair. "Now what is it you've done to yourself?"

A.J. summoned a weak smile. "Oh, hi, Mr. Meagher. I just turned the wrong way. I'd wish you a Happy Easter, but under the circumstances it seems . . ."

The Alexanders had never been a particularly "religious" family. When A.J. had been growing up most of the nationally approved holidays had been enjoyed primarily for their secular purposes. The most spiritual person she had ever known was her Aunt Diantha. Diantha's approach was sometimes unorthodox but always sincere. A.J. was trying to appropriate some of that spirituality into her own life, but it was not an easy process. It was especially not easy on days like this.

Mr. Meagher was watching Elysia as she dragged up another chair. "Yes, yes. A strange turn to the holiday and a bad business all around," he agreed absently. "And how are you feeling, me wee darlin'?"

Hadn't they just covered this? A.J. opened her mouth, but Elysia was there first.

"She's half-crocked on painkillers." Elysia perched on the edge of the chair on the other side of A.J.'s bed, and A.J. now had the uncomfortable feeling that she was holding court in her jammies. Granted, it had worked for John and Yoko.

"I'm not half-crocked, Mother. I'm very well aware that one of us needs to keep her wits about her."

"I do admit I've felt wittier." Elysia sighed, apparently trying to disarm her companions with an unconvincing show of vulnerability.

"You'd be best to tell me the whole story," Mr. Meagher said, looking from mother to daughter.

Elysia beckoned graciously to A.J. A.J. gave her a dis-believing look, and then launched into a terse recital of her morning's adventures. She concluded in a bitter di-gression, "And how the heck am I supposed to run a yoga studio flat on my back for who knows how long?"

Elysia said, "This is why you have Lily. You see? There *was* method in your aunt's madness when she made the two of you co-managers of Sacred Balance."

A.J. moaned.

"Is your back hurting, lovie?"

A.J. tossed her head on the pillow. "This is *just* what Lily has been hoping for."

"Lily has been hoping you would injure your back?"

"She's been hoping something would happen that would keep me—" A.J. broke off. "Never mind. Mother, stop stalling. I told my story. Tell yours. Who was the man killed in your front yard?"

Elysia looked uncharacteristically grave. "Dicky. Dakarai Massri."

The name was vaguely familiar. A.J. cast her mind back to several months earlier. "The man you met in Egypt?" The young, handsome man she had seen in so many of Elysia's vacation snapshots? She felt a sinking sensation. This was getting worse by the minute.

"Mmm." That was it. *Mmm.* What did *Mmm* translate to in Elysiaspeak? A.J. was almost afraid to ask.

"I thought he was some kind of archeologist. Why was he blackmailing you?" She had a sudden uneasy vision of her esteemed parent thrusting antiquities down her blouse while browsing historic sites.

"Oh, you know. The usual reasons." Elysia cast a slightly discomfited peek at Mr. Meagher who looked atypically blank-faced.

A.J. looked from one to the other of them. "Well, I mean . . ." This was unexpectedly awkward. "Was he threatening to expose you?"

"Yes." Elysia suddenly tittered. "*So* amusing."

"*Amusing*?" A.J. and Mr. Meagher chorused.

"Of course." Elysia studied their expressions. "My *dears*. I'm an actress. Do you honestly imagine I could be embarrassed by a few naughty photographs after some of the films I've made?"

"But . . ."

"If those blasted reviews didn't shame me—"

"Yes, but you *paid* him?"

"I did. It was great fun." Elysia sighed. "And he did need the money rather desperately, poor love. This is such a tragedy." She seemed quite sincere.

A.J. and Mr. Meagher exchanged worried looks. "Let me get this straight," A.J. said. "You met Dicky on your Egyptian cruise and had some kind of affair. Later he tried to extort money from you to keep him from releasing embarrassing photos. You paid him but . . . you're *not* actually embarrassed by the photos?"

"You do have such a lovely, succinct way of putting things, pump-poppet."

A.J. narrowed her eyes at her mother.

"Why'd you pay this villain?" Mr. Meagher cut in. "Why didn't you come to me?"

"*Why*? But you'd have put a stop to it." Elysia clearly thought this was too obvious to need spelling out. "I was enjoying myself."

Silence.

"How much did you pay him?" A.J. asked when she could.

"About ten thousand dollars."

"*Mother!*"

"Sweet Christ in heaven." Mr. Meagher sounded faint. He had lost color—not so easy with that tan.

"Oh, that was nothing." Elysia flipped a careless hand. "A bit more than a thousand dollars a month. He wanted much more, of course, but I—"

"You—?" echoed A.J. and Mr. Meagher. They exchanged looks again.

Elysia bit her lip looking a little abashed. "I'm afraid I did rather string him along a bit. Pretended to forget my payment dates, pretended to be hard up, that sort of thing."

In the astounded silence that followed, the kitchen timer went off—a loud and distinct ping from down the hall.

Elysia jumped up.

"Wait!" A.J. exclaimed, and her mother paused in the doorway. "You teased him? You deliberately *teased* a blackmailer?"

Elysia's scarlet mouth twitched with amusement. "You make him sound so sinister. He wasn't, you know. Not the brightest bloke, darling Dicky. But really rather sweet. And so lovely to look at. Charming manners and a *marvelous* dancer. I expect I did make his life a misery sometimes. He really wasn't cut out to be a blackmailer." She added thoughtfully, "Yes, I suspect he felt a little guilty . . ."

"One of his other victims must not have been as accepting of Dicky's bad habits." Mr. Meagher was game but he looked a wee bit shell-shocked.

"One of his other victims must have murdered him," A.J. said. "Do you know who else he was blackmailing? I thought he was Egyptian?"

"He was. But any nationality is capable of—"

"I *mean* what was he doing here in this country?"

"He'd moved here. He said he wanted to marry me."

A.J. gulped. She couldn't bring herself to look at Mr. Meagher. "Were you planning to . . . marry him?"

Elysia's pencil thin brows shot up. "He was a black-mailer, pumpkin. I would hardly bring him into the family."

A.J. muttered, "Who knows? You might have thought it was funny to torture him full time."

Elysia looked unamused. She stalked away down the hall on her way to check on the dinner.

Mr. Meagher wiped a hand across his face. He and A.J. risked looking at each other once more.

"It looks very bad," he said. "Very bad indeed."

"But she didn't kill him. She couldn't. She wouldn't."

"Aye. But . . . imagine hearing this malarkey . . ."

A.J. didn't want to imagine it. "She doesn't even own a gun." She considered this uneasily. "At least . . . I don't think she does." Now *there* was a scary thought.

Mr. Meagher didn't bother to answer. "The affair is bad enough. He was blackmailing her—she makes no bones about it—and he was killed in her very own garden."

"But that's just it. If she was guilty, she'd surely try to hide the fact that he was blackmailing her. And she'd hardly kill him in her front yard."

"This is your mither we're speaking of. Her lover was murdered on her front step and she's concerned with not burning the Easter dinner."

He had a point.

A.J. said feebly, in an effort to spare his feelings, "It sounds more like she was paying him to act as a professional escort than a lover."

Mr. Meagher seemed to have no reply. From down the hallway Elysia was humming.

They listened without looking at each other. "It's not possible," A.J. said finally.

Mr. Meagher vouchsafed nothing. A.J.'s heart ached for him. She had long suspected Mr. Meagher's feelings for her mother were more than that of a dear old friend.

After a few minutes Elysia returned to the bedroom. "Dinner is ready. Shall we have it here on trays or did you need to rest, pump-poppet?"

A.J. quit rubbing her head, all efforts to soothe the ache in her temples failing. "I don't think I'm going to get much rest, and I'm not hungry. Mother, do you have any idea who might have killed Dicky?"

"I suppose another one of his birds. Perhaps someone got jealous." Still maddeningly untroubled, she requested Mr. Meagher's help in the kitchen. He rose like a somnambulist obeying commands and went to do her bidding.

Shortly afterward they returned with plates laden with ham, cheese potatoes, Jell-O salad, and all the trimmings. Monster rose, wagging his tail hopefully—and was sent packing. Elysia and Mr. Meagher set up trays and arranged the plates and silverware and glasses. The food was all A.J.'s childhood favorites. The smell alone was wonderful, and she was surprised to find that despite all she'd been through that day, she *was* hungry.

A.J. used her nightstand to push herself upright. Sitting was the worst, but she could hardly eat lying flat. Tray settled at last across her knees, she asked, "*Were* there other birds—er, women?"

Neatly dissecting her ham into bite-sized sections, Elysia murmured vaguely, "Sorry?"

"Dicky. Did he have other lady friends?"

"Oh, he must've done. He could hardly afford to live on what I paid him."

A.J. thought of the Armani coat, the Rolex watch, the Gucci shoes. She suspected her mother was right about Dicky supplementing his income with other victims. Perhaps blackmail was like potato chips—no one could stop at one.

She probed cautiously, "And it didn't bother you that Dicky had other lady friends?"

Elysia looked up and laughed.

So much for that theory. "But you don't have any idea of who these women might have been?"

Elysia shook her head. "It's not the kind of thing he would share with me, you know. Not when he was trying to convince me we should plight our—er—troths."

Mr. Meagher said grimly, "You must know, Elysia, how very bad this looks."

Mr. Meagher rarely called Elysia *Elysia*. Even Elysia seemed to sense the gravity of the situation. Her eyes darkened. She said, "Oh yes. A.J.'s inspector will do his best to stitch me up for this, I've no doubt."

"You know, in fairness to Jake, you do make a lovely prime suspect."

"I know."

"It's not a compliment."

"A.J.'s right," Mr. Meagher put in. "You could well be arrested for this."

"I've no doubt I will be." Elysia nibbled on ham. "That *is* good. I am a bloody good cook!"

A.J. struggled to control her exasperation. "Did you tell Jake everything you told us?"

Elysia's mouth full, she nodded pleasantly.

Of course she had. For all her love of quotations, Elyisa had apparently never heard the one about discretion being the better part of valor. "What did he say?"

"What you would expect from a man with his limited imagination."

A.J. let that slide. "What about your alibi?"

Elysia raised an elegant shoulder. "He seems to think it's shaky. I lost my receipt—well, who holds onto the receipt for a single container of milk? Field Marshall Rommel suggested that I might have shot poor Dicky, tossed a tin of evaporated milk in a paper sack, and taken a drive around the valley."

"But won't they remember you at the store?"

"One can but hope."

"It can't have been crowded on Easter morning. And they'll have a surveillance camera, surely?"

"No, it wasn't crowded, but there's the question of when the murder occurred. The timing is going to be fairly tight. I expect the prosecution will argue that I killed poor Dicky and then went shopping to give myself an alibi."

"The prosecution." A.J. looked worriedly at Mr. Meagher. "But surely it won't go to trial?"

The lawyer's expression was not reassuring.

"What can we do?"

Elysia said, as though the answer were obvious, "We could always solve the crime ourselves."

Three

✦

Voices. Arguing.

A.J. opened her eyes. Moonlight illuminated her bedroom. Monster, on the foot of the bed, raised his head, listening. A.J. listened, too. The voices were not raised—in fact they were muffled—but all the same it triggered unpleasant memories of her adolescence. Her parents had enjoyed one of those can't-live-with-and-can't-live-without relationships. Although *enjoyed* was perhaps not the right word. They had certainly loved each other, though, despite everything.

She turned her head on the pillow. The clock on the bedside table read twenty past eleven. A.J. swore under her breath. It took great effort, but she managed to crawl—nearly literally—out of the bed. Hobbling across to the door—it felt like she was about to crack in half—she inched it open.

Light from the front room fanned the hallway. Jake's

voice was quiet but carried. "Listen, lady, the only reason you're not in jail right now is that you're A.J.'s mom."

"I certainly wouldn't want mere innocence to sway you!"

A.J. huffed an exasperated sigh and, hanging on to the doorframe, pushed the door wider. "What's going on out there?"

"I am *trying* to throw this brute out," Elysia moved into view. "What are you doing up at this hour?"

"I'm not six years old, Mother. I'm allowed up past ten o'clock—even on school nights." She stared past Elysia to Jake who stood by the front door as though uncertain of his reception. "I didn't think you were coming over this evening."

"Yeah. Well."

"I can see why you can't resist this silver-tongued devil."

"Mother." Jake's gaze held her own. A.J. said to her mother, "You don't need to stay. I'll be okay now."

Elysia did not exactly roll her eyes, but the effect was similar. "Far be it from me to play the third wheel, but are you expecting Herr Himmler to help you bathe in the morning, fix your breakfast, and the rest of it?"

A.J. blinked as the reality of her situation sunk in.

Her point made, Elysia said dryly, "I'll be down the hall if you need me." She and Jake passed each other in the hallway like a cat and dog pledged to an uneasy truce.

Jake reached A.J., who backed carefully into her bedroom. He heeled the door shut and took her—carefully—in his arms and kissed her.

"Are you okay?"

"Better now." She kissed him back. She was very glad

he was there, glad she was in his arms again, despite the strain of knowing that he suspected Elysia.

As though reading her mind, Jake said, "I didn't expect her here. I guess I should have. What did the doctor say?"

A.J. freed herself gently, making her way to the bed and lowering herself slowly and painfully to the mattress. "No twisting, no turning, no lifting. What you're seeing is basically my full repertoire."

"How long are you on bed rest?"

"For as long as it takes. I'm supposed to get a steroid shot on Tuesday if the inflammation is reduced enough."

Jake hovered over her. It was not in his nature to stand by helplessly, that was obvious.

A.J. bit her lip against a yelp. *This was so unbelievably frustrating!* When she was lying flat again on her heating pad she said, "It's not as drastic as it sounds. I used to have a lot of back trouble. The yoga has really helped. Until this morning." She added, "You're an awfully long way away over there."

He sat down gingerly on the side of the bed. "I don't want to hurt you."

"You won't." She held out an arm and he came to her, kissing her mouth lightly.

"Poor baby."

It should have been patronizing, but oddly . . . it wasn't.

She nuzzled him back. "How is the investigation going?"

"Not good. And before you say anything else, remember that I cannot discuss this case with you. Not at all."

"She's my *mother*, Jake."

"You think that escaped my notice? That's my point."

"You cannot honestly believe she did this thing."

"Just cool down for a minute and look at this objectively."

"I don't want to look at it objectively!"

He drew back. "And I don't want to discuss the case with you. So let's drop it." He added quietly, "Or I can leave if that's what you'd prefer."

Would she prefer that? As angry and worried as A.J. was . . . she cared for Jake. A lot. Having to choose between her boyfriend and her mother was a dilemma she'd prefer not to face.

"Don't go," she said.

Not that they were going to be able to get up to much mischief what with her mother, The Accused, down the hall and A.J. unable to move a muscle without wincing. It took a fair bit of mindful shifting and rearranging before they managed to arrange themselves comfortably.

A few minutes were spent tenderly kissing before Monster insinuated himself on the foot of the bed, circled twice, and folded up with a doggy grumble as he encountered Jake's feet. Jake groaned. A.J. started laughing.

When they had quieted, again finding easy—well, relatively easy positions—A.J. sighed. "This morning seems like such a long time ago."

Jake grunted.

"Everything was so simple. Happy." That morning had been lovely. Jake had spent the night and they'd risen together, breakfasting on warm, buttery croissants, bagels slathered with cream cheese, and Irish coffee. He'd given her a Mr. Goodtime Easter Bunny—sixteen and a half inches of hand decorated white and milk chocolate. Something about the self-conscious way her laconic tough guy had handed over the cellophane wrapped rabbit had touched A.J. in a way that her ex-husband Andy's charming tokens of affection never had. Maybe because she sensed these kinds of gestures were not typical for Jake.

Jake kissed her temple and said nothing. A.J. knew that he believed it was going to be a long time before her life was that simple and happy again.

Either because of the drugs or emotional exhaustion, A.J. slept deeply—and late—the next morning. When she finally woke, Jake was already gone. She didn't remember telling him good-bye.

She didn't feel too bad after a decent night's sleep, but a few agonizing minutes later it was clear she was not going into the studio that morning. And all the will power and positive thinking in the world wasn't going to change that.

Before she had much time to fret, Elysia poked her head surreptitiously around the door. "Morning, sunshine!"

"That's just cruel," A.J. informed her.

Elysia raised her brows. "Now, now. A positive attitude is everything, as the Bard says."

"Mother, you know perfectly well the Bard never said such a thing."

"I suppose it's more of an underlying thematic statement in his work." Elysia moved the phone from the bedside table to the bed, and A.J. grimaced, sitting up with difficulty.

She phoned the studio and spoke to Emma Rice, the geriatric Wonder Woman who doubled as one of the Sacred Balance Studio receptionists. A.J. answered the inevitable questions and offered reassurance. Emma put her through to Suze MacDougal, a junior instructor.

"I knew it," Suze exclaimed. "You're never late.

The shooting is all over the news. How's your mom holding up?"

Now there was a question for the ages. A.J. studied her
mother as Elysia bustled from bedroom to bathroom running a bath. For a woman suspected of murder, she seemed
pretty cool. But then no doubt she remembered a similar
episode on *221B Baker Street*, the legendary British television detective show she had graced for years, and was
acting out her role.

"Better than me, probably," A.J. admitted. She went on
to explain that she'd fallen and wouldn't be making it into
the studio. Suze commiserated with comforting energy.

When A.J. felt she'd stalled long enough, she asked to
be put through to Lily. Lily Martin was A.J.'s co-manager
at the studio; it was not a partnership either of them would
have chosen.

"Yes, A.J.?" Lily came on the line, brusque as always,
and A.J. had to wonder again at Aunt Di's purpose in pair-
ing them together. Yoga seemed like such an odd field
of endeavor for Lily. A.J. could more easily picture her
achieving her full potential intimidating marines in a
boot camp somewhere or training gladiators for the
Colosseum.

Although Lily had to be aware of the situation with
Elysia, she said nothing after that curt greeting, waiting in
silence for A.J. to come to the point.

"I fell yesterday and injured my back," A.J. told her.
"I won't be in the studio today. Realistically, I probably
won't be in this week." Even that might be optimistic, but
A.J. had faced all the reality she could deal with for one
day—and she hadn't even had breakfast yet.

"Oh dear!" Lily said, and A.J. couldn't help but think

there was as much excitement as surprise in that single exclamation.

Lily asked the appropriate and intelligent questions, and A.J. answered politely—it was probably the most cordial conversation they'd ever had. Lily, sounding eerily sympathetic, instructed A.J. not to worry about anything, and finished off the call urging A.J. to take care of herself.

A.J. pictured the other woman doing handsprings when she hung up the phone. Lily's delight was only too obvious.

"All taken care of?" Elysia returned to the bedroom.

"It won't be easy, but she's going to soldier on somehow." A.J. gingerly pulled herself into an upright position. She caught her breath as the pain seemed to radiate from her lower back all the way around to her abdomen and down to her buttocks.

"Well, who can say? Perhaps Lily will appreciate you after having to manage things on her own for a few days."

A.J. snorted.

"Now, now. Is this the spirit that won the war?" Still exuding unnerving cheer and optimism, Elysia helped A.J. into the bath, and A.J. thought how strange it was to rely on your mother for such things once you were an adult.

"Thanks," she said when she was finally lying back in her freshly changed sheets. "I appreciate it." She patted Monster who stood on the mattress gazing down at her, wagging his tail.

Elysia looked a little uncertain. "But of course. You know there's nothing I wouldn't do for you, Anna."

A.J. flicked her mother a shy look. "I know." It had

taken her most of her adult life to realize it, but she did know. She quickly changed the subject, demanding rhetorically, "What the heck am I going to *do* for a week?"

"Why, any number of things. Catch up on your reading, watch a little telly, eat. It'll be like a holiday."

"Sure, except for the excruciating pain part."

Elysia, bundling the used sheets from A.J.'s bed, frowned. "Are you in excruciating pain?"

"It hurts a lot," A.J. admitted although she hated to sound like a wimp.

She stared at the ceiling as her mother took the laundry out. Monster jumped stiffly off the bed and followed her down the hall.

When Elysia returned with A.J.'s breakfast, A.J. said, "I guess I could take a look at the book Aunt Di was working on when she—before she—"

A.J. had discovered the completed manuscript when she had first gone through her aunt's study. Every so often it occurred to her that she should do something with it, but she had been uncertain how to proceed.

"What a good idea!" Elysia said. She helped A.J. sit up, settled the tray over A.J.'s knees, and stepped back as though to study her handiwork.

"What was the book about?" she asked, watching A.J. sample scrambled eggs.

"It was a memoir. It seemed to be mostly finished. It might just be a matter of finding a publisher."

"Perfect. Where is this tome?"

A.J. told Elysia where to find the manuscript and Elysia brought the box with loose-leaf papers and notes and Aunt Diantha's rough draft. Studying her daughter's supine position, she said, "Perhaps I could pick up one of those laptop writing desks . . ."

"I already have a couple of trays, it's the having to lie flat part," A.J. said. She added thoughtfully, "You seem awfully interested in keeping me occupied."

"Idle hands are the devil's playpen, pumpkin."

"*My* idle hands are not the problem here."

Elysia's expression was wide-eyed and innocent.

"I know that look," A.J. said. "I don't trust it. Or you. Tell me about Dicky. How did you meet him? He was on the cruise that you took last year?"

"Oh, you don't want to hear about all that."

"You're right. But I think I'd better."

Elysia leaned against the footboard of the bed. "It's not particularly fascinating, you know. We met on the cruise, yes. He was doing a series of lectures on ancient Egypt. Nothing too heavy, of course. Mostly slide shows and chatting."

"He was employed by the cruise line?"

Elysia looked thoughtful. "I'm not absolutely certain. I believe technically he was employed by the Supreme Council of Antiquities, but had been seconded to the cruise line. They tried to break up the shuffleboard and miniature golf with a few cultural activities."

"How did you get involved?"

Elysia shrugged elaborately.

A.J. asked curiously, "Did you pursue him?"

"Not really. I wasn't looking for anything like *that*."

A.J. decided she'd be happier not knowing what *that* was. "So what happened? Just your ordinary average shipboard romance ending in blackmail and murder?"

"I believe so, yes."

"You're not being very helpful, Mother."

Elysia looked mildly pained. "It's not as though I anticipated this, pumpkin. I was on holiday and I was enjoying myself. Dicky was . . . charming. We had great fun together and then . . . we didn't."

Casting her mind back, A.J. recalled that Elysia had ended the cruise early, leaving the ship in Edfu, so perhaps the seeds of the affair's violent ending had been sown even then? Except that her mother could not possibly have had anything to do with Mr. Massri's demise, of that A.J. was certain.

"When did he start blackmailing you?"

"Weellllll," Elysia sounded vague. "Perhaps blackmail was putting it rather harshly. He began to hint that he had certain expenses."

"What kind of expenses?"

"The usual sort of thing. His tailor, his mechanic, his bookie. I didn't think much of it."

"His *bookie*?"

"Not back in Egypt, of course. But after he moved here, well, Dicky liked to play the ponies."

"And you paid him ten thousand dollars when he hinted he had these expenses?"

Elysia raised an elegant bony shoulder. "Not in one go. I'm liberated enough to pick up the chit a few times."

"Then what happened?"

"You know this part of the story, pumpkin. I learned that Nicole Manning had been murdered, and I left the ship in Edfu, hired a car for the return trip to Luxor, and flew back home."

Nicole Manning had been a local television celebrity. Her violent death had resulted in A.J. being unwillingly dragged into another homicide investigation by Elysia, who had developed an alarming taste for amateur sleuthing.

"That's the only reason you left the ship?"

Elysia nodded, but it struck A.J. as unconvincing. Perhaps Elysia had not found extortion all that amusing to begin with. Her mother had an ego like anyone else.

"But Dicky contacted you?"

"He turned up one afternoon at the house and said he'd moved to the States to further his career."

"Which career? Blackmailing?"

Elysia tittered—inappropriately, in A.J.'s opinion.

"Did he try to blackmail you then?"

"He didn't phrase it quite so crudely." Elysia smiled reminiscently. "We began seeing each other again."

"But you never said a word about him!"

"He wasn't the sort of person you bring home to meet your children."

"Do you have other children I'm not aware of?"

Elysia seemed amused, which did not do much for A.J.'s mounting exasperation.

"So how long did that go on for?"

"Oh, it was still going on." Elysia seemed mildly surprised at A.J.'s assumption. "We'd been seeing each other for about seven months. I knew I'd have to break it off soon, though, as he kept pushing for me to marry him."

A.J. shuddered. "I can't *believe* you were living this double life."

"It sounds much more interesting than it was."

"Is it possible he could have been killed by his bookie? Maybe he . . . what do you call it? Welshed on his debt?"

Elysia looked thoughtful. "He took his gambling debts very seriously, true enough. I wonder . . ."

"Or maybe his death had something to do with his job? His other job. Perhaps he was involved in faking or smuggling antiquities? It's big business, I know."

Elysia looked thoughtful. "It's interesting you should

mention that. Dear Dicky did hint once or twice that he knew something, shall we say . . . unsavory? And wanted to clear the slate. Prove himself worthy before our marriage."

"Mother, did you tell him you were going to marry him?"

Elysia said evasively, "I didn't say I *wouldn't*."

A.J. put her hand over her eyes.

"I was working up to it," Elysia said defensively. "But he was pinning so much on it, poor ducks. I hated to dash his hopes when he was just getting his life on track again."

When she could speak calmly, A.J. said, "Did he give you any hint as to what this unsavory thing was that he wanted to clear off his slate? Are you sure it had to do with antiquities?"

Elysia said apologetically, "You know, I didn't always listen as carefully to the dear boy as I suppose I should have."

"You don't say!"

Elysia rose and went to the window. She stared out for a few moments and then stiffened. She bit her lip, her attention still glued to whatever she was looking at.

"What is it?" A.J. asked uneasily.

"You won't like it."

"I'm getting used to that."

"I know you're in pain, Anna, but please don't take that tone with me."

A.J. gritted her teeth. "Who is out there, Mother?"

"Now don't overreact, pumpkin. The police have arrived."

Four

A.J. had managed to hobble down the hall when Elysia opened the front door. She could see two uniformed officers—looking very uncomfortable—and, behind them, Jake.

Elysia greeted them coolly. "Ah, Inspector. Did you bring your leg irons?"

"For the record, Mrs. Alexander, I'm not enjoying this."

A.J., hanging onto the wall for support, joined the tableau at the door. "Jake, this is *ridiculous*," she protested.

Jake moved past the uniformed officers and Elysia stepped back haughtily, but Jake was not reaching for her. His grip on A.J.'s arms was hard but supportive. "Look, I don't want to do this. It's my job, all right?"

"No, it's not all right. You're arresting my mother!"

He threw a look at the waiting officers, and lowered his voice. "I know exactly who she is. I don't have a choice here, honey."

Honey. Disconcertingly, it undermined her anger.

Elysia said briskly, "No need to fuss, Anna. Call Bradley and tell him to exercise option B." To Jake, she said disdainfully, "I'll be out from behind bars by lunch."

Jake said shortly, "It's already past lunch."

Elysia ignored this.

"I'll call him," A.J. said. She freed herself from Jake's hold, shuffling toward the phone in the hall as she threw back, "And you'd better not handcuff her!"

"Ooh, kinky," Elysia bit out.

Jake said wearily, "Elysia Alexander, we're arresting you on suspicion of homicide. . . ."

A.J. watched Elysia stalk down the porch steps followed by the bemused officers. Jake hesitated in the doorway, waiting for A.J. to say something or at least acknowledge he was still there. A.J. knew it, yet couldn't quite bring herself to soften toward him—largely because she was struggling to maintain her composure.

Then Mr. Meagher came on the line, and when A.J. next glanced around Jake was gone and the front door was closed.

Her heart sank, but there was no time to worry about what this disaster was doing to her relationship with Jake. She hastily filled Mr. Meagher in on the latest developments, and he grimly reassured her he was on the case.

A.J. hung up the phone and tottered back to the bedroom, shoved her barely touched brunch tray and Aunt Diantha's manuscript out of the way, and eased flat on the mattress once more.

She had no doubt that Mr. Meagher would get her mother out of the slammer in short order, but then what? If Jake had gone so far as to arrest Elysia, the evidence piling up against her must be fairly damning.

A.J. wasn't given to panicking, but the situation seemed bleak, despite Elysia's casual attitude. It was unbelievable to think her mother might actually go to trial—even be convicted—but unfortunately she had spent too many years married to a man who adored television crime drama not to know that these things happened in the best of families.

Let alone in eccentric clans like her own.

Monster came to the side of the bed and snuffled her face. "What are we going to do?" A.J. asked him.

His recommendation seemed to be that A.J. let him have her lunch if she wasn't going to eat it. A.J. vetoed this, and he climbed creakily on the bed, circled twice, and settled with a doggie *hmmph*.

If only she wasn't stuck flat on her back. A.J. swallowed hard as she recognized the direction her thoughts were turning. She had solemnly promised Jake not to dabble in anymore amateur sleuthing—it had nearly wrecked their relationship once. But she could hardly stand by, or even lie by, while her mother went to jail for a murder. And it was a cinch that Elysia was not going to patiently wait for Jake or anyone else to prove her innocent, in which case A.J. might be the stabilizing influence.

Except that her own stability was a little rocky at the moment. Of all the times to injure her back! Still she could use the phone and she could use her laptop. Maybe she could do a little checking into Dicky Massri—

She became aware that the doorbell was ringing. Monster jumped off the mattress and trotted down the hall, woofing. A.J. commenced the long and painful process of getting off the bed and on her feet. She had made it to the doorway of her bedroom when she heard a key in the front door lock. Her heart leapt thinking that it might be Jake.

That thought was instantly dismissed as highly un-likely and replaced by relief that her mother must have already been released—although a quick glance at the bedside clock indicated Elysia would barely have had time to be booked.

The door swung open, and the short, stout figure of Stella Borin appeared framed in the front hall.

"A.J.?" she called tentatively.

"Right here."

Stella was A.J.'s nearest neighbor. She lived about a mile down the road in the farm bequeathed to her by A.J.'s aunt. In addition to farming, she supported herself as a psychic, and although A.J. did not put a lot of stock in things like tarot cards and séances, she had to admit that Stella had, on one or two occasions, seemed to display an uncanny ability.

According to Andy, A.J.'s ex, the most uncanny thing about Stella was her dress sense, and this afternoon was no exception. She was wearing what appeared to be polka dot pajama bottoms beneath a plaid jumper, giving her the impression of a badly dressed piggy bank. Her gray hair was bound in two fat, short braids that seemed to stick straight out of the sides of her head, confirming A.J.'s long held conviction that no woman over the age of ten should wear braids. Stella eschewed makeup, and her hands looked as battered as a potter's.

"Jake called and told me what happened. He thought you might need some help this evening, at least till Bradley Meagher bails your ma out."

Ma.

Hard to imagine a term that less suited Elysia, but all

A.J. really noticed was the kindness of Stella running to her rescue—and that Jake had been looking out for her, even if he had tossed her mum in the hoosegow.

"Oh, you didn't have to do that," she said, hobbling down the hall.

Stella raised her bushy brows but didn't point out the obvious. It occurred to A.J., and not for the first time, that when she had lived in the big city she had barely known her neighbors, let alone relied on them in times of trouble. There was a lot to be said for small-town living—even if the cable did go out on a regular basis.

"Did Jake say anything about . . . ?" A.J. wasn't even sure what she was asking. She knew that Jake would hardly confide anything about the case against Elysia to Stella. She was grasping at straws, hoping that someone was going to reassure her that this was all a big misunderstanding.

But Stella must have read her correctly, because she said in her gruff way, "Don't you worry. Jake Oberlin is a good cop. He'll get to the bottom of this."

A.J. nodded. She was leading the way, slowly, to the front parlor, ignoring Stella's advice to return to bed.

"I'm going crazy, lying there worrying about this."

A.J. stretched out on the sofa. Stella asked if she'd like a cup of tea, and she assented, staring up at the ceiling. At least it made for a change of scenery.

Stella brought in a tea tray and A.J. sat up. Stella had found the frosted animal cookies that A.J. had been hiding from herself in the back of the pantry. A.J. took her cup of tea and sipped gratefully. There was something very comforting about a hot cup of good, brewed tea.

Stella selected a frosted white bear and remarked, "Just like your ma. She always did like her cuppa."

And her glassa. But thankfully those days were in the past. Elysia had been sober for over a decade now. A.J. gave in and chose a pink elephant cookie from the plate before her.

She asked, "Stella, can I ask you what happened between you and my mother?"

"When what happened?" Stella chewed rapidly, her expression blank.

A.J. clarified, "Whatever it is that happened, happened. What I mean is, I'm wondering about your history. Because I've sensed over the last year that there is one."

Stella picked up another cookie and crunched away. A.J. thought she would simply decline to answer at all, but at last she said, "You'd have to ask Elysia."

"I have asked her. She always brushes it off."

"There you go," Stella said. "Nothing to worry about then."

"Was it something to do with Aunt Di? With her leaving you Little Peavy Farm?" That was hard to imagine. Elysia enjoyed her worldly goods as much as the next material girl, but her infamous acting career had left her comfortably off in addition to the bundle she had inherited from A.J.'s father, a successful business entrepreneur. But perhaps Elysia felt that Stella had somehow taken advantage of Diantha's generosity? Or spiritual beliefs? Although that was also hard to imagine because Aunt Di had been nobody's fool.

"Noooo," Stella said thoughtfully. "Nothing like that."

A.J. sipped her tea and frowned over it, but although it was hard to accept, perhaps it wasn't any of her business. She changed the subject and said, "Did you happen to know this young man she's accused of shooting?"

"Elysia and I don't travel in the same social circles."

"I'm not sure Mother and this Dicky Massri traveled in the same circles."

Stella made a sound somewhere between a snort and a laugh.

"I think he was younger than *me*," A.J. said. "Aunt Di did the same thing—started a relationship with someone young enough to be her son. I don't understand it."

Stella eyed her thoughtfully. "That's because you've never been lonely."

"I've been divorced, that's pretty lonely."

"I mean years of being lonely."

Stella spoke so matter-of-factly that A.J. barely registered what she was saying. When she did, it was with a sharp tug of sympathy that she felt instinctively would make Stella uncomfortable. She hated to think of Stella being lonely, and she hated even more to think of her mother being lonely.

But surely there was a medium ground between senior bingo nights and Egyptian gigolos?

"I just don't understand why she couldn't have found someone more her own age. She wouldn't be in this mess now."

Stella said patiently, "Because falling in love is scary. Hot sex with a man toy is just tiring."

A.J. blinked at the idea of Stella having hot sex with anything, let alone with tiresome man toys. She said at random, "Mr. Meagher is really worried. He seems to think the police might be able to build a strong enough case to go to trial."

Stella selected another cookie, crunched in that same meditative way—like a thoughtful squirrel—and said, "I guess it's occurred to you that your ma really might have killed him?"

Five

❧

A.J. inhaled cookie crumbs and spent an agonized couple of seconds coughing before she managed a hoarse, "I'm sorry?"

Stella said, "Elysia's got a temper when she's riled."

"She's not violent." She closed off memories of her mother hurling glasses, plates, and, on one memorable occasion, a brass paperweight at her father during some of their livelier arguments. That had been back in the bad old days when alcohol had formed the foundation of Elysia's daily food pyramid.

Stella, unmoved, said, "She's always had her own ideas about the law."

"What does that mean?"

Stella shrugged. "I think Elysia believes laws are for other people."

A.J. knew her instinctive rejection of this statement was illogical. Certainly Elysia did often behave as though the laws of the land did not apply to her. Sometimes that zany attitude was sort of charming—and sometimes it wasn't.

"We're not discussing exceeding the speed limit here, we're talking about murder. And I can't see my mother committing cold-blooded murder. She just . . . wouldn't."

"Not cold-blooded murder, I agree," Stella said. "But if she felt threatened or she was angry enough?"

A.J. stubbornly shook her head despite uneasy memories of the things her mother had done back when she had been drinking. Those things could be attributed to the alcohol. And while it was true that Elysia did rather live in her own world, that was still a far cry from the sort of loss of control Stella was suggesting.

A.J. was marshaling her argument when the phone rang. Stella rose to answer it, returning a few moments later. "That was the *Stillbrook Streamer*. They were hoping for an interview."

"Yeah, well, hope springs eternal," A.J. said shortly.

"That's pretty much what I told them."

"Why doesn't Mr. Meagher call?"

It was a rhetorical question, but Stella replied seriously, "It's a homicide charge. They might not be able to get bail. Or the judge might decide to set it high, given your ma's financial resources and nationality."

A.J. stared in horror. "You don't think they'll *keep* her?"

Stella said gruffly, "I think Jake wanted me here just in case."

This time A.J. was less touched by Jake's thoughtfulness.

*   *   *

A.J. spent the afternoon reading through her aunt's manuscript.

> *No thinking person can deny that we live in a time of crisis. We look around and witness financial, environmental, and social upheaval. We turn on the television and see a world at war. Our ideals, our very faith in the greater good is challenged. Yet this is also a time of extraordinary spiritual opportunity. It depends on how we respond. At the core of the most painful experiences lie the seeds of philosophical awakening, of epiphany.*

A.J. reread the paragraph slowly. It was unexpectedly comforting in her particular time of trouble to read her aunt's words. Diantha's memoirs were almost like hearing her speak.

The phone rang off and on, but it was always members of the press. The *Stillbrook Streamer*, the *Star-Ledger*, *Chicago Sun-Times*, the *New York Times:* the papers mounting in importance as the news of Elysia's arrest hit the wires. Stella staunchly fended them off but it was clear that even her nerves were growing frayed as the afternoon wore on.

It was after five o'clock when Mr. Meagher finally called, and the news was not good.

"Well, you see, it's complicated, me wee girl," he began when A.J. picked up the phone.

"What does that mean?"

"We're . . . eh . . . probably looking at tomorrow."

"*Tomorrow*? She's going to have to spend the *night* in jail. But why?"

"It's complicated, me darlin'. There's already a lot of media attention. Too much in the opinion of that great fascist swine of a superior court judge. There's also the fact that your mither has considerable financial resources—as do you. They're viewing her as a flight risk."

"You mean they might not let her out at all?" A.J. felt a childish and utterly disconcerting urge to burst into tears. It had to be the combination of meds and back pain.

"Don't fret," Mr. Meagher reassured her quickly. "I'm pulling every bloody favor I ever did anyone in this miserable town."

A.J. realized then how angry Mr. Meagher was because she'd never heard him speak with anything but love for his adopted country and home. She swallowed down her anger and fear as it was clear he had plenty of his own to deal with.

"So . . . what do we do?"

"You just rest that back of yours and leave the rest to me. I'll have her out by tomorrow or me name isn't Bradley Jamieson Meagher."

A.J. thanked him sincerely and replaced the phone on the hook with an unsteady hand. Her anger at Jake was now sky-high even though a tiny voice in the back of her mind loyally pointed out that he probably hadn't had a choice. Part of her wrath was based on the knowledge that he apparently really did suspect her mother capable of such a crime. And even though A.J. had also experienced an uneasy twinge or two maybe partly because of that, it seemed a severe betrayal.

She picked at the chicken noodle casserole Stella had fixed for their dinner, listening with half an ear as the other woman talked about a séance she had conducted for a recently widowed woman.

"I know what people say, what they think, but it brings comfort to my clients to know there's something on the other side."

A.J. remembered what Stella had said earlier about being lonely. Loneliness led people into doing all kinds of dangerous and foolish things. Attending séances might even be one of the less foolhardy.

She studied Stella's weathered face. "Before I met you I thought all séances took place in auditoriums. Well, except the ones in movies."

"That's a stage mediumship séance. I don't have much faith in that. I prefer the personal touch myself."

A.J. remembered the séance they had held after Aunt Diantha's death. It had been inconclusive—and a little scary, frankly. But she had seen all kinds of movies where people tried to solve crimes by conducting séances. She tried to picture summoning Dakarai Massri's spirit. Did he even know who had killed him? Did people go into the afterlife as confused and misinformed as they were in the here and now?

Stella had plenty of ideas on that topic. She was still offering her theories over coffee and creamy rice pudding (Stella being apparently unfamiliar with the concept of low carbs) when Andy, A.J.'s ex, called.

"What the heck is going on down there? It's all over the TV that Ellie's been arrested for murder," Andy demanded, uncharacteristically not even pausing for the usual civilities.

Andy and Elysia had always been close—closer than A.J. and Elysia in fact, even after Andy had left A.J. to be with another man.

"On TV?" gulped A.J.

"Of course. Well, she *is* a cultural icon," he added with what A.J. couldn't help feeling was misplaced pride.

A.J. explained about Dakarai Massri, which took some doing. Andy listened in stunned—and uncharacteristic—silence.

"Your mother is accused of murdering a blackmailing Egyptian gigolo?" Andy repeated a little faintly when she had finished.

A.J. pleaded, "Can we refer to him as a blackmailing Egyptian antiquities expert? It doesn't sound quite so seedy."

"It doesn't?" Andy swallowed loudly enough for A.J. to hear it clear across the New Jersey Turnpike. "So what are you going to do? Prove she's innocent, I assume?"

That was another reason Andy and Elysia got on so well; they both fancied themselves master detectives, with A.J. as their unwilling Watson. An unhealthy diet of TV mystery shows had persuaded them both that anyone was equipped to investigate major crime.

"I don't think that would be a good idea," A.J. said firmly, just as though she hadn't been contemplating that very idea most of the afternoon. "It's Jake's case and you know how he felt the last time—"

Andy interrupted, "It's *Jake's* case? *Jake* arrested your mother? Your *boyfriend* arrested your—"

"Thanks, Andy, I already know that part, and don't tell me Nick wouldn't do the same to your mother if his bosses at the FBI gave the order."

"Well, yeah, but Nick doesn't like my mother."

A.J. had no response to that. Andy's mother was hard to like, although A.J. was sort of fond of her in spite of it all.

"It's ridiculous," Andy was protesting. "Ellie wouldn't hurt a fly. So what *are* you going to do?"

"I don't know. I've hired a lawyer. Well, Mr. Meagher is hiring a top notch criminal attorney for me."

"An attorney? You can't let this go to trial. You can't just sit there and let that bastard railroad Ellie!" Since

Andy actually liked Jake, his choice of epithet indicated how worked up over this he was getting.

"I can't do much about it at the moment." A.J. explained about putting her back out, and Andy was appropriately sympathetic—and momentarily diverted. She took the opportunity to ask after his own health; Andy had been diagnosed with MS the previous summer. It had been a rocky time, but thanks in part to yoga he had found a delicate balance between fighting to stay as well as possible and learning to accept what couldn't be cured.

"I'm holding my own," he said a little grimly.

"How are things with Nick?"

His voice was relaxed as he answered. "The best. The best they've ever been. Although it turns out he does have this freaky and totally unnecessary maternal streak."

A.J. chuckled. "I'm glad. I mean that things are good. You two deserve each other."

"I'm sure that's not entirely a compliment. So what about you and Jake? Has he popped the question yet? I mean, before all this happened. I assume you won't marry him if he puts Elysia in prison."

"No." A.J. added quickly, "I mean no, he didn't pop the question. Anyway it's way too soon for that."

"Not necessarily. Sometimes all it takes is one look." Andy and Nick had fallen in love at first sight, but that was still a painful memory for A.J. Her silence must have reminded him of this, for Andy said awkwardly, "But I can see how suspecting your mum of murder might put a crimp in things."

"A little. The scary thing is I'm sure they wouldn't have arrested her so quickly if they didn't have a mountain of evidence already."

"Circumstantial," Andy scoffed.

"I don't know if it's circumstantial or not. We haven't heard what all the evidence is. The murder happened in her front yard. She admits she was paying this man black-mail money."

"Yeah, but this is Elysia. That money was probably her equivalent of the normal person's entertainment budget."

"Ten thousand dollars?"

Even Andy didn't have an answer for that one.

Unwillingly, A.J. admitted, "Even if I wanted to, I'm not exactly sure where to start, um, investigating."

"Start with the victim," Andy said with brisk confidence, just as though he'd been solving baffling mysteries for the last decade or so. "Start with Ellie's Egyptian gigolo."

The next morning Stella drove A.J. into the borough of Rutherford to receive cortisone shots. Had A.J. been feeling better she might have tried walking the thirty miles; it could hardly have wasted more time, because Stella, a nervous and unhappy chauffeur, drove as though she had a jar of unstable nitroglycerin bouncing around in the truck bed. If A.J. hadn't traveled short distances with Stella before, she might have thought she was driving slowly out of consideration for A.J.'s bad back, but no such luck.

The slow drive prolonged the pain of sitting, which was, as much as A.J. hated to admit it, excruciating. But they arrived at long last at the clinic; A.J. changed into a hospital shift and lay very carefully down on the X-ray table, a small pillow under her stomach to curve her back. If this didn't work, she was considering trying acupuncture or another alternative medicine.

Her lower back was swabbed and then numbed with a local anesthetic. Then the surgeon used fluoroscopy—a live X-ray—to guide the needle toward the epidural space. A.J. closed her eyes, tuning it out. At roughly six thousand dollars a pop, she sincerely hoped this would do her good. Sometimes it did, sometimes it didn't.

Using the breathing techniques she practiced in yoga, she relaxed and tried to think positive, healing thoughts. She had been hoping that with yoga and proper exercise she might never have to go through this again.

After the epidural, she rested for twenty minutes and was then released.

Though not groggy exactly, A.J. had not slept the night before, and she was tired and emotionally drained—never mind the fact that her back was tender. She rested her head against the cab window as the truck crept toward home, Stella's deep voice a comfortable white noise in the background of her thoughts.

Her cell rang. A.J. fumbled it out of her purse and received word from Mr. Meagher that Elysia was being released on bail within the hour.

Stella obligingly, if slowly, changed direction, and A.J. worked to contain her impatience as the pickup truck moseyed on down the highway back to Stillbrook.

When they arrived they found the small town in something resembling a state of siege.

Normally the town of Stillbrook was a quiet and quaint little place, a harmonious blend of historic homes and village industry. Victorian architecture housed bakeries, boutiques, and art galleries—not to mention families that had lived in Warren County since Colonial times. In the center of town was a scrupulously neat village green, which was dutifully decked out in appropriate holiday garb at every turn of the calendar page. Currently, giant colorful Easter eggs, slightly drooping pastel balloons, and wide ribbons in pink and yellow and blue competed with the natural beauty of the blooming flower beds.

Not that the milling sightseers were paying much attention to scenic beauty—natural or otherwise. News vans were parked around the green oval of the park and a small mob seemed to have gathered outside the brick police station.

"Maybe they're planning to lynch her," Stella muttered, not sounding particularly distressed at the idea. But as they drew nearer, they saw that the crowd appeared to be mostly made up of reporters and photographers.

"This is crazy," A.J. muttered.

"Maybe so. It ought to make your ma's day." Stella searched for any space alongside the curb wide enough to wedge the truck into.

"But she hasn't made a film in over twenty years," A.J. protested, taking note of the national television logos on the long line of vans.

"Doesn't matter. Easy Mason was big news once upon a time. Every naughty film and risqué photograph she ever posed for will be turning up."

A.J. gulped. Not that Elysia had been a porn star, but she had certainly played more than her share of scantily clad ingénues and sirens, and the words *sex kitten* had been used more than occasionally in reference to her work. A.J. had outgrown her adolescent agony over her mother's colorful career; in fact she was even proud of her in a conflicted way that she'd probably never admit, but the idea of all those photos of Elysia wearing hot pants, shoulder pads, teased hair—and little else—resurfacing gave her a definite qualm. No one enjoys thinking of her mother as a sex object.

Stella parked, reached under her seat, and dug out a battered-looking straw hat. "You better wear this, just in case someone recognizes you."

Anything that ugly was more likely to draw attention than deflect it, but A.J. reached automatically for the hat. "Why would anyone care? It's not like I've been in hiding for all these years."

"Murder changes everything," Stella said darkly.

A.J. squashed the hat down on her head and they climbed out of the truck, making their way up the sidewalk and then across the street. She could hear the murmured inquiry as to who she and Stella might be before they reached the front steps. They worked their way through the crowd, cameras whirring, and a uniformed officer let them inside where Mr. Meagher met them, appearing tired and triumphant.

"They're bringing her in now."

Mr. Meagher looked as though he had literally done battle to get Elysia free. His tie was crooked and his usually immaculately coiffed silver hair was standing up in tufts.

"Is she all right?" A.J. asked tentatively.

"Spitting mad," Mr. Meagher admitted.

Stella inquired curiously. "How much was her bail?"

Mr. Meagher named a sum and Stella whistled. A.J. barely listened to this exchange, having heard the familiar brisk footsteps on the checkerboard linoleum floor.

A stolid-faced, plump female officer appeared, escorting Elysia. She was pale and her eyes looked smudged and dark-circled. Her hair was more than a little tousled, but otherwise she looked like herself.

"Ah, Stella. You didn't have to dress up on my account." Her gaze fell on A.J., taking a moment to recognize her in the oversized straw hat. "And you brought Pollyanna. How sweet."

"Mother." A.J. hugged her. Elysia squeezed her tightly back, and A.J. managed not to yelp as her injured back protested.

"You shouldn't have come down here yourself, lovie. Or were you actually hoping to see Der Fuh—"

Mr. Meagher hissed as loudly as a cobra-spying mongoose and Elysia broke off as Jake appeared in the lobby, carrying a sheaf of papers.

He stopped, nodded gravely, his gaze lingering on A.J.'s, before he apparently changed his mind and walked out again.

Elysia sniffed disapprovingly. "I need the loo." She turned on her heel.

A.J. exchanged looks with their companions and followed Elysia into the ladies' room, where she found her mother reapplying her makeup with fierce efficiency.

"Are you . . . ?" A.J. cut off what was obviously a silly question. She couldn't imagine how it would feel to be jailed, but she could imagine that once she'd been released, feeling clean and in control of her life again would be high priority.

"Bradley tells me there are reporters out there," Elysia said, combing through her dark hair in sharp, short strokes. She twisted it up into a loose chignon and studied her wan reflection narrowly.

"We can probably sneak out the back of the station," A.J. said. "I can ask the desk sergeant—"

"*Sneak out the back?*" Elysia stared at her. "I have no intention of sneaking out the back."

"I thought . . ." A.J.'s voice trailed off.

"You thought what?" Elysia raised her elegant eyebrows. "You thought I would sneak away in the night like a whipped cur?"

"Er, no. I thought you would prefer to slip out the back and avoid all the dumb questions and bad publicity."

"You. Thought. Wrong."

All riiiiiight. Clearly ready for her close-up, Mr. DeMille.

Elysia held her head high. A.J. could just make out the ghostly obscenities scrawled on the multi-bleached wall behind her. "I have no intention of going gently into that good night," she said clearly and coldly. "Far from it. In fact I'm going out there to give a press conference on the front steps of this dungeon."

A.J. sucked in a sharp breath. "I don't think that's a good idea, Mother."

"I didn't ask. You can sneak out the back if you like." Elysia moved to the door.

"Wait! I really think we need to—"

Elysia cut her off, throwing open the bathroom door, nearly taking out what looked like a teenaged hooker and her baby.

"My public," Elysia announced crisply, "awaits!"

Six

❦

"**Dear,** dear. After all, it could have gone worse," Mr. Meagher said absently, for the fifth or sixth time. They were tooling along the tree-lined highway, lush farmland, and green woodland flashing by as they headed for Starlight Farm. Monster, his head stuck out the window, sneezed loudly and wetly.

Other than Mr. Meagher and Monster, no one had had anything to say since they had left Deer Hollow. Actually, no one had had anything to say before Deer Hollow. In fact no one had had anything much to say since Elysia had delivered her scathing denunciation of her treatment at the incompetent hands of the Stillbrook Police Department—which she had concluded by challenging "the plods" to solve the murder of Dakarai Massri before she did.

It had made excellent copy—and had probably earned her the undying enmity of every single member of the Stillbrook Police Department from Chief of Police Harlan

Welles to Fred the janitor. Safe to say Elysia wasn't top-ping the charts with anybody pulling a salary in the legal and judicial branches either.

Not that she cared. She sat in the front seat gazing broodingly out the windshield at the vast and cloudless blue skies overhead. She had remained so since they'd said good-bye to Stella at the police station and driven to Deer Hollow to pick up Monster. A.J.'s back was begin-ning to give her, in Elysia's vernacular, "gyp." But it seemed easier to spend the night at her mother's than try and manage on her own. Mostly because it would be difficult to keep an eye on her mother long distance, and A.J. definitely felt it behooved her to keep an eye on Elysia. Especially now that Elysia seemed determined to take an active role in solving Massri's murder.

"Did you know they found an engagement ring in the remains of that Easter basket?" Elysia said suddenly, seeming to shake off her preoccupation.

"No," A.J. replied. "But that's good, right? That proves that there was no ill will between yourself and Dicky." She tried to read Mr. Meagher's expression in the rearview mirror.

"Those bloody fools gave me a glimpse of it. Three stones. Baguettes with a two-and-a-half carat center stone. A total of five carats. Do you have any idea what that would have cost the poor dear boy?"

"Do you remember how the poor dear boy would have raised the money?" A.J. inquired. "Because that's what got us into this jam." She really didn't think she could handle her mother getting sentimental over that lying, cheating, sneaking little blackmailer. No one deserved to be murdered, but A.J. was willing to bet Massri had reaped what he sowed.

Mr. Meagher cleared his throat. "The police theorize that Massri might have tried to blackmail your mother into marriage and that's why she shot him."

"That's ridiculous. That's not logical, it's just hokey melodrama."

"That's what we're dealing with," Elysia said. "The filth likes me for it, and that's that."

"The . . . filth?"

"Coppers," Mr. Meagher reminded her out of the side of his mouth. "Pejorative term."

"I remember now. I must have blocked it out of my mind. Mother, it's not going to help things if you keep antagonizing the police or the DA or the superior court judge."

"It's not going to help kissing their arses either."

A.J. caught Mr. Meagher's gaze in the mirror. He shook his head very slightly and, unwillingly, she subsided.

When they reached Starlight Farm, however, and she saw the crime scene tape in the front yard and took in the mess that the police had made searching her mother's home, A.J.'s anger at Jake surged again. If he didn't believe her mother was guilty, why was he going along with this garbage? Why wasn't he doing anything to help? Was he so ambitious that he was willing to sacrifice anything and anyone to his career?

"I'm going to sue the police department," Elysia said, moving down the hallway and straightening the series of eighteenth-century London watercolors as she went. "Starting with that great, bloody bully boy you call a boyfriend. And I shall enjoy wringing every last penny from their coffers."

A.J. ignored that. "Haven't they found the weapon yet?" she asked Mr. Meagher.

"Not yet."

"Well, surely *that's* a positive."

Elysia drawled, "They think I dumped it in the
Delaware when I was driving around the countryside with
my evaporated milk."

A.J. sighed and lowered herself to the long sofa, stretching out. "I have to lie down. My back is killing me."

Some of the hardness left Elysia's face. "I thought you
said you'd had an injection, pumpkin. Didn't it help?"

"I'm sure it will. But it takes a little while to kick in."
· She closed her eyes. When she opened them again
Elysia was setting a tray with a pot of tea and a plate of
lemon madeleines on the low table.

A.J. realized she must have dozed off for a few minutes
because Mr. Meagher was in the middle of saying something about the police checking into Elysia's bank records
and finding proof that she had been making payments to
Massri.

Elysia opened the silver cigarette box on one of the
side tables, seemed to recall that she had company, and
flipped it shut again. "Is this supposed to be a big break in
their case? I've *already* admitted it."

"The point is, Elysia, it looks very damaging." It was
one of the only times A.J. could remember Mr. Meagher
actually sounding sharp with her mother. Her mother
seemed to hear the difference in his tone, too. Her brows
drew together.

"I can't help how it looks," she snapped. "Nor can I
help people's narrow minds."

Mr. Meagher reddened. He replaced his teacup and
saucer on the table and rose. His accent was pronounced
as he said, "I must be on me way. I'll see meself out."

"Oh, Bradley—"

"Good night, ladies," Mr. Meagher said with injured dignity.

The quiet, careful closing of the front door was worse than any slamming.

Elysia groaned and dropped her face in her hands.

Jake phoned later that evening after A.J. had retired to Elysia's comfortable guest bedroom. "I'm at your house."

"I'm at my mother's."

"I figured that out. How's your back?"

"It's a little better, I think."

Abruptly they were out of things to say.

Into the yawning, black silence, A.J. said, "This is . . . awkward."

"I know. The DA plans on pushing all the way. He's convinced there's a real case here. And your mother didn't make things better with her grand performance this afternoon."

"She's scared, and she's angry."

"I understand that, but—"

"But?"

"Look, you don't have to take that attitude with me, A.J. I don't think your mother killed anybody. But that's beside the point."

As great a relief as it was to hear Jake admit even that much, she couldn't help responding, "It shouldn't be."

"This is my job."

"This is my mother."

"And I can't allow personal feelings to interfere with how I do my job. That wouldn't help Elysia."

A.J. communed within herself. "Intellectually, yes. I get it. But emotionally? This is an impossible situation. She's having a rough time and my fraternizing with the . . . the enemy isn't helping."

"So what are you saying?"

A.J. was silent. "One day at a time? I think we just need to take things slowly for a while. I mean, if this really goes to trial—"

His voice was flat. "Okay."

Was she glad or sorry that he accepted it so easily?

"One thing, though," Jake said quietly. "Elysia said a lot of inflammatory things outside the station today. She challenged the police department to find the 'real' killer, and I don't think I'm totally off base thinking she inferred she'd be poking her nose in if we didn't come up with a result she liked pretty quick."

"She was angry and emotional."

She heard what could have been a brusque laugh. "Sure she was. But that doesn't mean she didn't mean every word. Do *not* let her drag you into some dingbat amateur detective scheme. Or you're going to be wearing matching mother-daughter prison garb."

"Duly noted, Detective."

He sighed. "Okay. Well, keep me posted."

"Likewise."

She flipped shut the cell phone and gazed up unseeing at the shadowy corners of the moonlit ceiling.

One of A.J.'s unexpected newfound pleasures since moving to New Jersey was her morning yoga routine. Not only did she feel physically better for those few but intense minutes of stretching and limbering, but that period of quiet reflection centered her for the active day ahead. Although it had only been a couple of days since A.J. had injured her back, she was already missing her morning yoga session.

Accordingly, on the morning after her steroid shot, she went through a very cautious, abbreviated workout. She was uneasily conscious that the wrong moves could worsen her situation, but she was sure that if she proceeded carefully, all would be well. She had worked hard over the past months and didn't want to lose the ground that she had gained.

She started by spreading a quilt on the bedroom carpet and then lying flat on her back. She stretched her arms out from her side in a straight line with her shoulders. Exhaling, she started to raise both legs perpendicular to the floor, but she immediately felt the burn in her lower back, and had to abandon the pose.

Dismayed, but still determined, she rested for a few seconds and then rolled carefully onto her left side, raising her right leg—

The pain halted her.

No way was this going to happen. She was liable to do more damage even trying. For a few seconds A.J. struggled with her frustration and fear. Had one misstep undone all the diligent work of the last months?

She *refused* to give up.

She sat up, moved onto her hands and knees, and keeping her spine lengthened, she stared straight ahead, breathing normally. Or as normally as she could, given her state of tension.

So far, so good.

She started the arch of Marjariasana or Cat Pose—and again she had to stop at the blaze of fierce pain.

A.J. sat down, forcing herself to breathe evenly, to resist giving into her anguish.

Her body would not cooperate.

No. Wrong. Her body *could* not cooperate. This was not a matter of willpower or discipline. She could not force her injured nerves and muscles to respond the way she wished; to try to do so would merely cause more damage. Surely the lessons of the past year had as much to do with retraining her way of thinking as moving?

She drew a couple of long, calming breaths. When she had her emotions under control once more, she rose—carefully—refolded the quilt, and went to take a warm, muscle-relaxing shower.

When A.J. at last made her way to the kitchen, she found her mother whisking eggs for mushroom and cheese omelets while she watched a local TV station replay of herself on the police station steps.

"I don't suppose the tiger-stripe jeans matter, do you?" Elysia inquired, critically studying her miniature image.

"Better than prison stripes."

"Ha."

Suze MacDougal dropped by around lunchtime, full of grievances over Lily's high-handed behavior. Suze was one of the junior instructors at Sacred Balance. A short girl with spiky yellow hair and huge blue eyes, she bore an unfortunate resemblance to Dopey the dwarf, and perhaps she was a little ditzy, but she had a good heart and was a loyal friend and employee.

"Couldn't you just come in for a few hours? Even if you hung out in your office all day?"

A.J.'s spine gave a little twinge just considering the idea.

"I don't think I'm going to be a lot of use at this point. I'm going to have to take it easy for a while. Standing is hard, sitting is worse, and walking hurts like heck, to be honest. I'm supposed to lie flat until it stops hurting."

"For how long?"

As long as it took. Despite her disappointment over the morning's failed workout, A.J. was determined to focus on the fact that her back *was* definitely better. She was going to have to be patient—something that did not come naturally to her— and she was going to have to have faith. But she did not believe, refused to believe, that all the months of practice and discipline could be so quickly undone by the wrong move. This was a temporary setback, that was all.

She said staunchly, "It won't be too long."

"There's something going on, A.J. Lily's *up* to something."

"Like what?"

"Like suits in the studio."

"Suits?"

"Suits. *Suits*," Suze emphasized. "Executive types in suits being shown around the studio, kind of like investors getting the grand tour."

"We don't have investors. Sacred Balance is a privately held corporation."

"Exactly. And there's more."

A.J. rubbed her forehead. No question: so far the day was off to a not-so-great start. "Maybe they're potential clients, Suze. Maybe they were reporters."

"Mara Allen from Yoga Meridian called asking for Lily."

A.J. straightened, wincing. Yoga Meridian, located in the nearby town of Blairstown, was their biggest competitor; they had already lost two important clients to the new studio with its spa and salon facilities. "Called Lily about what?"

"No one knows. But she called *twice*."

A.J. felt an odd prickling at the back of her neck. "Even so, it doesn't necessarily mean anything."

"Okay, but why would Mara Allen be calling Lily? Think about it. Yoga Meridian is our only real rival. I mean, if they—if Mara—wanted to link up with Sacred Balance for some charity benefit or something, why wouldn't she contact you?"

"Because I'm out of the office."

"She called asking for Lily on *Monday morning*. Now how could she have known you were going to be out Monday morning when *you* didn't even know you were going to be out?"

"Who says Mara called Monday morning?"

"Emma."

A.J. thought this over. Emma Rice was not given to idle gossip. Nor was she someone who got her facts wrong.

Suze said eagerly, "And if it was something like hooking up for a charity benefit, why hasn't Lily called you to discuss it?"

"Because I'm on sick leave and it isn't anything urgent. Because, knowing Lily, she wouldn't think my input was necessary."

"Why hasn't she mentioned it to anyone at the studio?"

"Maybe there isn't anything to tell yet. Maybe it isn't anything at all. Maybe Mara was calling for information or to check a reference."

"What reference? The last time anyone left Sacred Balance—" Suze broke off uncomfortably. The last time there had been an opening in Sacred Balance's staff roster was Diantha's murder.

A.J. brightened as a delightful thought occurred. "Maybe Mara's offering Lily a job."

Suze's lips parted as she, too, was transfixed with momentary rapture. "Do you think so?" Her face fell almost at once. "But what about the executive types Lily was giving the grand tour to?"

"I don't know, but we can't—shouldn't—speculate. Is everyone talking about this at the studio?"

Suze looked uncomfortable. "Well . . . you know what it's like."

A.J. did. Only too well.

"I'll tell you what I think," Suze said. "You've only been out for two days. If Lily *is* up to something, she's moving pretty fast. There's some time factor involved." Suze stared at A.J. "Whatever this is, it's not good."

Seven

Wednesday stretched out, long and tedious. A.J. rested her back and caught up on her reading. She browsed articles on weight-loss vitamins, the medicinal value of whole foods, and the obesity epidemic. Epidemic was the word the article used, and as A.J. read, it appeared to be advisedly. According to the article, for the first time in history *two-thirds* of all Americans were overweight. Those were some pretty scary statistics.

Inevitably, all that reading about dieting made her hungry and A.J. snacked on the last of the lemon madeleines while she flipped through stories on learning to unwind, learning to get one's life back under control, and learning to balance work and play. All the while, she was conscious of Elysia prowling the house like a caged animal. Mr. Meagher had not phoned so far that day.

"Maybe there isn't any news," A.J. pointed out when her mother began another lap of the antique Savonnerie carpet.

"How can there be no news?"

"Well, they've already arrested and charged you. So now it's probably just a matter of the police continuing to collect evidence and build their case while your attorney collects evidence to mount your defense. It takes a lot longer than it does on TV."

Elysia disapproved of this. Several times already she had called the criminal lawyer Mr. Meagher had found her, but apparently he had no news either. No news was good news in A.J.'s opinion, although the fact that there was no news was not for lack of trying. Elysia received several requests for interviews from both print and visual news media. To A.J.'s fervent gratitude, she turned them all down.

"I do have one idea," Elysia said, taking the chair catty-corner from the sofa where A.J. reclined.

"What's that?" A.J. asked warily.

Elysia held up a key. "We could search Dicky's flat."

After what seemed like a long time, A.J. closed her mouth. "What are you doing with a key to Massri's place?" She held up a hand. "Never mind. Forget I asked."

Perhaps the possession of the key was a point in her mother's favor. After all, it would be a pretty stupid—or totally eccentric—murderess who decided to kill her victim in her own front yard when she had a key to the victim's home. In fact it would be a pretty stupid murderess who killed her victim in her own front yard whether she had a key to the victim's home or not.

"Does Jake know you have a key to Dicky's home?"

"It's none of his business." Elysia selected a cigarette from the silver box, but did not light it. She'd been talking about quitting for the last month or so but being charged with murder was probably not doing much for her resolve.

Was it Jake's business that her mother had a key to the murdered man's home? A.J. wasn't sure. "Did he ask?"

"No."

A.J. studied her mother's austere profile. "What on earth did you two talk about?"

"I assume you mean Dicky and I?"

A.J. nodded.

"We talked about all kinds of things. Oh, nothing of earth-shattering importance. We laughed a good deal. He was very good-natured. Very good company. He knew how to listen. Or how to pretend to listen, which is nearly as good."

Keeping in mind Stella's observations on loneliness, A.J. said, "But why *him*?"

"Oh, he chose me, pumpkin. I told you I wasn't looking for anything like that."

"Why do you think he chose you?"

At Elysia's look of affront, A.J. said, "He was blackmailing you, Mother. It obviously wasn't just about your sparkling personality."

Elysia half-closed her eyes, considering. "Mmm. Tactless but true. There were several of us on the cruise. Unattached women of a certain age. Dicky was very pleasant, very charming with all of us, but gradually he seemed to narrow his focus. I remember the others taking the mickey out of me about it."

"Do you think you were more receptive to his advances?"

"I don't know that I was," Elysia said. She seemed reflective not defensive. "Nor was I the wealthiest. I was, if I may say so, by far the best looking."

"*That* goes without saying."

"Thank you, pumpkin. Women my age do have a tendency to let themselves go. So I think it was probably a combination of factors. I was attractive, receptive, and sufficiently well off."

"Do you think it was the first time he'd ever tried anything like that?"

Again Elysia seemed to have to cogitate. "As much as I'd like to think so . . . no."

"Why?"

Elysia sighed. "Looking back, I can see that it all seemed to go rather like clockwork." She clarified, "As though we were on a timetable—his timetable."

"So you do think he was a professional blackmailer?"

"It obviously wasn't full-time. He was employed by the cruise line."

"But imagine what a nice supplementary income he could collect if he scored one blackmail victim per cruise."

"I'd like to think it wasn't quite as common as buses running . . ." Elysia made a face. "I suppose it was, though. He did seem to have it down to a science."

"How did he approach you? Once the deed was done, I mean. Did he present you with photos?"

"Yes."

"Then he must have had an accomplice. Unless the camera was in his bow tie?"

Elysia tittered at some mental image. Then she sobered. "He did have an accomplice. One of the stewards. A little rat-faced man. I'm quite sure they were in it together."

"Did the little rat-faced man emigrate, too? Have you ever seen him since?"

"I never saw any sign of him after I left the cruise ship."

"Maybe he didn't like the partnership being broken up?"

Elysia tapped the unlit cigarette meditatively. "I think that's weak, pumpkin. It's very hard to picture a man following another halfway across the world just to twep him for breaking up their partnership."

"Twep?"

"Terminate with Extreme Prejudice," Elysia said tartly.

"Ouch."

"Qeb, the ship steward, was quite a different sort of person from Dicky. Such a trip would have been extremely difficult and frightening for him. He was rather . . . rustic."

"All right. Scratch Qeb. So it must have been one of Dicky's other victims."

Elysia said nothing.

"Unless he had some other means of support? Obviously he couldn't continue to work for the Egyptian cruise line, but maybe he found something else?"

"I doubt it. I never saw any sign of gainful employment. Frankly, it would have been a pain working our trysts around a nine-to-five schedule."

"Yes, I'm sure most people agree with that. Mother, are you sure you have *no* idea about any of Dicky's other lady friends?"

"He wouldn't have introduced us, pumpkin."

"You never heard him mention anyone? Never saw a name on a note or an envelope?"

"I would hardly read his mail, Anna."

This had been a sore point for a time during the tumultuous years of A.J.'s parents' marriage. She said bluntly, "You would if you were sleuthing."

"Oh." Elysia's expression changed. "True. But unfortunately I didn't. I suppose I didn't want to learn anything that might spoil the fun."

"What about phone conversations? Or messages on his answering machine?"

Elysia brightened. "Actually, now that you mention it, I did hear a name once. Dora . . . Boombox. No. Bombeck? Hmmm. *Beauford*. That was it. She used to ring the poor boy up all hours of night and day. She was *besotted*."

"Besotted." Now there was a good old-fashioned word. "You mean she was stalking him?"

"I don't know if *stalking* is the right word. She did grow increasingly angry and she did seem to be making rather a nuisance of herself."

"Do you know if she ever threatened him?"

"He could be very exasperating."

"So she did threaten him? Mother, maybe this Dora Beauford had something to do with Dicky's death. Did you tell Jake about her?"

Elysia shook her head.

"Why not?"

"Because that was months ago, pet. I don't believe Dicky was still in contact with her."

"But you don't know. That's the kind of thing you're supposed to let the police determine."

"Well, if she was still in contact, they'll know by now. They took his cell phone."

A.J. nodded absently, thinking.

"Well?" Elysia asked after a time.

"Well what?"

Elysia studied her unlit cigarette tip. "Shall we try a spot of the old B&E?"

A.J. stared at her in consternation. "Please tell me you're joking."

"Joking? I'm most certainly not joking. We're discussing my life and liberty."

"It's your life and liberty I'm thinking of. Talk about finding the fastest possible way to get yourself thrown back in jail! I can't believe you'd even suggest it."

Elysia's brows raised. "Never mind the lecture, pumpkin. Yes or no?"

"It's *no*. Absolutely not. Under no circumstances are we sneaking into Dicky's flat."

Dicky Massri lived—formerly lived—in an innocuous two-story apartment building in Hackettstown. It looked like a hundred other places: hardy generic gardens surrounding pseudo-Colonial red brick and black shutters. It did not look like the lair of a master blackmailer.

"Are you sure this place doesn't have a security guard?" A.J. asked doubtfully, glancing up at the windows on the second story as they approached the complex.

Elysia didn't bother to answer that. "See," she threw over her shoulder as she led the way briskly up the cement walkway to the side entrance. "No crime scene tape."

A.J. followed her, watching uneasily as Elysia inserted the key in the lock and pushed open the door. Far across the expanse of patchy lawn she could see a gardener bouncing along on one of those ride-on mowers.

"You know the police have probably been all over this place by now."

Elysia tossed a furtive look over her shoulder and stepped inside the apartment. A.J. followed her inside, and

Elysia closed the door. The apartment smelled stale, empty.

A.J. looked around. They stood in a long, narrow living room. The walls were dove gray, the carpet white, the furniture dark and severe and modern. The only splash of color came from the primitive abstract paintings on the wall: orange, blue, and green swirls that reminded A.J. of the sort of things a hazmat team generally dealt with. It had the signature look of a mediocre interior decorator: overpriced and impersonal.

The entertainment system looked especially pricey. But there were only a handful of CDs: Englebert Humperdinck, Frank Sinatra, Dean Martin, Tom Jones. Music to seduce older ladies by. There were no DVDs.

"It doesn't look like he spent a lot of time here. Is this where you used to meet?"

Elysia shook her head. She seemed uncharacteristically quiet.

They wandered into the kitchen. Another long, narrow room. Pale green walls and white tile. White stove, fridge, dishwasher, microwave. A.J. opened a cupboard and there were two plates, two coffee cups, a few glasses.

"He certainly didn't eat here often."

"No. We usually ate out."

A.J. opened the fridge and found it empty of food beyond a jar of green olives, three bottles of champagne, and a damp looking takeout container of moldy looking koshary.

"Whatever he was spending his ill-gotten gains on, it wasn't the good life."

There was no answer. A.J. glanced around and saw that her mother had left the room. She found her in the bed-

•

room—inside the walk-in closet to be precise—and saw that in this room spartan simplicity gave way to sybaritic luxury. The queen-sized bed had a silver brocade bedspread and was piled high with jewel-bright velvet cushions. The closet was stuffed with clothes: tailored suits, silk shirts, designer sportswear, and cashmere sweaters. There were rows and rows of expensive shoes. Dicky had possessed far more shoes than A.J. owned, even back when she'd been a rising young freelancer.

Elysia methodically checked the pockets of the trousers and shirts and blazers. A.J. moved off to the bathroom and found the glass shelves packed with a variety of name-brand grooming products. Dicky also had more hair products than she did. A.J. counted shampoos and conditioners from L'Occitane, Calvin Klein, and The Salon.

Returning to the bedroom, she noticed a snapshot tucked in the corner of the framed mirror over the dresser. The family grouped in front of the neutral background appeared to be Egyptian: a dignified older man, a plump, comfortable middle-aged woman, two self-conscious teenaged girls, and a little boy. Judging by clothes and haircuts, the photograph seemed quite recent. Was this Dicky's family? She couldn't think of another reason for such a group portrait.

As she studied the photo, A.J. viewed Dakarai Massri for the first time as something more than a threat to her mother. She recalled how young he had been; she recognized that whatever his faults, he had been someone with hopes and fears, dreams and ambitions, disappointments and sorrows. He had a family somewhere and they had probably loved him and would soon be, if they were not already, grieving for him.

"What about this bookie of his?" A.J. called. "Do you think Dicky might have had gambling debts he couldn't pay?"

"He liked to gamble," Elysia replied absently.

"What did he gamble on?"

"Horses, mostly. But he spends—spent—a fair amount of time in Atlantic City."

A.J. sat down gingerly on the side of the bed. "I don't begin to know how we would locate a bookie or investigate Dicky's gambling habits."

"Hmm. I admit it'll take some thought." Elysia stepped out of the closet and looked around. "I don't see his laptop anywhere."

"Did he have a laptop?" A.J. asked sharply.

"One of those cute little notebook thingies."

"The police must have it. Did you write him e-mails?" A.J. braced herself for the answer.

"You know I don't use e-mail unless I have to."

That was true, and it was one bright spot. At least Elysia would not have left an electronic trail.

They went through all the drawers in Dicky's bureau and dressing table but turned up nothing more interesting than an overabundance of dress socks.

A.J. sifted through her share of the dresser drawers quickly. She wanted out of this apartment as soon as possible. All they needed was a nosy neighbor or a prospective tenant and they'd be trying to explain themselves to the local law—and good luck with that. "What about his friends? Did he have any?"

"I met his upstairs neighbor once," Elysia said. "They seemed to get on well enough."

"It's so weird. He's like the Man Who Never Was."

"I assure you, pumpkin, he most definitely *was*."

As A.J. slid the drawer back it seemed to stick. She pulled it out, tried again, and heard something tear.

"There's something here."

A.J. pulled the drawer all the way out and Elysia rushed to take it from her.

"You're not supposed to lift!"

Letting Elysia take the drawer, A.J. reached inside. Jammed into the wooden track was a crumpled greeting card. She freed it carefully, drew it out, and smoothed the stiff paper, examining it curiously.

Elaborate gold script on embossed white stock read *Happy Birthday to My Husband.*

Heart pounding in hope, A.J. opened the card. Beneath the usual lavish and saccharine sentiments was scrawled *xo* and a name: Medea.

"Hey, take a look at this." She held the card out to her mother.

Elysia took the card and opened it. She seemed to go very still.

"He was married," A.J. said.

Elysia said nothing.

"He was already married to someone else. Married to someone named Medea. If we could find this woman, this Medea, we would probably have the answer to who killed Dicky."

Still Elysia did not speak—and that was so odd that A.J. fell silent, too.

And in that profound silence she heard a key scrape in the front door lock and the sound of the front door opening.

"Hide!" gasped Elysia, attempting to shove the drawer soundlessly back in its track.

"Hide where?" squeaked A.J.

There was no more time than that. Elysia dove beneath
the bed. Her arm poked from beneath the bed skirt, beck-
oning wildly to A.J., but A.J. knew there was no way her
back would permit her to climb under the bed—not if she
planned on ever climbing out again. She backed into the
crowded walk-in closet, ducking behind the suits and silk
shirts, listening tensely. Yes, someone had definitely entered the apartment.

The scent of Dicky's aftershave was disconcerting. A.J.
tried to blank it out and concentrate on the voices. Blanketed
in sport coats and shirts, she could see nothing, and though
she could hear voices, they were too low to discern more
than that there were two more people in the apartment and
that one was—possibly—female.

Her first panicked thought had been that she and Elysia
had been discovered by the apartment complex manager,
but she realized now that that was probably incorrect. The
intruders sounded as though they might be arguing. Then
A.J. heard the distinct slide of blinds across the front
window.

Perhaps these were the hitherto unknown friends or
family of the dead man? *Oh God.* What if they had arrived
to pack all his things?

She heard the floor creak. A male voice close to the
bedroom door said, "I still don't see the point of this."

The answer was indistinct.

"Well, we better make this fast. That gardener is coming down this way."

A muffled response.

"How do I know? I don't want to take the chance of
being spotted walking out of here."

Over the pounding of blood in her ears A.J. could just

make out the hurried swing and bang of the kitchen cupboard doors. What were they looking for?

This was very bad. Unless they found what they were looking for in the kitchen—and given how bare the cupboards were, that was unlikely—they would undoubtedly search the bedroom and the closet.

"I think you're giving him too much credit," said the same voice irritably.

And then, very distinctly, a female voice said, "His answering machine is missing."

"The cops will have grabbed it." The man's voice was moving away from the bedroom doorway. A temporary reprieve, A.J. knew.

"A.J." hissed a frantic whisper.

A.J. poked a cautious head out of the closet and saw Elysia at the far wall with the window open. She beckoned frantically and A.J., ignoring the pain in her back, tiptoed as quickly and as silently as she could manage across the room.

Elysia shoved the window screen out of its track and into the shrubbery beneath. "Can you climb?" she mouthed.

A.J. had no idea if she could climb or not, but she was not about to be caught in that room. It had already occurred to her that if the intruders were not the apartment management or Massri's family, one or both of them might have had something to do with his death.

From down the hall the woman said, "Stop complaining. The faster we do this, the faster we get it over with."

"You should have been a philosopher."

The philosopher said something very rude. A kitchen drawer banged hard.

Elysia made a cup with her hands, and A.J., biting her lip against the flare of pain shooting down her hip and leg, stepped into the makeshift step and boosted herself up. Even though she was braced for it, the pain caught her by surprise. She closed her mind to it, and hauled herself out through the wide sliding window and lowered herself to the hedge below. It made for a prickly but reasonably sturdy landing, and she half-rolled, half-wriggled off, landing gracelessly on the walkway in a shower of leaves.

Elysia came scrabbling out the window a moment later, flopped onto the hedge, and dropped to the walk.

"Scarper!" she gasped.

One of her best ideas in a long time, that was A.J.'s opinion as she scuttled after her mother.

They hurried down the path to the parking lot. With all the gratitude of a shipwrecked sailor spotting land, A.J. recognized the blue and white Land Rover right where they had left it.

Elysia used her key fob to unlock the doors while they were still a yard away. They sprinted the last few feet and slammed inside the vehicle.

Hand to her throbbing back, A.J. gasped, "That was too close!"

Elysia smirked—in between pants—and turned the key in the ignition.

"Never again, Mother. I must be insane to have gone along with this. I must be taking way too many pain meds. I must be—"

"Don't be so poor spirited, pumpkin."

"If that had been the apartment manager, we'd be on our way to jail right now. In fact that's probably optimistic. Never mind getting caught, we could have been in real danger. For all we know one of those people was Medea."

Elysia wrinkled her nose. "I don't believe so."

"I didn't catch any names. Did you?"

Elysia shook her head. There was a dead leaf in her dark hair, which somehow made her certainty all the more annoying.

A.J. demanded, "Well then? *Why* couldn't that woman have been Medea?"

Elysia's wide green eyes met hers. "Because I know who Medea is."

Eight

⌒

"Yes?"

They were hurtling down Interstate 80 back toward Stillbrook, Elysia driving pedal-to-the-metal as though the combined law enforcement agencies of New Jersey were in hot pursuit.

She answered absently, "Yes what?"

"Who is she?" A.J. demanded.

"Medea Sutherland."

A.J. lowered her car seat trying to find some relief for her throbbing back. "Why is that name familiar?"

"You remember Maddie. She's an old mate of mine." Elysia sighed reminiscently. "I remember once when she made a guest appearance on *221B Baker Street* to help us solve the murder at the Peking Opera—"

"Oh my God," A.J. exclaimed. "*Maddie Sutherland*. I remember now. She's the one who used to make those Hammer Horror films."

"Yes. Among other things."

"The crazy one."

Elysia made a disapproving sound.

"Mother, she invited the *National Enquirer* into her home to interview the ghosts she thought lived there. That's pretty crazy by any definition."

"You do have such a long memory for other people's . . . foibles. Anyway, Maddie believed the house was haunted."

A.J. decided to overlook the "foibles" crack although her tone was crisp as she responded, "Then she should have called an exorcist or whatever they're called. Because it looked like either a publicity stunt or that she was stark, raving bonkers. Or both." She examined Elysia's uncommunicative profile. "What makes you think this Medea is your Medea?"

"When was the last time you met someone named Medea?"

"There must be women around named Medea. Especially in Greek communities."

"Be serious, pumpkin. Anyway, I recall Medea writing me a few years back to tell me she was getting married. And she does rather fit the profile of the kind of woman Dicky used to . . . romance."

"Crazy old ladies?"

"So amusing, Anna," Elysia murmured, sounding not the least amused.

A.J. considered the ceiling of the Land Rover as they raced along. "Maybe Medea knocked Dicky off when she found out he was two-timing her?"

The Land Rover suddenly reduced speed. "It's hard to imagine a less violent soul."

"Even so, the spouse or lover is usually the prime suspect. And your old mate Medea certainly always seemed a little . . . unpredictable."

"But I don't think they *were* still married." Elysia's eyes were in the rearview as a police cruiser drew behind. "Try to act natural, pet," she said out of the side of her mouth.

"Why?"

"The coppers are after us."

A.J. gulped. "How much more natural can I act than sitting here?" She did her best to appear to be innocently and leisurely enjoying the spring landscape as it slid by at a much more sedate pace.

She couldn't help worrying. Had there been some development in the case? Was there now an APB out on Elysia's car?

Neither had much to say for the next few miles, and then the cruiser suddenly put on his lights and zoomed ahead of them.

Elysia relaxed. "Bloody coppers," she muttered as the cruiser disappeared in the distance.

"This is such a disaster. Because *we* were in that apartment illegally I can't even tell Jake about the other intruders searching it."

"You could. He'll probably throw you in the hoosegow, but if you feel it's your civic duty . . ."

"Don't you see that if Jake knew about those two it would take some of the heat off you?"

"I wish that were true. But the fact of the matter is that, given Dicky's occupation, it's no surprise that people are attempting to search his apartment. The only surprise is we didn't run into more people searching it."

She had a point. A.J. reflected how alarming it would be to find out that someone with access to your deepest, darkest secrets had died—perhaps leaving those secrets where anyone might stumble over them.

She watched unseeing as trees and barns and road signs flashed by. A sign for a winery, a sign for Yards Creek Soaring glider rides, a sign for Yoga Meridian.

"Do you mind?" A.J. said on impulse. "I want to check something out."

Elysia threw her a curious look but nodded. They drove down Blairstown's Main Street. Though a little larger than Stillbrook, Blairstown had the same quaint, old-fashioned vibe to it—which wasn't surprising given that the area had been settled all the way back in the 1700s.

"Did you know they filmed scenes from *Friday the 13th* in Blairstown?" A.J. murmured as they passed the bright blue historic building Roy's Hall. "They always pick peaceful places like this for horror movies, don't they?"

"Still waters run deep."

As the Bard said? A.J.'s attention was caught by another sign advertising the yoga studio and she said quickly, "Turn here!"

Yoga Meridian was housed in what had once been a huge old Greek Orthodox church. The white stone building featured a large blue domed roof surrounded by three golden cupolas and several enormous stained glass windows. The large parking lot was packed.

"It's gorgeous," Elysia murmured.

It was, though A.J. couldn't bring herself to admit it.

"Remind me what we're doing here," Elysia inquired as A.J. got out of the Land Rover.

"Reconnoitering."

Elysia raised her eyebrows but said no more.

Inside the lobby—formerly the church nave—A.J. took in a series of slogans in bright, cheerful colors:

Come On, Stretch Yourself!
Yoga for Every Body!
Real Yoga for Real People!

What did that last one even *mean*?

She glanced at the list of offered classes. It was a smorgasbord of traditional and trendy. everything from Hatha Yoga to Laughter Yoga.

One thing that was no laughing matter was the prices. How could Mara Allen afford to stay in business? Especially with a staff this size?

She muttered, "We couldn't keep the doors open at these prices." That wasn't exactly true, but it was a source of pride to A.J. that Sacred Balance pay for itself without her needing to dip into the cash reserves of Aunt Diantha's other investments.

"If they bring in enough new customers it will be worth it, I suppose."

A.J. nodded. Perhaps that was Mara Allen's gamble. Or maybe Yoga Meridian was simply beating the prana pants off them.

Followed by Elysia, she walked through to the salon and spa center located in the former narthex of the church.

"It's nice, I have to admit," A.J. said grudgingly. "In fact it's more than nice. It's really well laid out, and the prices are more than competitive."

"Very." Elysia, watching her, asked, "What's wrong?"

"That's Michael Batz."

Elysia followed her gaze to where a young, athletic man with a head of hair like a Renaissance angel was working on the mat. "And?"

"He resigned his Sacred Balance membership about a month ago. He said he was taking a break from yoga."

"I wouldn't take it personally. No place is right for every person, after all. Sacred Balance probably had too many painful memories for Michael."

Remembering the role Batz had played in her aunt's murder investigation, A.J. nodded, but she was still unconvinced. That made three Sacred Balance clients that she knew of who had defected to Yoga Meridian in the past five weeks. If the exodus continued at this rate, they'd be out of clients before Christmas.

"A.J. Alexander," a carefully modulated voice remarked from behind them. "Welcome to Yoga Meridian."

A.J. turned. Mara Allen, tall and willowy in a white leotard, came to greet them. Mara had striking blue eyes and a long, curly, prematurely silver mane made famous by her TV spots.

"Hello, Mara."

"Namaste, A.J." Mara put her palms briefly together, prayer fashion. "This is an unexpected pleasure."

"Er, we were in the neighborhood. Truly."

Mara smiled graciously. "May I show you around our facilities?"

"That would be lovely." A.J. hoped she didn't sound as lukewarm as she felt. She suspected, given the little glint of amusement in Mara's eyes, that she wasn't fooling anyone.

"You've been so often on my mind, A.J." Mara led them through a bright airy atrium where students rested quietly on their mats amidst the forest of potted trees.

"Oh, really?" A.J. replied.

"Your determination and enthusiasm to carry on for Diantha, despite your lack of training or experience is really . . . heartwarming."

"Thank you, but I've worked hard to get the training and experience I need."

"Of course you have."

Mara flashed her professional smile and led them past the steam room and then up the graceful staircase to the "Meditation Arbor."

"It's my greatest joy to share the gift of yoga with my students so that we can bring our lives, bodies, and minds into balance."

A.J. smiled politely.

"Of course, *you* know that," Mara said. "I love the Sacred Balance philosophy. *Just do it.* It's so . . . succinct."

"That's Nike," A.J. said. "Sacred Balance's slogan is *It could happen*."

"Of course it could," Mara said encouragingly. "And here is the massage lab. If we weren't already booked into next week, I'd offer you both a complimentary Thai yoga massage."

By the time the gently condescending Mara had finished giving A.J. and Elysia their quick tour of the fabulous spa facilities, A.J. was struggling against uncharacteristic depression.

"Pretentious cow," Elysia said when they were once again outside the building and the soothing sound of flutes and running water had died away with the closing of the painted doors. "Remind me why we needed to subject ourselves to the sight of that many middle-aged bodies in leotards?"

"I don't know," A.J. admitted. "I just thought maybe I should scope out the competition."

"You're not worrying about Suze's mystery phone calls?"

"No. Yes. It's too soon to know for sure. If Mara really was calling Sacred Balance to set up something like a charity benefit, why didn't she mention talking to Lily?"

"Because Lily has already taken care of whatever the matter was?"

"You're probably right."

"Probably." Watching her, Elysia added shrewdly, "But never ignore your instincts, pet."

"Yes, but is it my instinct kicking in or my rampant paranoia?"

"Paranoia is useful, too. Ms. Allen did seem a bit . . . smug."

A.J. smiled faintly at Elysia's dead-on mockery of Mara's deliberately timed digs. "She did, didn't she?"

They drove back to Starlight Farm and picked up Monster.

Elysia wanted A.J. to stay overnight again. A.J. felt a little guilty about not keeping Elysia company, but as much as she loved her mother, it was not easy for them to be in each other's company for long stretches without butting heads. Elysia's legal woes were liable to continue for some time, and A.J. could not put her life on hold indefinitely. She would have to find a way to continue helping her mother while she got back to running her own life.

"What you really mean is you want to see Jake," Elysia said shortly.

"I can't not ever speak to him again, Mother."

"I don't see why not."

A.J. said patiently, "Because I care for him."

Elysia sniffed. "You could do so much better than that

flatfoot, Anna. I know that your experience with Andrew undermined your confidence, but there's no need to throw yourself away on the first man who shows an interest."

And here it was. A perfect example of why she and her mother could not share airspace long without a collision. "My feelings for Jake have nothing to do with Andy. Things were going perfectly well between us before this murder charge cropped up. In fact—" A.J. stopped, realizing that admitting to Elysia her hopes for her relationship with Jake was tantamount to placing a loaded gun in her mother's hands.

Elysia looked unconvinced. "Well, I can't help but feel it's a little disloyal to keep seeing the man who's determined to put me behind bars."

"Don't do this," A.J. said. Despite Elysia's light tone, it was obvious that she was serious. "Jake is just doing his job. He's already said he doesn't believe you killed anyone."

"He has a funny way of showing it."

"Arresting you was not his choice."

"That's easy to say."

A.J. took a deep breath and released it slowly. "I don't want to argue with you about this. You're my mother and I love you—and you obviously have my support or I wouldn't have risked my neck breaking and entering Dicky Massri's apartment with you today."

"Just entering." Elysia corrected.

"It's not funny, Mother. I also care for Jake. A lot. So don't ask me to choose because that is not a fair or loving thing to do to me."

Elysia made an exasperated sound. "Very well. But don't be surprised if *he* tries to force the issue."

The rest of the drive to Deer Hollow was completed in silence filled only by Tom Jones's *24 Hours*.

A cottontail rabbit darted out from the lush flower bed as A.J. let Monster out of the Land Rover, and the dog took off after it with unexpected energy. A.J. walked up the porch steps. A graceful statue of Kwan Yin stood amidst the purple and yellow irises lining the house. The sweet smells of evening drifted across the sunset-gilded meadow.

Inside the house A.J. played her messages while Elysia put the kettle on, but there was nothing from Jake. Nothing on A.J.'s cell either.

Well, he would be busy with the investigation, after all. And she was the one who had said it was an impossible situation and that they should take things slowly.

Her and her big mouth.

Elysia, watching her, said suddenly, "I've been thinking that perhaps I ought to contact Maddie."

For a moment A.J. couldn't remember who Maddie was, her own problems temporarily outweighing her mother's. Then it came back to her: Medea Sutherland. Her mother's wacko friend who was apparently up to her bushy eyebrows in this murder investigation. It was indeed a small world.

She sighed. "I think we should try to find a way to tell the police exactly what we discovered in Dicky's apartment and leave it to them from here on out."

"Oh, I'm sure the police already know about Maddie."

"Then what's the point of contacting her?"

Elysia looked vague. "This must be a distressing time for her. As her friend—"

"You don't even know for sure that she's Dicky's Medea."

"Trust me, pumpkin. I've one of my hunches on this."

One of her hunches? Next she was going to be referring to her little gray cells and twirling her imaginary mustache. A.J. managed to swallow several unproductive comments without choking, and said, "Mother, my relationship with Jake is complicated enough without this."

"I didn't say you had to be involved," Elysia said tartly. "I said *I* would contact my old friend and offer my condolences."

A.J.'s back was hurting. She was tired and she was disappointed that Jake had not called her—yes, despite the way they had left things the evening before. She missed him. A lot.

"If you think that's a wise idea," she managed to say evenly. She was proud of herself for not saying what *she* thought of the idea.

"Are you going to be all right?"

A.J. nodded. "I can manage. The shot helped." It would probably have helped a lot more if she hadn't tried diving out a window, but she managed to bite that comment back, too. Her mother hadn't kidnapped her; A.J. had been a willing—if not enthusiastic—party to the insanity.

Elysia patted her cheek sharply. "I'll call you in the morning, lovie. Don't worry about anything." And she was gone in a waft of mingled cigarette and Opium scent. The Land Rover roared into life in the front yard and then silence fell.

A.J. fixed dinner for herself and Monster. "It's just you and me tonight, big boy," she said.

Monster wagged his tail.

After dinner A.J. sat down with her aunt's manuscript.

What would Diantha have thought about the choices A.J. had met since inheriting Sacred Balance and the new life that had come with it?

Safe to say many of her choices would not have been her aunt's.

Life is loss. If we allow ourselves to care, to love, we must accept the pain that inevitably follows. Nothing lasts forever however much we wish otherwise. Yoga teaches us to concentrate on the here and now, on living within the moment. We focus on each breath we draw, and as we focus we become present and grounded in our bodies. Breath is the bridge between what is now and what is not. Grief is part of what is not, and when we are truly living in the moment we are releasing our grief and concentrating only what is now.

A.J. undressed and washed, climbing into the bed that had once been her aunt's. She listened to the sounds of the house settling down for the night, the crickets outside the window, the owl in the peach tree out back inquiring after his supper.

She wondered what Jake was doing.

Nine

The parking lot was full and classes were in session by the time A.J. arrived at Sacred Balance on Thursday morning. It appeared to be business as usual at the studio. She was glad of that, of course, but there was a tiny insecure part of her that wished things weren't running *quite* so smoothly without her.

She was moving slowly, but she was moving, and that was the good news. The bad news was there was no possible way she was going to be able to conduct her classes. That morning's attempt at Sun Salutation had made that much clear.

In a spirit of optimism A.J. had unfolded her yoga mat in the front room with its picture window view of the sun-flushed meadow. It was still a little too chilly these spring mornings to use the back patio as she did in the summer. A.J. sat down on her mat, breathing quietly.

Soft inhalations.

Soft exhalations.

She gathered herself to rise, and her back immediately spasmed. It was all A.J. could do not to cry. *Why* was this happening to her?

She struggled with her emotions for a few seconds and then was forced to admit that walking up the long staircase at Yoga Meridian had probably not been a good idea, and diving out the window of Dicky Masrai's apartment had probably been an even worse one.

Once again she was fighting the very tenets of yoga by trying to force her body to do as she wished rather than what was sensible.

Accordingly she arrived at the studio in a somewhat chastened frame of mind.

"Howdy there, stranger!" Emma greeted her from behind the front desk when A.J. pushed through the glass doors. "We weren't expecting you."

Emma was a short, slender, sixty-something black woman. Originally, concerned that Emma would not have the necessary energy or attitude for manning the front desk in a yoga studio, A.J. had been a little hesitant to hire her. It had turned out to be one of the best decisions she'd made. She was especially conscious of this as she remembered her visit to Yoga Meridian where every instructor and employee seemed to be under thirty and genetically airbrushed.

"I thought I'd try to catch up on some paperwork. I'm not really here," A.J. replied.

"Very metaphysical," Emma said. "Do I hold your calls?"

"No. Put them through."

There were not many calls, however, and A.J. was able to drink her tea and go through her e-mail in relative peace.

The harmonious sounds of cheerful voices and laughter in the main lobby informed her when the first sessions of the morning ended. She glanced up as someone—Lily—tapped on her door.

Ignoring that inward sinking feeling, A.J. smiled. "Come in," she invited. "How are things going?"

"Smoothly. Never better, as a matter of fact," Lily said with her usual tact. Belatedly, she asked, "How's your back?"

"It's getting there."

Lily's dark eyes appraised A.J. shrewdly. "I'm a little surprised to see you here, frankly. Are you sure this is a wise decision?"

"I won't be able to teach my courses, obviously, but there's no reason for me not to catch up on the administrative side of things."

Lily nodded, a little frown between her black eyebrows.

"Is there a problem?" A.J. asked, knowing it was a tactical mistake even as the words left her lips.

Lily drummed her fingers on the arm of her chair. "Since you've brought it up, yes," she said at last. "Don't you think it's a little absurd for someone with a bad back to be running a yoga studio? You're not exactly a great advertisement for us."

A.J. stared at the other woman in disbelief. "'Absurd'?"

Lily inclined her head.

"First of all, my back is much better these days, thanks to yoga, which should be some of the best advertisement around. Secondly, there's a lot more to the Sacred Balance philosophy than physical fitness."

"But that's my point," Lily said in the patient tone of one instructing a not-too-bright student. "Diantha left an

entire business empire. I don't see why you feel it's necessary for you to focus the majority of your attention on the
studio when there are so many other divisions that could
keep you entertained."

"Keep me *entertained*?"

Lily had the grace to look chagrined. "Maybe I didn't
put that as diplomatically as I could, but we both know
that the reality is—thanks to your inheritance—unlike the
rest of us, *you* no longer have to work. So doesn't it make
more sense for you to concentrate on some aspect of
Diantha's empire that you're better suited for? Your background is marketing. Wouldn't it be better for all concerned if you used those skills to develop and market our
sportswear and other merchandise lines—or the plans for
organic foods? Those things have all been completely ne-
glected since Di's passing."

"It was Aunt Di's wish that we co-manage. That we
work together in the studio."

Lily was shaking her head, repudiating this. "I loved
Di, but there's no question she was eccentric. And leaving
you Sacred Balance had to be one of the most eccentric
decisions of her life. In fact I firmly believe that if Di had
lived—"

"If I were you, I'd stop there."

Lily said coolly, "Why? We both know you can't fire
me. We're stuck with each other. Until one of us quits."

"I've offered to buy out your interest in the studio."

"I'm not going to sell out. This studio is my life."

"Then I'm not sure what it is you want."

The intercom buzzed and Emma said, "A.J., your
momma's on line one."

"Thanks, Emma." A.J. continued to wait for Lily to

state the true purpose of her visit, but Lily said nothing, simply staring at her in silent challenge.

The call rang through. After the second ring, A.J. said, "I have to take this."

Still weirdly, defiantly mute, Lily rose and left the office. She closed the door with a little bang.

A.J. realized her hands were shaking. Lily got under her skin like no one else on the planet, and A.J. wasn't even sure exactly why. She gave herself a moment and then picked up the phone.

Before she could speak, Elysia said, "Maddie has invited us to stay the weekend."

Her thoughts still on the argument with Lily, it took A.J. a few moments to register what her mother was saying. "Medea Sutherland has—Mother, what did you tell her?"

"Nothing any reasonable person could possibly object to," Elysia protested. "I merely said she'd been on my mind lately, which is perfectly true. She popped out with the invitation with nary a nudge from me. I think she's lonely."

Be careful what you wish for, Maddie, thought A.J.

"What did she say about Dicky?"

"Nothing. I didn't ask, and she didn't volunteer any information."

"But that's strange. Is it possible the police don't know about her?"

"I don't know."

A.J. gnawed uneasily on her lip. "Have you heard from Mr. Meagher?"

"No. I was thinking we could drive down tomorrow—Friday afternoon."

A.J. was shaking her head, rejecting this idea instantly. "I can't just take off for the weekend."

"I don't see why not. You can't be much use at the studio right now."

A.J. controlled her instinctive response. "Thank you, Mother. I don't just conduct classes, you know."

"But your minions are so well-trained, pumpkin. And it's nice for them to be out from under your iron fist once in a while."

"My *what?*"

Elysia chuckled.

Who wouldn't be looking forward to a weekend of this? And under the roof of a potential murderess, to boot. "Mother, I don't think you've thought this through. I know she's an old friend, but what if Medea did kill Dicky?"

Clearly amused, Elysia returned, "You don't remember Maddie very well, do you?"

"I don't remember her at all. I've seen her movies, though."

"Then you'll have to take my word for it. Maddie is no more a murderess than I am. But keeping me safe gives you an added incentive to come on this little jaunt, yes?"

As dearly as A.J. longed to say *no*, Elysia had a point, and unfortunately it seemed only too apparent that A.J. was not necessary to the smooth operation of Sacred Balance.

"What time tomorrow?" she grumbled.

"Let's say eleven. I'll treat you to lunch and we can discuss our strategy." Elysia was ever gracious in victory.

A.J. agreed morosely, hung up, and went to find Lily. She found that the other woman had left the studio for an early break, and thwarted once again, A.J. returned to her own office.

There had to be more she could do even if she was sitting on the sidelines. A.J. opened her laptop again and went into her mail program hunting for the e-mails her mother had sent while on vacation in Egypt. She found them without too much difficulty and read over them, curiously inspecting the attached photos with new attention.

Even now they did not seem particularly revealing. The main point of interest from A.J.'s perspective was that Elysia never mentioned Dicky, although he appeared in picture after picture.

Perfectly symmetrical bone structure, a wide, white grin, shining black eyes. No question Dakarai Massri had been a very handsome young man; A.J. had to give him that much.

She tried to cast her memory back to Elysia's first mention of Dicky. She thought it had been shortly after her mother's return from Egypt, but that had been a difficult and stressful time—right after Nicole Manning had been killed. A.J.'s memories were fuzzy; she'd had a lot on her mind. She recalled she had commented on the attractive young man who appeared in so many of Elysia's photos and Elysia had been vague—deliberately so, A.J. realized now. One thing she did remember was that Elysia had mentioned Dicky working for the Supreme Council of Antiquities.

Had he left the SCA after his decision to move to the States or had something happened at the SCA to precipitate that decision?

A.J. initiated a web search. She found the SCA without

much trouble. It appeared to be a completely legitimate
branch of the Egyptian Ministry of Culture originally established in 1859. Located in Cairo, the SCA was responsible for protecting and managing the cultural heritage of
Egypt. That meant everything from restoring historical
monuments to the recovery of stolen antiquities; she read
an article on the SCA's attempts to have the Rosetta Stone
and the bust of Nefertiti returned from the foreign muse-
ums currently housing them.

It sounded like important work. Not the kind of profes-
sion a scheming blackmailer would opt for, but perhaps
the SCA had merely been his day job.

Locating a phone number at the bottom of the official
website for the SCA, A.J. spent the next few hours trying
to find someone who knew of Dakarai Massri. Given the
six-hour time difference, some long distance problems,
and a bit of failure-to-communicate, she didn't get far beyond verifying that Dicky had indeed been employed by
the SCA for a time.

By the time she was finally willing to concede defeat
for the day, it was after two o'clock and she was starving.
She went next door to see if Lily was back from lunch.
Lily had returned but she was upstairs teaching another
class.

A.J. decided she could wait to have another unpleasant
run-in with her co-manager until Monday. Packing her
laptop, she went to the front lobby to tell Emma she would
be out for the rest of the week.

As she knew she wouldn't feel like cooking, she decided to stop for lunch on her way out of town, pulling
into the parking lot of the Blue Bridge Pub, a new place
she and Jake had talked about trying out.

The pub was surprisingly crowded—although maybe

it wasn't that surprising, as any new restaurant in Stillbrook tended to draw a lot of business for the first few weeks after opening.

A.J. was led to a comfortable high-back, leather-lined booth against the wall. She glanced over the menu, ordered Greek spinach salad with feta cheese and a hot oil dressing, and then studied the artfully placed copper dishes and molds adorning the dark-paneled walls while she waited for her meal.

Her idle gaze fell on a familiar set of shoulders and sleek, dark head. She registered the fact that the shoulders and head belonged to Jake at approximately the same moment she realized that he was having lunch with a slender, attractive young woman about her own age.

It gave her an odd jolt. Not that there was anything wrong with Jake having lunch with someone of the female persuasion. She certainly had male friends who she occasionally lunched with. She tried to think of one and came up with Simon Crider, one of the instructors at the studio. Well, and Andy, her ex-husband. Jake hadn't objected too much when Andy had spent several weeks with A.J. the previous summer while he was going through a rough patch.

She tried to scrutinize Jake's companion without appearing to stare.

The woman had wide light eyes and brown hair artfully streaked with blonde. Her smile was very white. She smiled a lot. While she was not pretty exactly, she had a certain wholesome sex appeal.

A.J. watched them for a few seconds with an odd, uneasy sensation. She told herself not to be an idiot, but there was nothing like having been the victim of a cheating husband to hone a woman's instincts, and even from behind, watching the curve of Jake's lean cheek crease in a slight smile, watching the attentive tilt of his head as he listened to the woman, A.J. knew this was not a long lost sister or a former partner from his days in uniform.

Of course, what she should do—the normal thing— would be to get up and walk right over there and say hello.

So why wasn't she doing that?

The waitress arrived with her lunch, and A.J. managed to eat a few bites of salad before her gaze was drawn inexorably back to Jake and his companion. They were laughing. The woman reached over and rested her hand briefly on Jake's arm.

A wave of cold nausea washed through A.J. She told herself not to overreact, but she knew her instinct was not wrong. There was definitely something between them.

She tried to decide what to do. If the situation between her and Jake were as usual, she would simply go over there and say hello. But with matters strained as they were . . .

As this thought took form in A.J.'s mind, Jake—as though feeling the gaze burning between his shoulder blades—glanced around. He did a double take. And then he rose and came over to A.J.'s table.

A.J. dredged up a smile.

Jake didn't even try. "I didn't see you come in," he said. He didn't seem guilty, exactly, but he did look uncomfortable.

"You were otherwise occupied." She winced internally at both the words and the light, cool tone. The last thing she wanted to appear was jealous or insecure. She and Jake did not have a commitment. They didn't even have an agreement not to see other people.

"I'm having lunch with an old friend."

A.J. considered and discarded a variety of responses. She settled on the all-purpose, "Oh?"

Belatedly, though only by a second or two, Jake asked, "Would you like to join us for dessert?"

"I don't think so." Somehow, despite A.J.'s best intentions, it came out sounding like an action hero's line seconds before he blew the bad guy away.

She couldn't read Jake's expression at all, and he seemed to be having a similar problem with her. He said, "Well, at least let me introduce you."

"Of course!" It came out far too brightly, but she was oversteering, trying to make up for the snippiness of her earlier response.

Scrubbing her teeth with her tongue in search of any stray bits of spinach, A.J. slipped out of the booth and followed Jake through the crowded tables.

"How is your back?" he asked as an afterthought. "Are you back at work now?"

"It's better," she said. There wasn't time for more as they had reached Jake's table.

Jake's companion smiled confidently up at A.J. Her eyes were a strikingly light shade somewhere between green and blue.

"A.J. this is J—" Jake broke off, looking confused, and the woman smiled that frank, white smile and offered her hand.

"Francesca Cox. But everyone calls me 'Chess.'"

"Nice to meet you, Chess." Chess? What kind of nickname was "Chess"? Affected was what it was.

"I've heard so much about you." Chess was smiling.

Maybe it was intended as a pleasantry—well, it was almost certainly intended as a pleasantry, what was the matter with her? She was *not* this insecure. But it did bother A.J. that Chess apparently knew all about her, and she'd had no idea of Chess's existence until that instant.

A.J. asked with all the cordiality she could muster, "Are you visiting or are you new to Stillbrook?"

"I've just moved here, yes."

"How nice! Welcome to the neighborhood." *Welcome to the neighborhood?* Break out the zippered cardigans. A.J. had morphed into Mister Rogers.

"It's a lovely little town," Chess said. She smiled at Jake. He, meanwhile, was doing his best impersonation of one of those Easter Island statues. Why *did* he look so . . . so stony if everything was on the up and up?

"It is lovely, isn't it? You should see it in the autumn. Where are you from originally?" A.J. inquired.

Chess's eyes flickered. "Oh, I move around a lot. I admit that's one of the charms of a small town like yours. The idea of putting down roots, of getting to know your neighbors, of building a real home: it's very . . . alluring."

A.J. heard herself give one of those terse murmur-laughs that sounded uncannily like Elysia when she was displeased and barely trying to hide it.

"What do you do, A.J.?"

Apparently Jake hadn't shared all the pertinent details if Chess didn't know something this basic. Then again, she was probably just making conversation. Someone needed to.

A.J. replied, "I run a yoga studio."

"Really? Now I wouldn't have guessed that."

"What do you do, Chess?"

"I'm a travel writer."

"That sounds like fun," A.J. said politely.

"It is mostly."

A.J. checked her wristwatch. "Gosh, is it that time? I've got to pay my check and run."

Literally.

Jake said woodenly, "I'll walk you out."

"Nice to meet you, A.J.," Chess said cordially.

A.J. paid her check and walked out of the dining room with Jake a silent presence behind her.

She knew it was unreasonable to be angry. She reminded herself that they didn't—did *not*—have an exclusive arrangement.

As they reached the lobby front door, she said, "Chess seems pleasant. How long have you known her?"

Never one to waste time on polite chitchat, Jake said, "I've been meaning to call."

A.J. couldn't read anything in his expression. "Well, things are weird right now. I realize that better than anyone."

"They are, yeah." He raked an impatient hand through his hair. "Look, we need to talk. Are you going to be home tomorrow night?"

She hadn't made her mind up about going with Elysia until that very instant, but A.J. suddenly realized how much she did not have the emotional energy for whatever this talk was about. "Actually, I'm going out of town."

His face tightened. "Come on, A.J."

"I'm not playing games," she said. "I'm going out of town with Mother."

"How far out of town?"

"Sussex County. Andover, to be precise. Don't worry. She's not trying to make a break for it. She's going to stay with a friend for the weekend, that's all." She added, "If you want to talk, we can always use the phone."

She didn't like the expression that crossed his face.

"This might be a little complicated for a phone call."

"Then I guess I'll see you when I get back."

Jake nodded, looked away. Staring into the distance he said tersely, "I'm not enjoying this, you know."

"I can see it. That makes two of us."

Ten

❦

A grinning skeleton leaned against the etched glass front of the long-case grandfather clock in the long reception hall of Medea Sutherland's restored Victorian mansion. The black-flocked velvet walls were lined with horror movie posters with titles like *The Devouring*, *The Girl in the Grave*, *She-Wolf*.

"That's Wee Geordie," Medea said cheerfully, following A.J.'s gaze.

"Please tell me you found him on a movie set somewhere."

Medea—Maddie Sutherland—laughed her unexpectedly raucous laugh. She was tall and mournful looking with gaunt features and black eyes beneath Joan Crawford eyebrows. In her black trousers and black turtleneck, she could have played the dour housekeeper in any number of low-budget scary movies, but in her heyday she had been cast exclusively as demon-possessed vixens or terror-stricken ingénues.

"A.J.'s afraid you dug him up in the garden," Elysia remarked, and Medea laughed that deep laugh again.

"I've found interesting things in the garrrden, but no skeletons so far. Not human ones, anyway!" While most of Medea's native Scottish accent had been trained out of her, she retained a small but definite Scottish burr, that charming way of rolling the *R*s. "Let me take you up to your rooms and then I'll give you a wee tourrr of the house."

One thing for sure, Medea seemed in good spirits. If she was aware of Dicky Massri's death, it clearly wasn't ruining her day. She led them briskly down the long reception hall adorned with artfully placed fake cobwebs, gilt-framed mirrors with cracked glass, and a huge chandelier with flicker bulbs.

A.J. exchanged a glance with her mother. Elysia seemed to be taking it all in stride. The house was immaculate, so it wasn't a housekeeping issue, just some very funky ideas about home décor. Medea had to be the oldest goth A.J. had met.

They reached the staircase to the second level and A.J. examined the gallery of old photographs and tintypes. "Are these your family?" she inquired.

"No, no," Medea replied. "I just like the look of their faces."

A.J. had no particular response to that, but if she had, it would have been lost as a small, furry creature came sliding down the banister. For a moment she thought it was a rat, although it looked more like a weasel. She let go of the banister and just missed stepping into Elysia, who had stopped on the stairs.

"What on earth?" Elysia stared as the black-and-white creature streaked past. "Was that a skunk?"

Medea chuckled at the very idea of such craziness. "It's a ferrrret."

"A ferret?"

"That's right, hen. Her name is Morrrag."

Morag the ferrrret had safely reached the lower level and scampered away into the gloom. A.J. and Elysia followed Medea as she continued the trek upstairs. They reached the top landing where the statue of a mournful marble lady weeping into a hanky seemed to be commiserating with A.J. over her weekend plans.

Medea led the way down the hallway to their separate bedrooms.

"You share the bath. It adjoins both bedrooms." Medea opened the white door leading into the large bathroom, but A.J.'s attention was riveted to the graveyard scene painted across the far wall. No, not painted. The wall was covered in a full-sized decorative vinyl photograph of a mournful graveyard.

"Uh . . ." she began, but she was talking to herself. The other two women had moved down the hallway to the next bedroom. She dropped her carryall with relief. She had insisted on carrying it upstairs, but it hadn't done her back any good.

The rest of the room was relatively ordinary: forest green walls and white trim, a large canopy bed with bone white draperies, green and white globe lamps, and a large mirror with a dragon frame and candleholder.

A.J. followed her mother and Medea; she was almost looking forward to seeing the next stage set—because that's what these macabre rooms seemed like: elaborate, tongue-in-cheek movie sets.

Elysia's room was minus a mural but the gloomy paintings on the gray walls more than made up for it. The bed in her room was lacking a canopy, but it was an enormous, black, iron affair that suggested a torture device or a birdcage—although the fluffy duvet was a cozy touch. There were a couple of gargoyle wall sconces and a table by the bay windows that seemed to be of a gargoyle in the pose of *The Thinker*. A.J. couldn't help feeling that anything a gargoyle put that much mental energy into would not be good.

Medea was still talking cheerfully about the repairs and renovations to the mansion, most of which she had done herself.

"Very thrifty, petal," Elysia remarked, when she could get a word in edgewise. "Er, what's happened to . . . what's his name? Your lord and master. Will we meet him this evening?"

Medea's sharp features darkened. "I told you about that, surely?"

"No. What?"

"I didn't tell you? I thought I wrote you?"

"I'm sure I'd have remembered."

"I divorrrced him, the villain."

"Oh dear," Elysia said mildly. "That was sudden. What happened?"

"It wasn't nearly sudden enough. Ought to have known better at my age."

"What happened?" Elysia persisted.

Medea straightened the head of a small, grinning gargoyle wall sconce. "He was nothing but a forrrtune hunter."

As Elysia made the appropriate noises, her gaze found and held A.J.'s. "That's terrible. What was his name again?

Dick . . . something, wasn't it? How long did the marriage last?"

But Medea shook her head sharply, the subject seemingly closed. Elysia raised her shoulders in a ghost of a shrug.

Medea, once again in tour guide mode, led them back downstairs pointing out the architectural points of interest in the house as they went. One thing A.J. liked was that nearly every room had bookshelves, mostly filled with works of science fiction, fantasy, and horror.

"Back in 1890, the house had both electric and gas lighting. Lightbulbs weren't fully developed, you see, and didnae cast enough illumination to be the primary source of light. You can see the old gas lines all through the house."

Medea pointed to a place on the hardwood floor where the heating pipes fed the radiator in the parlor.

"Those don't still work, do they?" Elysia asked, sounding alarmed for the first time.

Medea laughed heartily at the idea. "The old gas lines were disconnected long ago, although I'd have liked to have the old gas lamps working in a few spots. It'd throw a very nice warm light."

Ah yes. The better to illuminate the fake cobwebs and plastic spiders.

"You don't have a television?" A.J. inquired.

"Och, I don't have time for such nonsense! There's too much work to be done and too many good books to read."

"Ah," Elysia said. Once again her gaze met A.J.'s, and once again A.J. knew exactly what her mother was thinking. Assuming they had the right Medea, Maddie was not aware that Dakarai was dead or that Elysia was suspected of killing him—*unless* Medea had killed him herself and was playing a clever game with them. A.J. didn't quite rule that out. Medea certainly had a dark and playful side; *eccentric* was a pallid word for it.

Medea finished showing them the house—the restoration work she had done was truly impressive even if her ultimate aim seemed to be to turn the place into an upscale haunted mansion—and then they went into the back garden, followed by the ferret Morag.

"Isn't this lovely," Elysia murmured faintly. "A shade garden."

It was indeed dark and shady in the very large and very overgrown garden. The gateposts were made of small wooden coffins topped by resin wolf skulls. There were no flowers, just grass and ivy and green vines. It looked like the sort of garden Edward Gorey might have designed had he abandoned illustrating and gone into the landscaping business. A variety of dark stone urns, pointy obelisks, and odd statues were strategically placed. A.J. recognized what appeared to be a likeness of the Minotaur and, across the lawn, a bronze version of Kali. Toward the back of the garden was a large plot lined by a knee-high, wrought iron fence as though for a vegetable garden, although it was too dark for most vegetables to thrive. Mushrooms might do well. Toadstools.

They watched the ferret scurry across the grass and disappear through the fence.

"She's visiting Angus," Medea said with grim satisfaction.

"Angus?"

"My Persian cat. They were grrreat friends. Angus crossed last month."

A.J. stared at the fenced square and then it clicked.

A miniature graveyard; a pet cemetery. "That's a grave-yard?"

"Aye." Medea placed the pitcher of lemonade she had carried outside on the table and the three of them sat down and watched Morag weaving her swift way through the statuary and greenery. "The final resting place for ma wee furry friends." Gloom settled on her like rain clouds on Ben Lomond.

"This is pleasant," Elysia chimed in, in an apparent effort to dispel the doldrums. She sipped her lemonade. "I'm glad you invited us, petal. Makes a nice change, doesn't it?"

She looked straight at A.J., delivering her cue. "Yes!" A.J. said enthusiastically to cover the fact that she had been thinking she was out of her mind to have agreed to this weekend.

"It's nice to have company. It's a bit lonely sometimes out here on my own," Medea admitted with seeming reluctance.

Elysia said casually, "I can relate only too well. It's lovely having A.J. living so close these days."

"Did you finally give up the house in London?"

"No. I've been thinking of letting it go, though."

This was news to A.J. Although she and her mother had been getting along very well since she had moved to New Jersey, the idea of being permanently in each other's pockets was a little disconcerting. Or was it? Maybe it was . . . reassuring. It was just that she was not in the habit of relying on her mother, having spent most of her life learning to not rely on her.

The two older women chatted about people and places unfamiliar to A.J. It was not that she was disinterested, but she had a lot on her mind. Her attention wandered.

She tuned back in to hear Elysia inquire casually, "What was his name, petal? Your handsome young villain?"

Medea's face took on that unattractive flush again. "Dicky. Dakarai, actually. He was Egyptian."

Elysia's gaze slid to A.J.'s. A.J. knew exactly what she was thinking. "Dakarai" was not like John or Kevin or Bill. The idea of two Egyptian men named Dakarai running around New Jersey romancing wealthy widows was pretty hard to believe.

"It's a shame," Elysia said. She suggested casually, "You met him on that cruise you took a few years ago, didn't you?"

"Aye."

Bingo.

Gloomily, Medea reached a hand out to the ferret, who had scampered up the table legs and popped through the umbrella hole in the table. Now the ferret was investigating the lemonade pitcher. She nipped gently at Medea's fingers. "You miss him, pet, don't you?" Medea flicked the ferret's nose and then reached for her lemonade with the air of one drowning her sorrows.

Elysia was shooting a certain commanding look A.J.'s way. A.J. couldn't figure out what her mother wanted. She raised her shoulders and Elysia gave her The Look again.

Hoping she was on the right track, and not exactly sure what her mother was up to, A.J. said, "Why, that's an odd coincidence!"

Elysia offered a tiny smile of approval before saying, as though the thought had never occurred, "Yes, that *is* strange. You wouldn't happen to have a photo of him, would you?"

"Angus? Aye."

"Not Angus, petal. Dicky. Your ex."

Brow furrowed, Medea gave it some thought. "Why?"

"Because a *most* unpleasant thought has occurred to me."

It looked like the unpleasantness was catching. For a lengthy few seconds Medea stared at Elysia, then she scooped up the ferret and nodded at A.J. and Elysia to follow her.

They trooped back into the house and Medea led the way to a side room painted in yellow and black—a color scheme that had all the appeal of a swarm of bees. She dropped Morag to the carpet, and the ferret darted away behind what appeared to be a marble statue of Medusa—or perhaps it was another goddess having a really bad hair day. Medea rummaged through the drawers of a tall secretary. Sheets of sandpaper and bills fell out along with photos and note cards.

"Here we are." Medea handed the photograph to Elysia who stared at it for several seconds. She handed it to A.J.

The photograph showed a tanned and happy-looking Medea in the loose embrace of a handsome and virile-looking Egyptian young enough to be her son. The young man also looked happy, though not nearly as radiant as Medea.

Though the photo was a few years old, there was no mistaking Dicky Massri, and though she had been prepared for it, A.J. murmured, "Good lord."

Elysia said crisply, "Petal, I have some disturbing news."

Medea's brows drew together as she waited for Elysia to find the words. A.J. could see her mother considering and abandoning various approaches.

"There doesn't seem to be an easy way to say this," she said at last. "I knew this young man of yours. Knew him rather well." When Medea still said nothing, Elysia clarified, "I met him when I was in Egypt last summer."

Medea's eyes seemed to start from her head. She opened her mouth and then closed it.

"I'm afraid I made the same mistake that . . . er . . . you did, petal."

Silence.

"He could be a charming scallywag." Elysia half-swallowed the word. A.J. almost felt sorry for her although she couldn't help feeling her mother had brought it all on herself. "I didn't go so far as to *marry* him, but—"

Elysia broke off, interrupted by Medea's roar of laughter.

They dined beneath a flickering chandelier that looked like it was straight out of the Vincent Price Collection. Keeping in mind that Medea had done most of the home repairs herself, A.J. couldn't help an occasional uneasy glance at the bronze rosette medallion in the ceiling, sincerely hoping it was not going to give way anytime soon. She could have sworn she heard the occasional faint cracking of plaster—or perhaps the whisper came from the ghostly woodland scene that decorated the walls of the long, narrow room: tall pale trees and silvery mist on another of those decorative wall coverings.

But while Medea might have had a macabre sense of interior design, there was nothing wrong with her culinary instincts. Dinner was fabulous.

Barley soup with porcini mushrooms started off the

meal, followed by seared scallop salad with asparagus and scallions. The main course was roasted veal loin with mashed potatoes. For dessert there was bittersweet chocolate tart with coffee mascarpone cream.

Between courses A.J. heard abbreviated versions of her mother and Medea's wild youth as fledgling actresses in the early seventies.

"Och, hen, remember that time you and Dennis Waterman . . . ?"

"And who was being linked with Patrick McNee in the press, petal?"

These recollections were followed by gales of laughter.

"What about Bradley Meagher? Is that old fox still waiting in the wings, then?"

Elysia's smile faded. "No, no. Actually, we're just good friends."

Medea snorted. "Tell me another." She studied Elysia with an unexpectedly worldly gleam in her dark eyes, but then changed the subject. "D'you ever think of going back on the stage?"

"All the time!"

More hilarity.

A.J. sincerely hoped Medea was not a murderess because the more she saw of her, the more she liked her. Yes, she was an oddball, but some of the most interesting people were.

Quietly sipping her wine, which was also excellent, A.J. observed both women. Medea, still recovering from the shock of learning that Dicky was dead, downed scotch all through dinner, growing progressively more cheerful and bright. Elysia stuck to sparkling mineral water despite the glasses of wine Medea pressed on her. A.J. experienced the usual tension of watching her mother around alcohol, but Elysia showed no sign of struggling against temptation.

Over dessert she skillfully managed to steer the discussion back to Dicky, and Medea, now well and truly lubricated, seemed to let her guard down once and for all.

"No fool like an auld fool!"

She and Elysia shared a giggle over memories A.J. suspected they would regret her overhearing. She tried not to listen too closely, but it wasn't easy.

"He was a delicious young rascal," Elysia admitted. "And those back rubs!"

Medea murmured agreement and A.J. resisted the temptation to cover her ears and say "Lalalalalalalala!"

"Hard to believe it's been two whole years." Medea sighed. "Sometimes I think . . . well. Water under the bridge."

"Speaking of water," Elysia said lightly, "how did you happen to pick that particular cruise?"

Medea shook her head. "I didn't. I won it. All the arrangements were made for me."

"That's an awfully nice prize. What contest was that?"

Medea sketched a broad, vague gesture. "Some sort of sweepstakes thingie."

A.J. asked Elysia, "You didn't win your cruise trip in a contest, did you?"

"No. Everyone I knew seemed to have been on a cruise, and I was thinking it might be fun to get away for a time. I think my hairstylist recommended the cruise line." She said to Medea, "Are you saying the sweepstakes prize covered the cost of everything?"

"It covered the cost of the cruise. I had to pay my own airfare."

"Was there anything odd about the cruise?" A.J. inquired.

Medea shook her head. "Not that I recall. Other than falling in love and getting married, no." She sighed nostalgically. "Wonderful nosh."

"How exactly *did* you happen to fall in love?"

Elysia and Medea exchanged looks. "No sense of romance this younger generation," Elysia said sadly. "A.J. uses her Palm Berry to schedule her beau."

"I don't use a Palm Berry, Mother. Whatever the heck that is. I use my Palm Pre. Anyway, I'm just wondering how Maddie managed to get married in a foreign country when she was only there for a cruise?"

"Eight sunny days and seven starrry nights," Medea said. "That's how it happened. After the cruise ended, I stayed on in Egypt until we could be married in a civil ceremony. Then I came home; I was in the middle of renovating the house. Dicky was supposed to follow when his immigration status was resolved."

"What happened?"

"He continued to come up with excuses for why he couldnae come—meanwhile always asking me for more money. Finally, I had to face facts. The young scoundrel had no intention of joining me here."

"So you divorced him?"

"Aye."

"How did he take your decision?" A.J. questioned.

Medea's mouth twisted. "He tried to talk me out of it. Then he suggested that he fly here for a visit so we could try to work things out."

"Didn't you want that?"

"I wanted it. I sent him the airfare, but he never booked the flight. When I taxed him with it, he said he'd had to give it to his mother for an operation."

"The old ailing mother routine," Elysia murmured. "He really hadn't much imagination."

"Shameless is what he was." Medea was grim. "So I made my mind up and I divorced him."

"Did he ever try to blackmail you?" A.J. asked.

Medea looked confused. "Over what?"

Good question. They had been legally married, after all. "I don't know. Did you ever hear from him again?"

"No. That I never did." Medea's expression was bleak.

"Did you want to?" A.J. asked, surprised.

Medea's gimlet dark eyes studied her. "Aye." She reached for her scotch.

Eleven

❦

"I believe her." A.J. paused in the doorway adjoining the bathroom and Elysia's bedroom. She brushed a fake spiderweb out of her face.

Elysia, sitting at the gargoyle table next to the window that looked over the back garden, briskly laid playing cards across the marble tabletop. "About what, pumpkin?"

"I don't think Maddie killed Dicky."

Elysia made a small, dismissive sound and set the remaining cards in the deck aside. "Of course she didn't kill Dicky."

"There's no 'of course' about it, Mother. She certainly had motive. A much better motive than you. And she's eccentric. She makes you look like a solid citizen."

Elysia sniffed and turned a card over.

"It's possible that she caught sight of him one day, realized that he had moved to this country after all—and was up to his old tricks—and in the shock of the moment, killed him."

"In my front garden?"

"It's possible."

"I thought you said you believed her?"

"I do."

"You saw the way she reacted when I told her Dicky was dead. It was obvious the news came as a complete bombshell."

"Maybe. But she's an actress, after all."

"She was never *that* good an actress," Elysia stated with ruthless candor.

A.J. shrugged, stuck her toothbrush back in her mouth, and returned to the sink to finish cleaning her teeth.

"What are you doing, anyway?" she called after she had rinsed, spat, and dried her face.

"Playing solitaire."

"Why?"

"I often play solitaire when I can't sleep."

A.J. returned to her mother's bedroom door. "Do you often have trouble sleeping?"

Elysia shrugged a bony shoulder and scooped up a couple of cards.

A.J. studied her, troubled. There were so many things about her mother that she still didn't know after all this time. But then they had been strangers to each other for nearly thirty years.

"Can I ask you something?" she asked.

Elysia raised her brows, her attention still apparently on the cards.

"When you and Daddy split up for that year and we stayed in Stillbrook . . . what happened?"

Elysia's hand froze on the card she was selecting. Then

she picked it up, checked it, and laid it back down. "You know what happened. We decided that we had made a mistake and we reconciled." She added firmly, "And we lived happily ever after."

A.J. checked this against her adolescent memories. It was true that no matter how miserable her parents were, they had always been more miserable apart.

Her recollection of that particular time was especially vague. She had been the usual gawky, self-absorbed, and insecure teen—and that year had been hell on earth. Stillbrook had been the place her family came to vacation; living there, attending school there, was a very different thing. Without her father's stabilizing presence the only person she'd had to rely on was Aunt Diantha.

But there was no point dragging up these dreary memories. The past was just that; she was committed to living in the moment.

So A.J. was surprised to hear herself ask, "What happened between you and Stella Borin?"

Elysia continued to check cards and turn them back over. At last, she said evenly, "Do you really want to know?"

"Yes."

"Your father had an affair with her."

"With *Stella*?"

It was like being told you were related to Porky Pig— absolutely and ludicrously beyond the realm of possibility. But one look at her mother's face told her it was not a joke.

"With the Stella Borin who lives down the road from me?" As though her mother might have confused her Stella Borins.

Elysia reaffirmed crisply, "Your father had an affair with Stella Borin."

"How?"

Even Elysia was thrown by that one. "*How*? All the usual ways, I suppose." She sighed. "Your father owned Starlight Farm before we married. His family used to come up for the summer when he was a boy, and when he became successful he bought Starlight Farm. That's how we met. I was on holiday, staying with Di." A faint reminiscent smile touched her mouth.

A.J. said tentatively, "And he knew Stella from . . . before?"

"Yes." Elysia made a face. "I can only imagine she was very different in those days."

Maybe. Maybe not. Stella might not have been a beauty queen, but she was kind and loyal and direct. She was also refreshingly uncomplicated, and that alone had probably held charm for A.J.'s father. Not that A.J. was foolish enough to say so.

What she did say was, "And you think they had an affair?"

"I know they did."

"Daddy admitted it?"

"Of course not."

"Stella admitted it?"

"Not on your life."

"Then . . ."

"My hunches are never wrong." That seemed to be the Master Detective's final word on the subject. Elysia went back to cheating at solitaire. But as A.J. turned to her own room, Elysia said levelly, "I forgave your father because I knew that I—or more precisely, my drinking—was to blame. I never had any doubt that he loved me, but I was not . . . easy to live with."

That was putting it mildly. Still, it was a shock to think of her father . . . in fact it seemed wiser to set that aside for later examination. A.J. had asked. Now she knew. It certainly explained that while Elysia could forgive A.J.'s father, she still felt strong enmity for Stella. Elysia had never been of the forgive and forget philosophy.

"Good night, Mother."

"Nightie-night, lovie."

Returning to her bedroom, A.J. lay down on the large canopied bed and cautiously attempted her evening asanas. She did some very careful stretching, then, tucking her knees into her chest in Happy Baby pose, she inhaled and spread her knees, gently pulling her flexed legs toward her underarms. She could feel the tug on her lower back and across her shoulders but there was no pain, just slight discomfort.

Shins perpendicular to the mattress, A.J. contracted her feet, pulling gently and creating resistance as she drew her knees toward the sheets. So far, so good.

Pressing her buttocks into the mattress, A.J. lengthened her spine. She relaxed her neck and the base of her skull. Holding the pose, she breathed deeply and evenly for one full minute.

When A.J. finally relaxed in the sheets, she felt triumphant. She'd done it. She had finally managed to successfully complete a full series of asanas for the first time since injuring her back. Yes, these were by far the easiest of the asanas, but she *was* healing. All her previous work had not been in vain. It was simply a matter of patience and care. Body and mind at peace, she closed her eyes and let herself drift to sleep.

"**Wake** *up!*" a voice hissed against her ear. A.J.'s eyes jerked open. She was confusedly aware that she was in an unfamiliar bedroom, that it was very late, and that her mother was whispering to her.

"Wha—?"

"Shhhh! There's someone in the garden!"

A.J. sat up fast, biting back the exclamation of pain at her unwary movement. Elysia was already over at the window, peering through a crack in the heavy draperies.

A.J. joined her, her own eyes searching the wooded darkness below. "Is he still there?"

"I think so." Elysia shifted so that A.J. could peer out, too.

"Where?"

"By that far wall."

A.J. stared but it was impossible to discern one distinct shadow among so many. "Are you sure?"

Elysia nodded. Her own gaze seemed glued to the yard below.

Long seconds passed. A.J. became aware of how cold the wooden floor was beneath her bare feet, how much her back hurt, how tired she was. "Are you sure you weren't dreaming? I don't see anyone out there."

Her mother reminded her of a bristling terrier, tense and pointy profile silhouetted by starlight. She didn't say anything.

"Are you sure you weren't—?"

Elysia made an exasperated noise. "I'm going down to check."

A.J. grabbed her wrist. "What do you mean, you're going down to check? You're not going out there! If you really think someone is lurking in the garden, we'll call the police."

Elysia tried to free herself. "That's the last thing we

want to do. We need to follow this person, whoever he—or she—is."

"You're not on an episode of *221B Baker Street* now. If someone really *is* down there, they could be dangerous. This could have something to do with Dicky's death."

"*If* someone is down there?" Elysia said dangerously.

"I haven't seen anyone so far."

"He probably sneaked off while we stood here debating it!"

"If you're sure someone is—or was—down there, I'll call the police." A.J. turned away and this time Elysia grabbed *her* wrist.

"You can't call the police without talking to Maddie."

"What? Why not?"

"It's . . . bad form. Bad etiquette."

"Says who?"

"It simply is. It's up to one's host or hostess—"

"Mother, this is ridiculous. If there's a prowler, we need to call the police. I can't believe we're even discussing this. You can go wake Maddie up while I phone."

"No, no," Elysia insisted. "We'll need to ask her first."

"I thought you were worried about this possible prowler getting away?"

Elysia's shoulders relaxed as she glanced back at the window. "I think it's moot at this point. I think he's gone."

"You're not making any sense." A.J. stared at her mother's shadowed face. "You don't want the police to know about Maddie."

"She's the only lead I have," Elysia said fiercely. "If the plods come barging in here and start interrogating her, she'll clam up. I know her. She doesn't like or trust coppers. And if that happens we'll lose the only connection we have to Dicky's blackmailing history."

A.J. couldn't believe they were truly having this debate. "We can't conceal a witness."

"She's not a witness."

"A suspect. Whatever she is, we can't conceal her."

"But we don't have to hand her over to the coppers."

A.J. looked worriedly from the window to her mother's rigid form. "We're not detectives. We don't know what we're doing. We might make things worse for you."

"This prowler probably had nothing to do with Dicky. He's probably just an ordinary, garden variety burglar."

"Well, he's certainly been in the garden long enough." A.J. grabbed her bathrobe from the foot of the bed. "Okay, let's wake Maddie and she can decide if she wants to call the police or not."

They hurried out into the hall, feeling their way in the dark. Something warm and alive scurried out from under A.J.'s foot. She stifled a yell.

She gasped, "That ferret!"

A small narrow form glimmered palely along the floorboard and then darted down the staircase ahead of them.

They reached the top of the stairs, groping cautiously for the railing. A.J. asked, "Where is Maddie's room in relation to ours?"

"I'm not sure." Elysia brushed past her, moving swiftly down the staircase. "You have a look for it while I check out the garden."

"What? We've already been through this!" But A.J. was talking to the empty darkness. She swore and made her halting way down the stairs in pursuit of Elysia, who had fled like a ghost through the uncertain light.

There was no sign of her on the ground floor. A.J. stumbled through the squares of moonlight and shadow until she found the dining room. She snatched the poker from the fireplace and continued through the empty rooms and out onto the sun porch. She closed the door softly behind her to keep the ferret from getting out.

A few yards ahead, she could see the spectral form of Elysia moving along the pet graveyard. Granted, most specters could not afford vintage Olga peignoir sets. The garden was damp, the leaves glistening in the faint starlight. The night smelled of wet earth and moldering leaves; it smelled creepy, like fresh graves.

A.J. caught up to Elysia. "For the record? That was *not* cool."

"It's all right," Elysia told her. "There's no one here." She was peering at the wet grass. "Do you see anything? Footprints? I can't tell in this light."

A.J. glanced at the grass. The lawn was of the thick and durable variety. They'd have to get down on their hands and knees with a magnifying glass to examine it for crushed blades, and that was not about to happen.

"Maybe it was the ghost of Angus the cat," she said sourly.

"Now don't be shrewish, pumpkin," Elysia said vaguely, moving through the overhanging tree limbs. The long, pale skirt of her nightgown trailed along the lawn as she moved away. "You were simply outmaneuvered."

"Outmaneuvered? This isn't a game."

"There's a gate back here," Elysia's voice floated back, sounding surprised.

A.J. followed her through the trees, still giving vent to her feelings. "You have no idea who was out here. It could have been some kid taking a shortcut home after a party or it could have been a serial rapist trying to get into the house. You didn't know what you were going to find when you came out here."

She fell silent, staring at the wooden gate in the back wall. Hinge creaking, it swung gently in the breeze.

Twelve

A.J. woke to sunshine and birdsong. Despite the disturbed night she'd spent, she felt refreshed, energized—and brave enough to try the Marjariasana again. That particular asana, the Cat Stretch, was especially good for easing and preventing back pain.

She knelt on her hands and knees, forcing herself to breathe normally, to stay relaxed, and to keep her spine straight. She looked straight ahead, focusing on her breathing, her muscles.

Crouching inward, she exhaled and arched her spine upward like a frightened cat. She held the pose for a few seconds, breathing softly and evenly.

Her back twinged, but it seemed to be the stiffness that came from disuse rather than actual pain. She moved very carefully, very slowly as she returned to her original position and exhaled.

A.J. knelt for a second or two simply listening to what

her body was telling her, and what her body seemed to be saying was, it was okay to move forward into the next asana.

Still on her hands and knees, A.J. dropped her back and raised her head as high as she could, extending her neck like a curious cow.

Both these asanas were very popular with the young students in the Yoga for Kids and Itsy Bitsy Yoga courses she taught—though they were usually performed accompanied by appropriate sound effects. However she could imagine what her mother would make of her mooing next door.

A.J. returned to her original position, relaxed with slow, even breaths, then lowered herself to the floor to lie in Corpse Pose.

Her patience and care were paying off. Her back was definitely improving.

As A.J. studied the artfully draped cobwebs overhead, she thought about the talk she'd had with her mother the previous evening and the disturbing news that her father had apparently had an affair with Stella Borin.

Apparently being a key word. As far as A.J. was concerned there was still some doubt that any affair had taken place since the two offending parties had never admitted their guilt. But maybe it was more comfortable, safer, for her to believe that?

Still . . . it was hard to give credence to such an idea when she vividly remembered how very much her father had loved her mother.

Men tended to do that: love Elysia. A.J. thought of Bradley Meagher. If half the things Medea and Elysia had said last night at dinner were true, poor Mr. Meagher had been waiting loyally, patiently, in the wings all these years only for Elysia to turn around and have an affair with an unprincipled young man half her age.

A.J. had a sudden, unpleasant notion. What if the investigation into Dicky's death was not so much about Dicky's romances as Elysia's relationships with the men in her life?

After showering and dressing, A.J. tapped softly on the door of Elysia's bedroom. There was no answer. She poked her head inside, but the room was empty.

She went downstairs, following the sound of voices to the kitchen.

"There you are, sleepyhead," Elysia greeted her. She and Medea sat at the oval table drinking coffee and eating slices of frosted pound cake. "Maddie was telling me about her prowler. It's a good thing we didn't call the police."

"Ooh, the pull man is harmless. His name is Bill Zemda. He lives with his parents. He was in a car crash a few years ago." Medea touched the side of her head to indicate non compos mentis. "He uses the gate at the back of the garden to visit the statues at night."

Elysia was looking unbearably smug. A.J. contented herself with a crisp, "Well, we didn't know he was harmless at the time, did we?" She took the cup Medea handed her and fixed herself coffee.

"Someone seems to have woken up on the wrong side of the bed," Elysia remarked.

A.J. jumped as the ferret, Morag, suddenly poked her head around a canister of tea. The other two women laughed heartily at this sign of nerves.

A.J. began to long heartily for her own home and hearth.

Carrying her coffee cup to the table, she took a place
across the table from her mother. Medea cut a thick slice
of cake, ignoring A.J.'s request for a sliver.

A.J. resigned herself to her fate and sampled the cake.
It was very good: lemon flavored with a hint of thyme.

"Maddie and I've been chatting about old times,"
Elysia remarked.

What else? A.J. managed a polite, "Oh yes?"

"And for more than long enough," Medea said briskly.
"We don't want to waste the entire weekend chin-wag-
ging. What *shall* we do? I wouldn't mind a wee game of
golf, myself."

A.J. bit her lip to keep from grinning at Elysia's expression as her plans for further interrogation were gently
thwarted. Not that she was thrilled at the idea of golf herself; her back was better, but a round or two of golf seemed
like pushing her luck even if she liked golf, which, frankly,
she didn't. She'd always left the golf course deal making
to Andy.

Besides, as she had been showering that morning,
A.J. had discovered her own clue, which she wanted to
follow up. She suggested, "I was sort of hoping I could
work in getting my hair cut this weekend, if I can squeeze
in somewhere."

Elysia opened her mouth in protest, and A.J. added,
"And maybe we could have lunch out?" That would kill
two birds with one stone and still allow her mother the
opportunity to question Medea.

Elysia, catching A.J.'s gaze, subsided, saying mildly, "I
suppose I could use a trim myself. We could make an
afternoon of it. Girls' Day Out?"

"I could see if they'll take you at the place I go," Medea

remarked, clearly a little puzzled by all this urgently required grooming.

A.J. and Elysia gave this idea a thumbs up and Medea went to phone her hairdresser. The minute she was out of the room, Elysia leaned forward and said softly, "What are you up to? What's this sudden desire for a haircut? You usually wait till the birds abandon their nest to fly south for the winter."

"Ha. I do need a haircut," A.J. said. "But when I was taking my shower this morning I happened to notice that all the soaps and shampoos in the bathroom are from The Salon."

"We all spend too much on hair product," Elysia conceded, disappointed. "I thought perhaps you were on to something. You had that gleam in your eye."

"You're not following me. I'm not talking about salon products, I'm talking about products from *The Salon*. That's where you go, right? And those are the products you use?"

Elysia assented, cutting herself another slice of cake.

"Isn't everything geared to women over fifty?"

"I believe so, pumpkin. No need to rub it in."

"It's probably just a coincidence, but Dicky had products from The Salon at his town house."

Elysia looked up—and now there was a gleam in her eye.

A.J. asked, "Were they yours? Did you ever spend the night over there?"

Elysia said gently, "Are you sure you want to hear this? You didn't enjoy last night's show-and-tell session, I know."

A.J. thought she had hidden her reaction better than

she seemingly must have. She said sturdily, "I'm a big girl, Mother. I can handle the fact that you have a . . . social life."

"Can you?" Elysia seemed amused at some thought she didn't share. "In any case, you can relax. I never spent the night at Dicky's, and I certainly never brought my own grooming products."

"Then Dicky was definitely entertaining another lady guest; someone about your age and probably in your income bracket. We're narrowing in on her. The Salon isn't a national company. You don't find its products in every beauty parlor or in grocery stores or even on the web except through their own website. I know because I tried to find some of that royal jelly skin cream I borrowed from you. You have to purchase directly from The Salon or from their website."

Elysia considered this without comment.

"And The Salon is locally based, which means it's likely that so is this woman—whoever she is."

Elysia said reluctantly, "It does look that way."

"It has to be that. There is no other explanation. Unless Maddie is lying—and neither of us thinks she is—Dicky *was* seeing someone else. And this woman is probably the woman who killed him."

"The shampoo could have been left by an earlier girlfriend," Elysia pointed out. "Someone no longer in his life."

"I suppose so . . ." A.J. put her fork down. "No. No, that won't fly because The Salon's packaging changed recently. That's something I noticed when I was searching their website for the royal jelly. I couldn't remember exactly what it was called and I kept looking for bottles and jars that resembled yours. The bottles that I saw had the new packaging and logo."

Elysia said unhappily, "Maddie could be lying about the last time she saw Dicky."

A.J. didn't want to believe that; she really did like Medea and didn't want to believe she was a murderer. "I think it's more likely there was a third woman. Madame X."

"*Or*," Elysia said suddenly, "Dicky was using the products himself."

A.J. blinked. It wasn't impossible. True, The Salon products were not geared toward the twenty-something male demographic, but that didn't mean a twenty-something male might not use them. Although she had only seen him briefly, Dicky appeared to be *very* well-groomed. Nearly as well-groomed as Andy, A.J.'s ex.

Perhaps one of Dicky's lady friends had introduced him to the products?

"I guess that's possible," she admitted, reluctantly. "I don't think it's likely, but I'm not sure how to rule it out."

Elysia ran a thoughtful hand through her dark waves. "We could always ask."

"It's possible someone might remember him. I doubt if they have a lot of young men buying blue rinse conditioner."

Medea returned to the kitchen and announced that they had appointments at The Salon for after lunch. Since golf was now out, she seemed less enthusiastic about leaving her mausoleum and suggested A.J. and Elysia drive into Newton on their own, browse the shops, have lunch, and then head over to have their hair done.

A.J. and Elysia quickly vetoed this. "It will do you good to get out, petal," Elysia said cheerfully. "No point hanging about brooding about the long-lost past or where to find replacements for brass keyhole covers."

"I suppose you're right," Medea muttered, clearly unconvinced of any such thing. "Now if we were going for a game of golf—"

But Elysia ruthlessly overrode any possibility of golf, and in the end Medea allowed herself to be persuaded. Leaving Morag to guard the house, they drove into the town of Newton in Medea's giant old black Bentley.

The historic town of Newton, or "the Pearl of Kittatinny," was a lovely old town located in the Northwest Skylands. Granted, it was a little limited as far as arts and entertainment day-tripping went. There was the Snowmobile Barn Museum, which all three women agreed to give a wide miss to, and the Newton Fire Museum. The town boasted no fewer than four terrific golf courses. A.J. and Elysia again had to overrule Medea, who opted they skip the hair appointments for a few rounds. There were a number of cute shops and boutiques, and some charming cafés and restaurants.

After a leisurely lunch at Andre's Restaurant and Wine Boutique, they drove to The Salon, a large white building with ionic pillars lining the front like a Greek temple. It wasn't an ugly building, but it stuck out like a sore thumb amidst the historic architecture of Newton.

Medea and Elysia were greeted like old friends by the salon owner, Gloria Sunday.

"Elysia, *darling*." Gloria was so exquisite she could have been made out of porcelain. Her makeup was flawless and her champagne-colored hair was so shiny and perfect it could have been a wig. Maybe it was. No concession had been made to her age, which was probably in her seventies. "*So* lovely to see you."

Elysia and Gloria air-kissed and then Gloria turned to Medea.

"Medea, *darling*." Gloria's smile faltered, but then recovered. "At least you haven't gone to a competitor. That's a mercy. Tim awaits you." She gestured to a slim young man with a goatee and a gold earring.

"Och," Medea said, "I wasnae going to—"

She was whisked away, still feebly protesting. Gloria smiled a tiny, satisfied smile.

"My daughter, Anna," Elysia said.

"Anna." Sherry-colored eyes flicked over A.J. appraisingly, lingering on her hair. Gloria's smile stayed firmly in place, but it seemed to require effort.

Elysia added, "She inherited my late sister's studio."

The sherry-colored gaze sharpened. "*Ah.* Of course, of course. *Welcome*, my dear. We have you down for the Athenian."

Hopefully the Athenian was a "what" and not a "who." A.J. said, "I just wanted a trim, really."

Elysia and Gloria laughed gaily at the very idea, Gloria appeared to consider and then she gestured like a sorceress summoning a genie. "Alessandro, I think."

Alessandro turned out to be a very handsome young Latino from Brooklyn. He had a sultry smile and a short ponytail. When he shook A.J.'s hand he clasped it warmly in both of his.

"This is a treat for me," he told A.J. as he settled her in the reclining chair next to a shampoo basin shaped like a golden shell. "I can't think of the last time I worked with someone who wasn't suffering hot flashes."

A.J. couldn't help wondering what charming lies he told the menopausal someones. That it was a relief to work with someone mature?

"You don't have many male clients?"

"We don't have any." Alessandro sounded definite. A.J. glanced around the salon. All the patrons were indeed female. And all the stylists were male. Young, handsome males. Gloria seemed to have isolated and identified her target market, and, judging by appearances, business was booming.

Alessandro certainly seemed worth his weight in gold. He had magical fingers, and as he skillfully massaged A.J.'s neck and scalp, she began to toy with the notion of hiring a masseuse for Sacred Balance. They had recently hired a physician for their Sitka Yoga program, so why not a masseuse? Especially since Mara Allen had one for Yoga Meridian.

Not that A.J. wanted to fall into her old competitive mind-set. Yoga wasn't just about stretching the body; surely she had managed to stretch her mind a little over the last year? Still, she had no intention of lying there in Corpse Pose while Mara Allen took over her business.

After the shampoo, Alessandro painted a purple glaze on A.J.'s hair and left her browsing a copy of *Vogue* under a dryer. She turned the magazine pages and surreptitiously studied the busy salon. Nearly every chair was full this Saturday afternoon. And every chair was manned—no pun intended—by an enthusiastic young sir chatting and charming his client. Alessandro was correct. With the exception of herself, none of the clients looked under forty-five.

A.J. spotted Medea beneath a veil of black hair. A few stations down she spied her mother; recognized the expression and the moving lips: Elysia was interrogating her smiling stylist.

Over by the elegant front desk—seemingly designed to look like a marble and gold sacrificial altar—Gloria was speaking earnestly to a tall, thin, courtly-looking older man.

Alessandro returned and escorted A.J. to the "styling pavilion." Here A.J. was given a flute glass of champagne to sip while Alessandro asked her a variety of questions about her job, morning routine, and exercise habits in order to determine the best possible haircut for her.

Back when A.J. had been an up-and-coming freelance marketing consultant she had paid major dollars to have her long, chestnut hair highlighted at the John Barrett Salon on Fifth Avenue. She really hadn't taken time to get a serious cut and color since she'd moved to New Jersey. Maybe it was time for a new look.

Alessandro certainly seemed to think so and made numerous suggestions—most of them good. One thing for sure, he wasn't just a pretty face. He did know his craft, and in between the amiable third degree he snipped and trimmed, eyes narrowed as he measured one side of A.J.'s hair against the other.

"So you're just having a girls' day out, Anna?"

"Yes, Call me A.J." She watched the silver flash of scissors. "How long have you worked at the salon?"

"Just about a year. And your mom used to be a movie star?"

"In Britain, yes." A.J. preferred not to go there. Elysia had a startlingly large cult following among young males. Her gaze fell on Gloria who was still talking to the handsome, but increasingly restive-looking, older man. "Who is Gloria talking to?"

"That's her partner Stewie Cabot. Are you married, A.J.?"

"Nope. Not anymore." She smilingly batted the ball back in Alessandro's court. "Are Gloria and Stewie involved?"

"Nah. No way. Stewie's gay." Alessandro chuckled. "You're engaged, I bet?"

And so it went. Alessandro was charming and attentive and never shut up. No, that wasn't true. He listened very carefully to all of A.J.'s answers to his questions—and he had many questions. Somehow his interrogation managed to skirt the line of actually being intrusive; Alessandro seemed merely young and guileless. Maybe A.J. was conscious of how many questions he was asking because she was doing her best to question *him*.

While they fenced, Alessandro snipped and styled. At the end of two and a half hours A.J. had a short, feathery cut that was stylish but wouldn't require too much work with her active lifestyle.

"It's lovely," she admitted, holding a hand mirror to examine the close cropped back of her head.

Alessandro handed her his card. "My pleasure. I would love to see you again, A.J. Anytime."

A.J. thanked him. When they shook hands, Alessandro gently, meaningfully squeezed her hand.

Elysia stood at the front waiting for her. Her eyes widened at A.J.'s approach. "You look absolutely fabulous, pet." She bade A.J. turn, which A.J. did.

"The rolling eyes make you look a bit unhinged, but otherwise, a truly lovely job."

A.J. noticed that Stewie, Gloria's business partner according to Alessandro, was smiling as he observed them.

"Gorgeous," he agreed, joining in the conversation. "Of course, it helps when we have such lovely raw material to work with." He turned to Elysia and expertly delivered the finishing stroke. "Your baby sister?"

They chatted with the smooth and personable Stewie for a few minutes and then he excused himself to speak to a customer on the phone. Shortly after, Medea joined them.

One glance at the older woman's face told A.J. something was very wrong. Medea was visibly shaken, her face white and her eyes red-rimmed.

"What's wrong?" Elysia demanded. "You're not happy with the cut?"

Medea shook her head. Paying the cupid-cute male receptionist for her cut with shaking hands, she pushed out through the amber crackle-glass doors. Elysia and A.J. had to hurry to keep up with her.

"What is it? What's happened?" Elysia persisted.

Medea gave another swift shake of her head. They reached the underground parking garage, Medea walking so swiftly the other two had to trot to keep up.

They found the Bentley amidst the rows of shining, silent cars. Medea unlocked the doors and they got in.

Slumped behind the wheel, Medea took deep, unsteady breaths.

Elysia put a hand on her shoulder and Medea's face twisted up.

"Maddie, petal, *tell me* what's wrong."

Medea let out a long, shaky sigh. "Peggy Graham is dead."

Thirteen

"Who's Peggy Graham?" Elysia asked blankly.

"Peggy. Peggy Graham."

"Yes, got that much, love. *Who* is Peggy Graham?"

Medea hiccupped a half-sob. "A friend. I've mentioned Peggy, surely?"

"Er . . . refresh my memory."

"Peggy and I sat on the League of Historical Societies."

As she began to speak of her acquaintanceship with Peggy, A.J. suddenly remembered the name of the woman who had been harassing Dicky before his death. Had the police investigated Dora Beauford at all? Did they even know of her existence?

Preoccupied with her own thoughts, she only vaguely heard Medea's shaky, "Well, she's killed herself."

Following a shocked silence, Elysia said, "When?"

"Nearly a month ago. They're saying she took sleeping pills."

"Do they know why?"

Medea shook her head.

Elysia bit her lip. "I'm so sorry, Maddie."

"It's not true! She wouldn't have!"

Elysia patted her back. "Perhaps she was ill. Perhaps—"

"No."

"Then it was an accident."

"No!"

Elysia stared at her. "What are you suggesting?"

Medea, face working, stared out the window.

"Are you saying someone killed her? What *are* you saying, Maddie?"

"I'm saying it was murder."

"Murder? Who killed her?"

"*They* did!"

"Who?" A.J. and Elysia chorused.

Medea shook her head fiercely.

When she said nothing else and made no further move, Elysia said, "You'd better let me drive, petal. You've had a shock."

"I'm fine." Medea seemed to shake off her paralysis. She started the car engine. She drove carefully, slowly, out of the underground garage and turned onto the main street.

Elysia asked at last, "When was the last time you saw Peggy?"

Medea's gaze stayed glued on the busy road before them. "It's been a wee while."

Why the guilty look?

"Had you and Peggy been friends long?"

"Years." Medea swallowed. "Six years. We weren't . . . as close as we once were."

"Had something happened between you?"

"No. Not really." But Medea didn't sound convinced. "People change. Friendships . . . alter."

Yet Medea and Elysia had stayed close even when they were not in regular contact.

A.J. questioned, "Do you have any reason to believe someone wished Peggy harm?"

Medea opened her mouth and then closed it again. "No."

It was probably the least convincing thing she'd said so far. "If you know something about your friend's death," A.J. said, "the best thing to do is tell the police."

Medea shook her head fiercely.

Elysia said, "Or tell us. You said 'they.' Who did you mean?"

Another fierce shake of Medea's head.

Did Medea actually have someone in mind, or by "they" did she merely mean the usual suspects everyone referred to by "they"?

"Do you know if Peggy did take sleeping pills?" Elysia asked, thoughtfully. Clearly her sleuthing instincts were roused, but that really wasn't saying much since Elysia hoped for mystery like most people hoped for winning lottery numbers.

"I don't know. I don't remember her ever saying so."

"Did she take any kind of medication?"

"I don't know. The usual things for blood pressure, I suppose."

"She wasn't in ill health that you knew of?"

"No."

"Or depressed?"

Medea shook her head.

A.J. said slowly, "I think suicide always comes as a

shock to other people. Couldn't it just be something like that?"

"I . . . I wouldn't have thought so."

"Where are you going with this, pumpkin?" Elysia inquired, clearly displeased at the suggestion of an accidental death when there was a possibility of foul play.

"I don't know," A.J. admitted. "Sleeping pills seem like an unreliable way to kill yourself. But they also seem like an unreliable way to commit murder."

"Sleeping pill overdose is the method most commonly used when women wish to commit suicide."

"How do you know that?"

"I remember once on *221B Baker Street* . . ."

A.J. quickly put up a hand. "Point taken. Anyway, I'll grant you sleeping pills are the kind of thing that could, in theory, be tampered with."

"I'm not following. If someone already wished to kill herself why would you need to tamper with the sleeping pills?"

"Well, but what if someone didn't? What if—"

"Stop it!" Medea cried suddenly, jamming on the brakes. "I canna bear it."

A.J. and Elysia lurched forward and then subsided into stricken silence. Medea shuddered over the steering wheel while cars behind them honked in outrage.

"Let me drive," A.J. said quickly. She scrambled out of the car, holding the door so that Medea could trade places with her in the backseat.

When they were once more on their way, Elysia turned to the backseat. "Maddie, my dear . . ."

But Medea was shaking her head fiercely. "Let me be, Elysia."

The short drive back to the house in Andover was ac-

complished in a tense silence that gradually grew heavy
and then settled into abstraction.

Reaching the house, Medea apologized for her behavior and then excused herself, claiming she had a terrible
headache. Promising to be down in time to fix dinner, she
went upstairs with the ferret clinging to her shoulder.

A.J. and Elysia retreated to the kitchen. Elysia made
tea and they sat at the oval table, talking quietly.

"Are you sure we're not in the way here?" A.J. said.
"Maybe she'd prefer to be on her own right now."

Elysia waved this off.

"Well, at the least we should probably order takeout or
a pizza so she doesn't have to cook for us."

"I can't possibly think of food at a time like this."
Elysia sipped her tea, then put the cup down in its saucer.
"Anyway, she likes to cook. Cooking will keep her mind
occupied."

A.J. opened her mouth, then gave up. She said instead,
"She seems very upset considering Peggy wasn't a close
friend."

Elysia said tartly, "The fact that they weren't as close
as they'd once been doesn't mean she didn't still feel affection for her."

"Did it seem like there was more to it than that?"

"What do you mean?" Elysia's blue eyes studied her.

"Did she seem . . . I don't know . . . guilty to you?"

"No."

The phone rang. They both jumped, then turned, listening. The phone did not ring again.

Elysia amended, "I think everyone feels guilty when a
friend or someone close commits suicide. You think you
should have seen the signs, should have noticed something was wrong, should have prevented it."

"I can see how that would be true. It's just that Maddie's reaction isn't what I'd expect. It seems . . . extreme."

"Mmm."

A.J. instinctively dropped her voice even lower. "That comment about 'they killed her.' Did you have the impression she meant a general 'they' or that she had someone specifically in mind?"

"What specific 'they' could she have meant? Peggy's family? Maddie said she was unaware that Peggy had problems with anyone."

A.J. nodded though Maddie's opinion didn't necessarily mean much since she hadn't been in contact with her friend for some time. "She didn't want to confide in us. That was obvious."

"True."

A.J. said grimly, "We've already got one murder case that we're not equipped to handle. We don't need to take on another."

"No," Elysia said reluctantly. "I suppose you're right."

They chatted a little longer about various things. A.J. went to call Sacred Balance and make sure all was well.

A brief phone call to Emma Rice seemed to confirm Lily's assertion that A.J.'s presence was not essential to the success of Sacred Balance.

"You know where to reach me if there's a problem," she told Emma.

"There's nothing here we can't handle for a day or two," Emma said with disheartening confidence. "You don't need to worry about us. You just take care of yourself."

Elysia and A.J. spent the remainder of the day quietly.

A.J. enjoyed herself exploring the bookshelves in Medea's library. In addition to Tolkien, Pratchett, Lewis, and Rowling, there were a number of young adult fantasy novels that A.J. remembered from her teen years: *The House With a Clock in Its Walls* by John Bellairs, *A Wizard of Earthsea* by Ursula K. Le Guin, *So You Want to Be a Wizard* by Diane Duane.

For a time she lost herself in the exotic worlds of mages and magic. She was startled to realize how swiftly time had passed when her mother joined her at six o'clock suggesting it was time to start discussing possible plans for dinner with their hostess.

A.J. glanced at the clock behind the statue of Medusa and nodded, surprised that Medea had not put in an appearance before now. Elysia went upstairs.

She returned a few moments later. "Maddie's not in her room."

A.J. set down the copy of *Jonathan Strange & Mr. Norrell.* "Where would she go?"

"Nowhere. Her car is still in the garage."

If Elysia had already checked the garage, she was obviously uneasy. A.J. joined her in a quick, quiet hunt through the house.

They reunited in the dining room. A.J. shook her head. Elysia's face tightened. They both jumped at the clatter of a chafing dish on the heavy sideboard. Morag the ferret poked her head out from under the lid.

"Did you check the back?" A.J. inquired.

"I glanced out the window. I didn't see her on the patio."

"Maybe she's working in her garden. I find it soothing sometimes just to pull weeds."

Elysia led the way out to the back porch. It was empty, but A.J. spotted a dark form lying on the grass inside the garden.

"Mother!"

At the sharpness in A.J.'s voice, Elysia turned, following her down the steps as she hurried across the lawn.

A few steps away, A.J. slowed and then stopped. Elysia joined her and they gazed in stricken silence. It was obviously too late. Medea's harsh features were waxen and empty of all emotion. She looked like one of her own macabre statues—except for the blood-soaked blouse and the bullet hole in her chest.

Fourteen

⚯

The on-scene investigation was winding up when Jake arrived.

A.J. spotted him striding tall and assured through the crime scene personnel busily searching Medea's Victorian house of horrors for the gun that had killed her. Jake paused to show his ID to a uniformed officer who pointed out Detective Lennon. Lennon was heading the investigation.

A.J.'s heart did a glad leap before she remembered that all was not well between her and Jake—and even if all was well, he would not be happy to find her in the middle of a murder investigation. She could understand that since she wasn't happy to find herself in this situation either.

She couldn't help staring as he and the silver-haired Detective Lennon began to speak.

She and Elysia had informed the police about the nocturnal visit of Bill Zemda the night before, pointing out the garden back gate, but so far no one seemed interested in anything but A.J. and her mother's movements.

"I see your inspector is here," Elysia stated. She was pale but composed.

"I think he's your inspector at the moment," A.J. said grimly.

Apparently finished speaking with Detective Lennon, Jake glanced around the room, spotted A.J. and Elysia, and made his way over to them.

Elysia said coolly, "Inspector."

"Endora."

A.J. covered an inappropriate laugh in a small cough.

"You okay?" Jake asked her, his features softening infinitesimally.

She nodded. It would have been nice if he had folded her in his arms—she could have used a hug right about then. Even a smile would have been welcome. Neither looked likely. Jake appeared tired and somber.

He said shortly, "Next question. What the—what *exactly* are you doing here?"

"Excuse me," Elysia said, starting to turn away.

"Not so fast," Jake said. "You're part of this equation. Of that, I have *no* doubt."

"You're so wise," Elysia cooed. "Unfortunately, nature calls and I must obey." She sauntered away to the downstairs powder room.

Jake turned back to A.J., his expression, if possible, grimmer than before. "Okay, let's try this again, what are you doing here?"

She definitely didn't appreciate him using his cop voice with her, but she managed to say evenly, "I told you I was going out of town for the weekend."

"And out of all the hotels and motels and homes of

friends and family you could have picked to visit, you just happened to choose to stay here? At a house where a homicide was due to take place?"

"Naturally we didn't know about the homicide ahead of time or we'd have booked the Best Western. Or maybe even tried to stop it. Or do you now suspect me, as well as my mother, of murder?"

Jake looked around as though he thought they might be overheard. "Listen to me because I'm only going to say this once more. Despite the fact that I think she's a nutcase, I don't believe your mother killed Dakarai Massri. But that's just my personal belief, and it doesn't mean a damn thing. I have to do my job. And that job is to investigate Massri's homicide."

"Can't you recuse yourself?"

"I don't want to recuse myself. I fought like hell to stay on the case!"

"Terrific. And I'm supposed to be, what? Happy about that?"

Jake said between gritted teeth, "I fought to stay on the case to make sure the investigation was thorough and careful and impartial. To make sure that nothing was missed or overlooked. I fought to stay on the case to *help* your mother."

A.J. didn't know what to say. Her idea of helping was such a different thing, but she could see that Jake's approach was practical and maybe even of more use than blind loyalty.

Into her silence, he said, "So you want to tell me what you're doing here, because I find this too much of a coincidence to swallow."

A.J. recognized that the time had come to lay her cards on the table. Well, maybe not the full deck, but then she wasn't sure that, given recent events, she was playing with a full deck. In either case he wasn't going to like it, but Jake would like lying even less. She recalled a certain conversation a few months earlier. No, lying was not an option.

"It's not a coincidence that we're here, but it might be a coincidence that Maddie is dead."

"What does that mean?"

"That this might not have anything to do with Maddie's murder, but . . . she used to be married to Dicky Massri."

She had the satisfaction of seeing Jake's jaw drop. He said at last, "That . . . hasn't turned up anywhere yet."

"They were married in Egypt. There were immigration issues, though—among other things. They divorced nearly two years ago."

"Go on."

"That's basically it. Mother remembered the marriage—" Despite her best intentions, at the last instant A.J. couldn't admit to breaking and entering Dicky's apartment. "We thought that there might be a lead here. Something that would, at least, cast doubt on the case you're—the police—are building."

"And?"

"I don't know. Maddie swore she hadn't stayed in contact with Dicky. Unless she was one heck of an actress, she didn't even know he was dead. But it's obvious that she and Mother weren't the only two women he had romanced with an eye to . . . um . . . fleecing."

"Is that what their generation calls it?" Jake was still dour. "Was Maddie being blackmailed?"

"No. I'm sure she wasn't. I don't think she even knew he was in the country. The scam with her was to marry her and then keep asking for money. Eventually she got fed up and divorced him. Like I said, I'm convinced she didn't even know Dicky was dead."

"How did she take that news?"

A.J. cast her mind back. "She was shocked. She didn't shed any tears over him, but she wasn't gloating either." She admitted, "In fact Maddie burst out laughing when she learned Mother had been involved with Dicky. Granted, she had a very odd sense of humor."

"Did she have any theories about who might have popped her ex?"

A.J. shook her head. "No. The last she'd heard he was still in Egypt. But something did happen today, and I think it has to tie in with her death. Anything else is too much of a coincidence."

"Go on."

"She found out that a friend of hers, Peggy Graham, had recently committed suicide. Except Maddie didn't believe it was suicide."

"No one ever does. What makes you think it ties into her death?"

"She was so shocked at the idea. She even said at one point she thought it might be murder."

Jake's green eyes narrowed. "Did she have any grounds for such a claim or was she just talking?"

"I don't know, but she was killed only a few hours later."

"Who overheard her say she didn't believe Graham's death was an accident?"

Reluctantly, A.J. said, "Just Mother and I, although Maddie was obviously upset when she left the hairdresser's."

"That wouldn't be unexpected. She'd just heard of her friend's death."

"There was a phone call while Mother and I were talking in the kitchen after Maddie had gone upstairs to rest."

"Who called?"

"That's the thing. The phone only rang once."

Jake rubbed his forehead. "In other words, someone could have just dialed wrong. So far none of this is getting us anywhere."

"What if Maddie went upstairs and phoned someone? And that one ring was the person calling her back to arrange a meeting of some kind? If Maddie was waiting for the call, she'd have snatched it up immediately, which would explain why there was only one ring. You could check the phone records, right?"

"Yeah," Jake said slowly. "So you think this person called Maddie back to arrange a meeting of some kind and then killed her?"

"I think it's a possibility."

"And they killed her because she didn't believe Peggy Graham committed suicide?"

"I don't know why she was killed. Maybe it's something else entirely. She was pretty wealthy. Maybe it's something as mundane as that. But there's some connection here. I know it."

Jake looked skeptical. "Did this Graham woman know Massri?"

"I don't think so. But I don't know." A.J. considered this idea more carefully. "It seemed like maybe something had happened between Maddie and Peggy. She said they weren't as close as they used to be."

"Wouldn't she have mentioned it if this Graham woman was seeing her ex?"

"Probably. I know there is one obvious connection."

He waited. A.J. knew how it was going to sound before she said unwillingly, "They all went to the same hairdresser."

For what seemed like a very long time Jake didn't move a muscle. At last he said, without any inflection at all, "Seriously?"

"I know what you're thinking," she said quickly. "I know how it sounds. But there's something there. I mean, just the fact that Maddie was killed after we went to The Salon. That can't be a coincidence."

"It could, actually."

"But it's not. Jake, Maddie was shocked when we left the salon, but she was also frightened. And angry."

Jake wearily rubbed his forehead. "You're grasping at straws."

"I'm not. This is fact. Maddie and Peggy both went to the same hair salon. The same salon Mother uses, by the way." A.J. very nearly slipped and added that Massri—or someone visiting his apartment—had also used The Salon products. As far as she was concerned that was the clincher in her argument, but unfortunately she couldn't reveal she had been in Massri's apartment.

"A.J.—"

"There's another fact," A.J. said stubbornly. "Two of these women, Mother and Maddie, went on Egyptian cruises. Maybe Peggy did, too. You could check, couldn't you?"

"Honey. A.J. I know you want to help your mother. But this is . . . silly. This Graham woman and the vic—er, Ms. Sutherland—were friends. Just like your mom and Sutherland were friends. They all probably shopped at the same stores and dined at the same restaurants, too. For all we know they might have read the same books or watched the same TV shows or listened to the same music. It doesn't prove anything."

"You're not giving this fair consideration, Jake. There's more to this than it sounds."

With an obvious attempt at patience, he said, "These women are about the same age and the same income bracket, correct?"

"I have no idea what Peggy Graham was like."

"Let's leave Peggy Graham out of it for a second. Your mother and Sutherland fit the same approximate profile. They're friends. They talk. One likes where she gets her hair done, she tells her friends. One has a good time on a cruise, she tells her friends. There's no mystery—or even surprise—to any of this."

When A.J. didn't have an answer, he said more gently, "Let's look at it from a different angle. Say there is a connection here. Say that somehow the beauty parlor and the Egyptian cruise are all linked together. Maybe the salon is getting a kickback for every client they refer. What does this have to do with Massri? How does this lead to murder? How does it lead to suicide?"

"That would be your job to figure out," A.J. said shortly.

"Okay, and what am I supposed to be figuring out?" He was equally curt. "What angle am I pursuing here? What is it you suspect the beauty salon of? Overcharging for haircuts?"

"Maddie was frightened and angry when we left The Salon. She wouldn't say why, but she was. And obviously with good reason."

"If she wouldn't say why, then maybe she wasn't frightened. Maybe she was just shocked and upset to hear that a friend had committed suicide. Isn't that possible?"

"She was murdered only a few hours later. I thought you didn't believe in coincidence?"

He was silent. Finally, he said, "I don't. I'll look into Peggy Graham's death. And I'll check out the hair salon. Maybe there's something hinky there. Maybe it's mob funded. Maybe . . . I don't know. I'll look into it." He met her eyes. "But I don't think you should pin your hopes on that line of investigation."

A.J. nodded.

"And I think you should also be prepared for the fact that the victim's connection with Massri and her homicide while your mother is a guest in her home is liable to look pretty bad for Elysia."

A.J. swallowed hard. "You think she'll be remanded to custody?"

"I'm not going to lie to you. I think it's very possible. The DA really thinks we've got the makings of a watertight case. On top of that, after last year's allegations of nepotism, he wants to make it clear to the media that no favoritism will be shown to anyone, including celebrities."

"So he's making an example of my mother?"

"He's not making an example of her," he said wearily. "He wants it played by the book. And if this was anyone *but* your mother, I wouldn't hesitate a second to put her back behind bars."

A.J. nodded tig htly.

"I'm going to be a while here. I'll call you tomorrow, okay?"

A.J. nodded again. Jake's cell phone rang.

"Excuse me." He moved away. A.J. watched his expression change and her heart sank. Something told her this call was not business—maybe it was feminine intuition, but the expression on his face told her the call was personal, private, and not unwelcome.

For a few seconds she stood frozen.

"I suppose you're driving back with that brute?"

A.J. started. She hadn't noticed Elysia's return. "No. Are we cleared to leave?"

"According to Detective Lennon, yes. And I don't know why we wouldn't be. We've been interrogated, tested for gun powder residue, and had our luggage pawed through in search of the murder weapon."

"It's not personal, Mother. They do have to investigate us."

"I know," Elysia said bitterly. "But it's not pleasant either."

A.J. did not see Jake again before she and Elysia packed the Land Rover and left.

As they pulled around the crime scene vehicles, lights flashing in the twilight, A.J. said, "I'm sorry, Mother. I know you were friends a long time."

Elysia nodded, for once having nothing to say.

The trimmed yards and tidy houses rolled by in the deepening twilight, some dark, some lit by cheerful lamps. Comfortable facades that hid . . . well, that was the point. Who knew what lived behind the pleasant surface?

"Mother, when we were talking with Maddie about Dicky, you said something about your hairstylist recommending the Egyptian cruise line. Was that your stylist at The Salon?"

"Yes."

"Who's your stylist there?"

"I'm not really locked into any one stylist," Elysia said indifferently. "I tend to go with whoever is available."

"Do you remember who recommended the cruise line?" Out of the corner of her eye, A.J. noticed her mother's purse—which was positioned behind the driver's seat—give a sudden jump. This so distracted her, she nearly missed Elysia's answer.

"Alessandro."

"The Alessandro I had today?"

"That's the one. He's very popular, from what I understand. I think Roberto actually gives a better cut, but he's not as personable."

A.J. ignored the summation of stylist social skills that followed. When Elysia finally paused, she said, "I'm beginning to think there really might be something to this idea that The Salon is somehow mixed up in all this. Alessandro spent most of his time with me asking me all kinds of personal questions: was I married, did I have a boyfriend, did I have kids—"

"He probably wants to date you."

"I didn't get that impression." Elysia's purse gave another, more forceful jump. "Mother . . . your purse is moving."

"That will be Morag waking up, I imagine."

"*Morag*?" A.J. reached behind the seat and dragged the purse over. Sure enough a pair of tiny beady eyes met hers.

"You stole Maddie's ferret? *Why*?"

"What was I supposed to do? I could hardly leave the wee beastie there. She'd have been handed over to animal control."

"You don't know that. Besides, you can't take evidence from a crime scene."

"I sincerely doubt anyone was going to devote themselves to finding her a good home. The way those idiots kept leaving all the doors open it was a mere matter of time before she got out in the street where a car or a dog might kill her. As for evidence, I don't think Morag is concealing the murder weapon. Nor do I think she's going to make much of a witness."

"That's not the point."

"Or perhaps you think she's a suspect?" Elysia tossed over her shoulder, "Morag, did you do it?"

"Very funny."

Elysia shrugged.

"What are you going to do with a ferret?"

"I've no idea. I only know that little creature was . . . very dear to Maddie. And Maddie was very dear to me."

A.J. had no answer to that.

Fifteen

"**Springtime** in New Jersey" sounded like the start of a joke, but the truth was that this part of the Garden State really did look like a garden at this time of year. The countryside was lushly green and bright with wildflowers.

Despite the tragedy of the weekend, as A.J. drove to Sacred Balance on Monday morning, she felt her spirits rise fractionally.

She was the first one in when she reached the studio. As she turned on the lights and set about preparing her morning tea, she considered Lily's closed office door. A.J. had a key to every office, every desk, every file cabinet in the building. It had never occurred to her to use them— she had no desire to spy on her employees—but for the first time she wondered if trust was not a mistake where Lily was concerned.

It was a depressing thought.

She went in her own office and signed onto her laptop. There was an e-mail waiting for her from the SCA.

A.J. read it quickly. It was polite and noninformative. Dakarai Massri had left the employ of the Supreme Council of Antiquities to pursue other opportunities in September of the previous year.

There were not many lines to read between on that, but she did her best as she absently listened to the comfortable bustle of the staff filing in.

She heard Lily go straight into her office and close the door. A.J. looked at the photograph of her aunt and sighed.

Suze came in.

"Thank *God* you're back. One more day of the Yoga Overlord's reign and I think there would be a revolution."

"What's been happening?"

"You mean aside from the fact that she tries to run this place like a prison camp?"

"It can't be that bad, Suze. Everyone was happy with the way Lily managed when Aunt Di was alive."

"That's because Lily didn't act like she does now when Di was alive. She wouldn't have dared. Di was totally hands on."

Meaning A.J. wasn't hands on enough? Sometimes it was hard to tell whether these observations were criticisms or simply observations.

"What exactly is Lily doing that's so bad?"

"It's not one gigantic thing. You know how it is with her. It's constant. It's exhausting."

"Have there been any more mysterious visitors to the studio?"

Suze shook her head. "Not during my shifts. Not that anyone has mentioned."

Suze went off to prepare for her class, and A.J. went next door to Lily's office.

She tapped on the door.

"Enter," Lily commanded.

A.J. opened the door. Lily looked up from her laptop. "Yes?"

A.J. had to squelch her instant annoyed response. Lily probably didn't even do it on purpose; it was just her manner, but in one curt word she managed to imply that A.J. was interrupting, irritating, and an idiot.

A.J. said with false brightness. "Hi! How was your weekend?"

"Good. Apparently much better than yours, according to the news. Murder does seem to follow you everywhere you go."

A.J. kept smiling although her face was starting to hurt. Better hers than Lily's though. "I thought maybe we could finish Thursday's discussion."

Lily made a point of looking at the clock. She rose. "Unfortunately, I've got class in ten. Perhaps later." She added, "That reminds me. Do I need to get someone to cover your classes today?"

"No, I'm back full time."

Lily smiled politely. "Great. Well, if you'll excuse me?"

She went out and A.J. went back to her office to practice deep breathing exercises.

The morning routine began.

Not long after A.J. finished her tea and e-mail, Emma Rice tapped on the door of A.J.'s office.

A.J. looked up smiling. "What's up?'

Emma came in and shut the door. At her serious expression, A.J. said, "Please tell me you're not thinking of quitting."

"Now there's a coincidence. That's exactly what I was going to ask you."

A.J. examined the older woman's lined face. "What do you mean?"

Emma said forthrightly, "The rumor is you're planning on selling Sacred Balance and moving back to New York. Is there any truth to it?"

"No. Absolutely not. Who started that rumor?"

Emma shook her head.

"Well, it's not true," A.J. said again, firmly.

After a moment, Emma said, "Your word is good enough for me, honey. But you might want to reassure some of these other folks before they start looking for jobs."

A.J. was startled. "Is it that bad?"

"Oh, yeah."

"Thanks for the heads up."

A.J. taught her morning class without incident; she was careful not to push herself too far. She was surprised at how happy she was to be teaching, how much she had missed it over the past week. Give up the studio and move back to New York? No way.

After her Yoga for Kids course, she went down to Lily's office to try again to meet with her, but Lily was locking her door, clearly on her way out.

"Sorry. Early lunch meeting," she said in answer to A.J.'s visible surprise.

"All right. Can we talk after lunch then?"

"I'm always available." Lily said it with absolute sincerity, so apparently she believed it. And it was true that Lily had never ducked confrontation before. But something was most definitely up. A.J. trusted her instincts on that.

A.J. went back to her office, glanced over the monthly reports, and decided she, too, could do with an early lunch. She asked Suze if she wanted to grab a quick bite between sessions, and they drove into town, bought sandwiches and drinks at a café, and took their lunch to the park to eat by the duck pond.

Preoccupied with her thoughts of Lily, it took A.J. a while to notice that Suze was not her usual bubbly self. Not at all, in fact.

"Everything okay?" A.J. asked.

"Sure!" But the bright tone didn't match Suze's expression.

A.J. examined the younger woman's glum profile. "Emma told me there are rumors flying around the studio."

Suze snorted. "You can say that again. And it's all Lily's doing."

"Do you have any proof of that?"

"Who else would it be?"

A.J. couldn't help but think there was some truth to that, but she wanted to try to keep an open mind. "What exactly is she saying?"

"She's not saying anything. Not to me, anyway. She just looks mysterious and smug whenever anyone asks her anything outright." Suze's wide blue eyes slanted A.J.'s way. "The rumor is you're considering selling your share of Sacred Balance to Lily."

"Oh, really," A.J. said very quietly.

Suze looked uncomfortable. "Please don't tell anyone you got that from me."

"Don't worry. And for the record, it's not true."

Suze looked relieved. "I knew it wasn't."

They ate for a time in silence, then Suze asked, "Is it over between you and Jake?"

A.J.'s avocado and tomato sandwich turned to moth-balls and lodged in her throat. She managed to choke it down and say, "Not that I'm aware of. Why?"

Suze's face looked as red as if she'd stepped into boil-ing water. "Uh . . ."

"Tell me."

"It's probably nothing," Suze said quickly. "It's just we had a new potential client come in last week. Chess Something-or-other." Suze firmed her voice with effort. "She mentioned that she and Jake were seeing each other."

At last A.J. managed to say colorlessly, "I see."

Once again A.J. reminded herself that she and Jake had never been exclusive, they'd never even discussed it, which seemed a bit odd in retrospect. But just because Jake was going out with someone else didn't mean . . .

At that point logic fled and it was all she could do not to be sick in the rhododendrons.

"A couple of people have mentioned seeing Jake—"

"Jake and I aren't exclusive," A.J. said quickly. Saving her pride seemed to be paramount now. More than that she couldn't bear to think about.

"Right, right," Suze said quickly. She was being care-ful not to look directly at A.J., for which A.J. was grateful.

They ate their sandwiches in silence for a minute or two and then Suze asked indignantly, "Who is she, anyway?"

"An old friend of Jake's. An old girlfriend, I guess. Francesca Cox. She's a travel writer."

"Oh *brother*," Suze said and her tone was so scathing they both started giggling shakily.

They finished their lunch with minimal discussion, walked back to A.J.'s car, and returned to the studio.

The rest of the day was uneventful. Around three o'clock A.J.'s cell rang and her heart leapt as she recognized the number as Jake's.

"Hi!" she said cheerfully.

"Hey." He sounded guarded. Or was she now overanalyzing every inflection and tone?

"What's up?"

"Are you free for dinner tonight?" He added quickly, "Just someplace casual."

"Sure." Her heart sank at the "someplace casual." Not that all their meals out were grand affairs, but something about the phrasing triggered recollections of friends' horror stories about getting dumped in public.

"I'll pick you up at seven."

"I'll be there," she said a little grimly.

A.J. left work on time, determined not to fuss or primp for this date that might not be a date. Which might in fact be her pink slip.

All the same, she dressed carefully and spent extra time on her makeup and hair.

Monster lay on the bed and watched her try to decide between a Tuleh floral ruffle-trimmed blouse with apple green skirt ensemble and a black, ivory, and moss dash-print shift.

"What do you think?" A.J. studied the dress, frowning.

Monster thumped his tail.

"You always say that." She put both selections back and pulled out a clean pair of jeans and a white T-shirt featuring the Paris Opéra. "It's just Jake," she informed the dog, and once again Monster's tail dusted the quilt.

Yeah," A.J. muttered, "but you've always had a thing for men in uniform."

Monster raised his head, jaws open in a silent doggy laugh.

A.J. pulled on the jeans and T-shirt, added a pair of vintage crystal teardrop earrings, fluffed her hair, and went to wait in the front parlor, resisting the desire to have a glass of wine while she waited. That was one habit she was determined never to get into: drinking to calm her nerves.

She hadn't long to wait before Jake's sports car pulled up to the front yard. He got out wearing his favorite off-duty snug jeans and the Gucci dress shirt she'd bought him for Christmas: fitted black cotton with tiny little red polka dots. He'd done his best to tame his unruly dark hair, but he was past due for a haircut—probably too busy trying to throw her mother in the slammer to find time for the barber.

A.J. made a face at her thoughts. Okay, so it was sort of a date, anyway. But Jake looked awfully solemn. Solemn and really good-looking.

She sighed, put on her game face, and briskly opened the door, which seemed to catch him off guard. Maybe she did sort of throw it open a bit more dramatically than intended.

"Hey!" he said, taking a cautious step back.

"Hey!"

Jake sort of hesitated, but then he moved to kiss her, his light salute hitting somewhere between her mouth and cheek.

"Your hair looks cute."

"Gold star for noticing the hair," A.J. said. She was proud of herself for managing to sound so much calmer than she felt.

"Are you ready?"

"As ready as I'll ever be."

He blinked at what probably sounded like a certain lack of enthusiasm, but led the way without comment, opening the car door for her, closing it, and going round to his side.

"I thought maybe Bill's tonight?" he suggested tentatively.

"Sure."

His brows drew together. "Everything okay?"

"Sure!"

He nodded, not entirely convinced, and turned the key in the ignition.

A.J. felt a strong sense of nostalgia as they walked through the front doors of Bill's Diner, a nostalgia that had nothing to do with Buddy Holly singing "Love's Made a Fool of You" on the jukebox or the wall display of vintage lunch boxes. The first meal she and Jake had shared had been at Bill's. She wondered if they had come full circle.

They hid behind their menus for a while, then Jake laid his down and A.J. followed suit.

"How is the investigation going?"

"We don't have the ballistics report yet, but the informal consensus is the weapon used to kill Massri was probably the same used to kill the Sutherland woman."

"Then Maddie's death is connected to Dicky's, and *not* to Peggy Graham's."

"If ballistics confirms, yeah, it looks that way." He drummed his fingers restlessly on the table, caught A.J. watching, and stopped.

"Is Mother going to be arrested again?"

"Not at this time. The weapon still hasn't been found and she tested clean for gunshot residue particles." His eyes were very green beneath the dark straight brows. "Also, one of the neighbors reported seeing a blue sports car racing down the alley behind Sutherland's house around five o'clock, which would have been the approximate time of the shooting."

"Did the neighbor hear a shot? Because we sure didn't."

"No. She just noted the sports car. Very few cars use that alley so it stuck in her mind. But she wouldn't have heard anything. We found a silencer in the garden near the back gate. It must have been improperly attached to the barrel of the murder weapon."

Was that a clue? A murderer who wasn't familiar with how to attach a silencer was certainly not a professional assassin.

"Did the neighbor get a license or see the driver?"

"No. That would have been nice, but no. All the same, it does open the possibility to another suspect."

"I would hope so! Mother doesn't have any motive for killing Maddie."

Jake said patiently, "Motive is pretty much subjective, but that does seem to be the general opinion. No one can see any reason for Sutherland's death—certainly not for your mother contriving her death."

"What about the phone call—the single ring when Mother and I were talking in the kitchen?"

"That's another point in your mother's favor. There *was* a phone call. It was placed from a phone booth in Andover. The caller spoke to someone at the house for two minutes and thirty-six seconds."

The waitress appeared at their table and they gave their

orders. When the waitress departed, A.J. asked, "What about outgoing calls?"

"No luck there. The last two phone calls were to a hair place."

"The Salon!" A.J. exclaimed.

"Right. One was about ten o'clock Sunday morning. The other was at five after three in the afternoon. Roughly two hours before Sutherland was shot."

"But don't you see that's significant?" A.J. demanded. "I told you I thought there was a connection between The Salon and Massri's death. And now here's a direct link to Maddie's death."

Jake looked pained. "A.J., the first call was to set up hair appointments for all of you. The second call was Maddie asking whether she'd left her glasses at the salon. And before you ask? Yes, she had."

"Did you—?"

"I did. I went and picked them up myself."

A.J. racked her brains for a way to bring up what she believed to be the most damning fact: The Salon hair products at Massri's apartment. "You know," she said slowly, "Mother brought up a good point."

He sighed.

"I'm serious. She mentioned that the last time she was at Dicky's she noticed he had products from The Salon in his bathroom."

"You've *got* to be kidding me."

"No. Listen to me. The Salon only caters to women— and women of a certain age. Since the shampoo and conditioning rinse didn't belong to Mother, who did they belong to?"

"Shampoo and conditioning rinse," he repeated without inflection.

A.J. said steadily, "That's what Mother said."

He stared at her for a long moment. "I see. Well, first of all, we have only your mother's word she didn't bring those things into Massri's home. She could be making that up now in an effort to throw suspicion off herself."

A.J. opened her mouth, but he cut her off.

"Or maybe another woman did bring those items into Massri's apartment. Maybe he was having an affair with another woman and your mother discovered it and killed him."

A.J. couldn't seem to unlock her gaze from Jake's green one. "She didn't."

"I'm just telling you how it might look if you went around sharing this brand-new information too freely."

She opened her mouth, closed it, opened it again, and said, "You won't even consider the possibility that if there was another woman involved, she might have killed Dicky?"

"We haven't found any evidence of another woman being involved with Massri."

"Well you didn't find evidence that he'd been married to Maddie either."

His jaw tightened, and she knew that one had hit home.

"Fair enough. But how about this for an explanation? How about Massri bought the products himself?"

"I told you, The Salon caters to women."

"Hey, for your information, Avon makes bath oil that works great as a bug repellent. I use it camping, although I guess you've probably noticed I'm not generally at home to the Avon Lady."

Feeling deflated, A.J. sat back in the leather booth. She said stubbornly, "I don't believe it's a coincidence."

Seeming to feel he'd already won that round, Jake asked more tolerantly, "You don't believe what's a coincidence? That Maddie and Massri bought hair products from the same place? That's not that amazing of a coincidence, believe me." She could feel his gaze on her face. He said, "We've turned up another possible lead, though."

At her look of inquiry, he said, "Massri was fired from his position at the SCA. We haven't been able to pinpoint exactly what happened, but from everything *not* being said, it sounds potentially serious."

A.J. said slowly, "So you think it's a legitimate lead?"

"It's too soon to tell if it will pan out, but I think it casts reasonable doubt on the case we're building against Elysia." He threw her a look from beneath his brows. "Obviously that's off the record."

"When isn't it? Anyway, for the record, Mr. Meagher has already been looking into Massri's connection with the SCA."

He gave her a funny look, but whatever he might have said was interrupted by the reappearance of the waitress with their dinners.

They ate for a time in silence that gradually, at least in A.J.'s mind, took on the weight and substance of a funeral pall. With every bite it was clearer and clearer to her that Jake had not invited her out for the pleasure of her company or to discuss the case against her mother. She began to wish that he would just get it over.

The waitress returned to clear away their plates and offer dessert menus.

"Did you want dessert?" Jake asked, frowning over the menu. A.J. nearly laughed. He was clearly desperate not to have this discussion whatever it was.

"No thanks."

He ordered apple pie and stuffed the menu back in the metal holder.

A.J. waited.

He looked at her and this time he held her gaze. "Look, I owe you an explanation."

Inhale.

Exhale.

A.J. nodded.

Almost impatiently, he said, "We never specifically said anything about not seeing other people." He stopped. A.J. nodded. She managed to keep control of her face, but her stomach dropped. Officially she had only been dumped once in her life. That was when Andy had left her for Nick. It had been devastating; devastating enough that just the memory of it could give her dry heaves. Though thankfully not at the moment. The situation was shaping up to be humiliating enough as it was.

Jake's gaze rose from the wet ring on the table. He said, "But whether we said anything about it or not, I haven't been interested in dating anyone else."

"Me neither," a surprisingly calm voice said on A.J.'s behalf.

There was another pause, and then Jake said, "I'm not good at this kind of thing. What I'm trying to say is—what I'm trying to explain is—"

He stopped in awkward silence.

A.J. got out, "Honestly? It would be easier on me if you'd just say it."

Jake nodded. "I told you that I was engaged once."

"Jenny. Yes, I remember."

"What I didn't tell you—because I've never told anyone—is that Jenny disappeared two weeks before our wedding. No word, no explanation, nothing."

"You mean . . . something happened to her?"

Now there was a dumb comment, but Jake just nodded. "Yes. But not what I thought. I thought . . . I don't want to tell you the things I thought. That she'd had some kind of accident or had been kidnapped—or was dead. Maybe even worse."

Worse than dead? Then A.J. remembered that Jake was a cop and had probably seen things that she didn't want to know about—things that might be worse than being dead.

She tuned back in to hear him saying, "I spent weeks, months trying to find her. Trying to . . . find an answer."

"Did you find one?"

"Yes. I did. Or, more exactly, the answer found me. She'd gone into the WPP."

"The what?"

"The Witness Protection Program. Jenny worked for a real estate agent who turned out to have mob ties. Anyway, one night when she was working late, she saw her boss killed by none other than Jackie Palermo."

The name was vaguely familiar to A.J. Was Palermo a mob boss? Somebody connected to organized crime, she was pretty sure.

"Palermo's goons spotted her, but Jenny managed to get away, and she went straight to the cops who put her in contact with the feds. She agreed to testify, but Palermo put a contract out on her. To keep her alive, she was moved into the WPP."

"She didn't leave word for you?"

"No. It was deemed too risky. Palermo had a lot of clout, a lot of contacts—there was fear that it might reach all the way into the police department."

A.J. began to understand why Jake was such a fanatic

for the truth, the whole truth, and nothing but the truth. As
the last puzzle piece fell into place, she said, "Chess is
Jenny."

Jake nodded.

"I don't understand why she didn't get word to you.
You were her fiancé. Spouses are moved into the program—well, I mean, from what I've seen on TV."

He said shortly, "She wasn't thinking clearly. She
wasn't prepared for that. Who is?"

Clearly a sore spot. She said mildly, "Okay. Just
wondered."

Jake was instantly apologetic. "No. It's a valid question. I asked it myself plenty of times. Why did she let me
go through all that time believing the worst?"

"Would you have gone into the program with her if
she'd told you?"

He stared at her. "I . . . don't know," he admitted. "It's
so long after the fact it's hard to say what I'd have done
then." He sighed. "Anyway, I thought I'd never see her
again."

"So . . ." For the life of her, A.J. couldn't think of what
to say. Her first instinct was to ask if Jake had proof that
Jenny was telling the truth, but she knew Jake well enough
to know he didn't accept anything at face value. Jenny
must indeed be telling the truth. It was an amazing story,
and A.J. knew that she should probably be ashamed that
her primary reaction was the essentially selfish one of
wondering whether she was losing Jake to his ex-
fiancée.

At last she managed—almost steadily, "Are you still in
love with her?"

"No. I don't know." He stopped, wincing. "I don't
know what I feel. I thought I'd never see her again. I never

had the chance to say good-bye to her. Everything ended and I had all these unresolved feelings. Can you understand that?"

And the problem was, A.J. could. She could totally identify with those feelings. In fact the only hard part was picturing Jake having them. He always seemed so tough, so in control.

He said suddenly, urgently, "The thing is, I have feelings for you, too, A.J. I care for you. A lot. More than I thought I was ever going to care for anyone again."

If he told her they would always be friends, she was probably going to bean him with the saltshaker. But he didn't say it. He didn't say anything else. He just stared at her in that grim, pained way, waiting.

Waiting for what? Waiting for A.J. to say something? Waiting for her to break it off?

"Where does this leave us?"

"I don't know. I just know that I had to tell you. That I couldn't leave you wondering what the hell was going on with me."

She nodded absently. "Are you . . . seeing her?"

"Yes. I'm seeing her. I'm not dating her. I don't know what I'm doing, frankly. We're just talking."

Reliving old times? Trying to figure out if there was enough there for a future? Aware of Jake's gaze, A.J. said slowly, "I'm not sure what to say."

They stared at each other across the gulf that had unexpectedly appeared between them.

How simple it would be if A.J. could just give Jake an ultimatum. *You'd better make your mind up quick, buster!* Or if she could hate him for being confused and torn now. But neither of those was a realistic option. She cared too much for him to risk throwing down an ultimatum. For both their sakes—for all their sakes—he needed to make the right decision now. And, yes, while way down deep inside she was hurt and a little angry that Jake couldn't see that she was the best thing that had ever happened to him, apparently she had learned enough during the last year or so to recognize how unfair and unrealistic that attitude was.

In fact it was impossible not to be sympathetic to the pain he must have felt when Jenny—Chess—had disappeared. It was also impossible not to feel anger at the other woman. No matter what the circumstances, to have left Jake without a word was beyond cruel. And if Chess hadn't known him well enough to trust him with her life, she hadn't any business getting engaged to him in the first place.

So A.J. swallowed her pride and ego and fear. She said with calmness she was a million miles from feeling, "Thank you. For being honest, I mean. I care too much about you—and about us—to try and push you. For a decision. I know you'll tell me once you know, once you've worked out, what you're feeling."

He reached across the table, offering his hand. A.J. rested her hand in his palm, and to her astonishment, he raised their joined hands and kissed her fingers. It was the last gesture A.J. expected, but she found it incredibly moving—maybe because it was so obviously sincere.

She laughed shakily. Jake released her and they both reached hastily for their coffee cups.

Sixteen

❧

The next morning, Tuesday, A.J. and Elysia drove back to Stillbrook to see Bradley Meagher at his home office. Mr. Meagher greeted them cordially enough although he seemed just a little stiff with Elysia.

He led the way down a short hallway to his office in the basement of the gracious old Victorian house. It was a comfortably cluttered room with a collection of mismatched and battered furniture. Framed law degrees and honorary diplomas adorned the walls. The remnants of a TV dinner sat on the table next to a long leather couch. A white cockatoo in an enormous old-fashioned birdcage scooted along his perch and harshly called out, "You da bomb!"

Mr. Meagher threw the bird a beleaguered glance and stepped behind his large, cluttered desk. Something about that move and the funny, half-awkward look Mr. Meagher threw Elysia as he sat down put A.J. in mind of someone retreating behind the safety of a barrier.

"Well now," Mr. Meagher said briskly, staring down at the file on his desk. He began to bring them up to date on the progress in the DA's attempt to build the case against Elysia.

Yes, A.J. was now convinced that Mr. Meagher was uncomfortable with Elysia and wishing to keep both physical and emotional distance between them. A glance at her mother's face confirmed her suspicion. Elysia was watching Mr. Meagher with a perplexed expression. Perplexed and perhaps a little hurt.

"The forensics report confirms that the gun used in Maddie Sutherland's murder was almost certainly the same as that used in young Massri's."

A.J. remembered that Mr. Meagher must have, given the recollections of her mother and Maddie during their dinner together, known Maddie as well. He seemed businesslike and unmoved by her death. But perhaps they had not cared much for each other? Or perhaps he hid his feelings well?

"Have they found the gun?" A.J. asked.

"No, that they haven't."

Elysia drawled, "I'm surprised Herr Bormann—"

"That'll be enough of that, me girl," Mr. Meagher broke in sharply, his face flushing. "One reason you're out on bail now is Jake Oberlin spoke up for you. The DA and nearly everyone else involved in the prosecution of this case thought you too great a flight risk."

There was a hint of color in Elysia's ivory face, too. She lifted a slim, dismissing shoulder, but said grudgingly, "If that's true, I suppose I owe him thanks."

"*If* it's true?" Mr. Meagher repeated. "'Tis not meself who plays games with the truth!"

Elysia's eyes narrowed. "What's that supposed to mean?"

Mr. Meagher appeared to struggle with himself.

"Hey, dude!" cried the cockatoo. "Let's party!"

Mr. Meagher muttered a curse and rose to throw a faded blanket over the cage.

For the first time, A.J. forced herself to objectively consider whether Mr. Meagher might have had a motive to kill Dakarai. She dismissed the idea quickly, remembering Mr. Meagher's obvious shock at discovering that Elysia had been having an affair. Of course, he could have been acting; A.J. had seen plenty of TV movies where just such scenarios played out, in which case Mr. Meagher might have framed Elysia in the hope of driving her to turn to him for help.

Still. *Mr. Meagher?* That was pretty hard to believe—and not just because A.J. was very fond of the old rascal.

She observed him surreptitiously as he returned to his desk, and decided the idea was simply too far-fetched. Mr. Meagher probably did nurse unrequited feelings for Elysia, but that was still a long way removed from knocking off her gigolo lover. For one thing, Mr. Meagher was far too practical. He'd be bound to see that getting rid of Massri wouldn't help his own situation, nor was Elysia likely to change her feelings for him this late in the game simply out of gratitude.

Actually, now that she thought of it, A.J. wasn't exactly sure what her mother's feelings for Bradley Meagher were. She was clearly fond of him, considered him a friend . . . but observing the uncertain way Elysia was studying her old friend, A.J. wondered if Elysia herself had ever worked out exactly what she felt for Mr. Meagher.

"Mr. Meagher, what's our next move?" A.J. asked. "Surely the fact that the police haven't found the murder weapon works in our favor?"

"That it does. The problem remains that there is no other viable suspect."

"But all that means is the police haven't found him—or her—yet. Have you been able to get any further with the SCA?"

"Not so far," Mr. Meagher said grimly. "I'm planning to make a regular nuisance of meself until someone in that bloody country and organization will talk to me."

"I think it *is* a valid lead. Even Jake told me that the police have finally begun to explore the angle that Massri might have been involved in illegal activities regarding antiquities. There must be something there or they wouldn't be bothering to dig any further when they've already charged Mother."

"Now, now. The police prefer that the right villain go to prison for the crime," Mr. Meagher remonstrated automatically. But he was clearly considering her words. "If new information *has* come to light—"

"Well, it must have, although I have no idea what it would be. Jake didn't confide more than that to me."

Mr. Meagher's brows rose. He reached for a legal pad and began making notes. Unfortunately there wasn't a great deal more that A.J. could tell him.

"I'll talk to Jake Oberlin," he assured A.J. "Put a wee bit of pressure on him."

"Just make sure he understands that this was a line of investigation you were already pursuing," A.J. said, remembering some uncomfortable moments in the past between her and Jake.

Elysia sniffed dismissively but withheld comment.

"What about gambling debts?" A.J. suggested suddenly. "Mother, did you tell Mr. Meagher about Dicky betting on horse racing?"

Mr. Meagher looked up. "He played the ponies? Did he indeed?"

"Yes," Elysia said reluctantly. "But it really wasn't the sort of thing you're hoping for. Perfectly decent people do gamble for fun now and then. It doesn't always lead to losing one's home or having men named Guido turn up with baseball bats."

"True," A.J. conceded. "But Dicky *wasn't* a perfectly decent person. He was a blackmailer and probably a thief and he took advantage of vulnerable old ladies." Seeing her mother's indignant expression, A.J. added, "As well as you."

Elysia subsided, mollified.

A.J. stayed in town to have lunch with her mother—Mr. Meagher excusing himself on the grounds of a prior commitment—and then drove out to the studio. The lobby was relatively quiet as classes were in session. A.J. greeted Emma and went straight to her office.

She had switched on her laptop and was glancing through the morning mail when she realized Lily had followed her into her office.

Lily said, "So nice of you to join us."

"I'm sorry?" This was a little bizarre when she had been trying all day yesterday to get Lily to schedule time with her.

Lily smiled a tight little smile. "You seem to be keeping banker's hours these days. We had a problem with the upstairs restrooms this morning."

What the—? Did A.J. look like Josephine the Plumber?

But no, that wasn't fair. As co-manager, A.J. did have a responsibility to be at the studio at least as often as Lily.

"What was the problem with the upstairs restroom?"

"One of the toilets shattered."

"One of the . . ." A.J.'s voice faded out. "The seat shattered?"

"The entire toilet. Base and all. There was water everywhere."

A.J. nodded and kept nodding. She was very much afraid she might laugh. She said gravely, "And so you called a plumber, I assume?"

"That's right. But it's more serious than that. The toilet is a symptom not the disease. I believe we need to have a meeting with every overweight student and reevaluate the progress each has made since joining Sacred Balance."

Uh. . . .

A.J. said mildly, "Perhaps the toilet was defective?"

"The plumber didn't believe that to be the case."

Had Lily finally snapped or had she? It was very hard to believe they were having this conversation. Was Lily suggesting that students who broke their diets or missed their daily workouts shouldn't be allowed to use the restroom? What *was* she suggesting—beyond the fact that A.J. was not pulling *her* weight?

"I see," A.J. said. "Well, it happens that I agree with you that we should be monitoring the progress of those students who joined us with weight loss goals in mind."

"Yes, *we* should."

Ah. There it was. The accusation unveiled at last. "Lily, there is a *lot* going on in my life right now in case you hadn't noticed."

"Yes, and very little of it seems to have to do with yoga or Sacred Balance."

A.J. swallowed her ire. Lily was perfectly correct. Yoga

was pretty much the last thing on her mind these days. "You're right," she said pleasantly. "But that's a temporary state of affairs. Anything else?"

Lily seemed taken aback by A.J.'s calm response. After a stiff second, she said, "For example, this vacation you took last weekend. If you were well enough to be up and about, you should have been up and about *here*. Where we were short-staffed."

Whatever A.J. had been expecting, it wasn't this.

"Last weekend was hardly a vacation. My back wasn't at the point where I could have conducted classes. You know that."

"Aren't you the one who told me your value to this organization went beyond teaching classes?"

A.J. felt herself redden. There was an element of unpleasant truth to Lily's observation. *Much* of what Lily was saying was true. But it was only part of the truth and didn't take into account the tireless and enthusiastic effort A.J. had put into Sacred Balance over the past year. She replied, trying not to sound as testy as she felt, "That's true. I did choose to spend the weekend with my mother. This is a stressful time for her."

"More stressful now, I'd say." Before A.J. could respond to that, Lily said, "Why not be honest? You enjoy owning the studio, you don't enjoy running it."

A.J. managed to control her instinctive reaction, settling for a terse, "Not true."

"Of course it is. You don't have to work. Sacred Balance is just a hobby for you. You're dabbling in managing the studio, and that's not fair to the rest of us."

"I don't know where this is coming from because I'm at this studio working my tail off nearly every single day.

I'm here more than any other staff member—and that includes you."

"Maybe at first, but nowadays you're more interested in playing amateur sleuth than teaching yoga."

"You have zero idea what you're talking about."

"I'm not the only one to notice, A.J."

"Really?" A.J. sat up very straight. "Well, if anyone else has concerns, they can address them to me directly."

"You wouldn't be so defensive if you didn't recognize the truth of what I'm saying. Look, I know you care about the studio. I know you view it as some kind of spiritual trust left to you by Di, but if you really want what's best for Sacred Balance, you'll hear me out."

Here it was. A.J. had known that Lily was angling toward a particular end. She braced herself for what was without a doubt going to be unpleasant.

"Go on."

"Mara Allen of Yoga Meridian contacted me a few weeks ago. She and her investors are interested in making an offer for Sacred Balance."

"Sacred Balance isn't for sale."

"That's emotion talking, not reason. Mara is willing to pay a lot of money for Sacred Balance. Furthermore, she's willing to let me continue as manager of the studio—I could keep on any instructor or staff member I chose. No one would have to lose their job."

"No one has to lose their job now. Including me."

Lily's thin mouth twisted. "Yoga Meridian, and Mara, have a lot of money behind them. Her investors are willing to pay a more than fair price."

"Lily, as you keep pointing out, I don't need the money."

"It's not just about you, A.J. It's about what's right for the rest of us, too. What you don't seem to understand is, if you're going to be so blindly stubborn about this, we're going to lose Sacred Balance completely. We can't compete with Yoga Meridian. They've got everything we've got plus a day spa and hair salon. Every day we lose more customers to them."

"That's ridiculous. Yes, we've lost a few customers, but we've gained new customers, too. The turnover is normal. It balances out."

"You can't really believe that. You need to look past your own ego and face facts before we lose Sacred Balance completely."

A.J. took a deep breath and then expelled it slowly.

Inhale.

Exhale.

Inh—

"Okay. You've made your pitch and I've heard you out. I'm not selling Sacred Balance to Mara Allen or anyone else. This subject is now closed."

"Don't be so sure," Lily flared. "The choice isn't just yours. I'm willing to sell my share in Sacred Balance to Mara." Lily's black gaze met A.J.'s defiantly.

"You don't *have* a share!" Despite her good intentions, A.J.'s voice rose. "You're a co-manager, not a co-owner. You don't own any part of this studio."

"Try running it without me."

"I would *love* to try running it without you!"

They glared at each other. Then Lily rose with a nasty little smile.

"Maybe you shouldn't be so hasty, A.J. I very much doubt that you're going to want to hang around this little town managing a yoga studio now that your boyfriend has dumped you and your mother is about to be convicted of murder."

For a moment A.J. was so angry she wasn't sure she could get the words out without choking on them.

"If I were you, I'd get out of my office."

Lily's dark eyebrows rose haughtily, but get she did. A.J. slammed the door after her. The satisfying bang shook the pictures on the wall, and the framed photograph of Diantha fell over on its face.

"Well, what were you thinking?" A.J. inquired of the photo as she propped it back on the desk.

Aunt Diantha's serene smile had never been more enigmatic. Feeling sheepish at her loss of temper, A.J. took a few moments to regain her calm.

After all, what was the big deal? Surely, she should be used to Lily by now.

She went to the window and stared out at the pine trees and meadow. Her anger slowly subsided to be replaced by sheepish humor. Oh, if only she could phone Jake to share that line about toilets being a symptom and not the disease!

She was grinning ruefully as her door opened and Suze peeked in. She whispered, "Are you okay? We could hear you all the way in the front lobby."

"If she ever gets knocked off, I'm going to be the prime suspect."

"Take a number."

They both laughed uneasily.

"Is there anything I can do?" Suze asked.

"Keep her out of my way."

Suze nodded although they both knew that was a polite

fiction. Nobody was going to prevent Lily from going where she liked and saying whatever she chose to.

When A.J. cooled down she called Jake partly because she had remembered that she had never got around to mentioning Dicky's possible gambling debts, and she was quite sure her mother had never shared that information, and partly because—painful though it was to admit—she missed him and wanted to hear his voice.

"Hey," he said. He sounded preoccupied but not unhappy to hear from her.

"Every time we talk I forget to mention this, but Mother told me a while back that there's a possibility that Dicky had gambling debts. He used to bet regularly on horses, and she said he spent a lot of time in Atlantic City."

"Is that so?"

"Yes. She didn't know for certain that he ever had any problems meeting payments or anything like that, but . . ."

Jake waited for her to finish, and when she didn't he said, "Okay. Unfortunately it's not a whole lot to go on. Any idea where in Atlantic City he used to place his bets?"

"I don't know. She didn't know. She didn't go on those trips. She tries to avoid casinos and that kind of environment."

Aware of Elysia's history, Jake said, "Right. Well, it's another rock to turn over. Maybe something slimy is waiting there."

"And Mother remembered something else."

He didn't quite sigh, but he sounded wary as he said, "Which would be what?"

"A few months ago, when Mother and Dicky started up

again, she said he was getting abusive phone calls from an ex-lover. A woman named Dora Beauford."

"Why didn't she mention that sooner?"

"She doesn't think there's a connection because the woman hadn't called Dicky for a while—at least, not that she knew. I don't know that that's necessarily true. Dora might have stopped calling because he blocked her phone calls. The fact that Mother wasn't aware of her doesn't necessarily mean Dora wasn't still stalking him."

"Dora Beauford you said?"

"Right."

"I'll check it out."

After a hesitation, A.J. asked, "How's it going?"

"It's going. Look, A.J., I'm in the middle of something. I'll give you a call later, okay?"

"Of course!" she said quickly.

She clicked her cell shut and put her face in her hands.

The intercom buzzed.

"Miz Alexander," Emma announced.

Glad for any distraction from her crumbling personal life, A.J. snatched the phone up. "Mother?"

"I found her!" Elysia said triumphantly.

"Found who?"

"Peggy Graham's sister."

"I didn't know you were looking for her."

"Of course I was looking for her. Who else would know whether Peggy killed herself?"

"How did you find her?" A.J. questioned uneasily.

"Oh, you know," Elysia said airily. "The thing is, pumpkin, she's agreed to meet with us this afternoon."

"Meet with *us*?"

"Who else?"

"The police, for one."

"Well, we should find out whether she has anything to say before we turn her over to the law, don't you think?"

Mindful of Lily's accusations—and Jake's warnings—A.J. said, "It doesn't work that way. I think maybe we should leave this to Jake."

"It's always worked this way for us in the past."

"Mother, you make it sound as though we ran some kind of formal criminal investigation agency. The truth is, we've just poked around in other people's business until they got fed up and reacted—sometimes, if you'll recall—violently."

Elysia scoffed at this reminder. "What does it matter what the catalyst for truth is?"

"It matters if we blow Jake's case or get ourselves killed."

"I. See." Could there be two more ominous words in the English language?

"I just think—"

"'Sharper than a serpent's tooth it is to have a thankless child.'" Elysia interrupted with one of her favorite quotes from Shakespeare—one that A.J. hadn't heard for a few years, and would have been happy to have kept it so.

"Mother."

"Say no more. If you're going to abandon me in my hour of need, I shall have to manage on my own. Fortunately I still remember a trick or two from my days on *221B Baker Street*."

A.J. groaned. Lily was going to love this. "What time is this meeting?"

"I'll pick you up at the studio just after three," Elysia said immediately, cheerfully.

Seventeen

⎯⎯∞⎯⎯

"Peg was headstrong. Didn't like not getting her way."

A.J. and Elysia were sitting in Matt Crowley's large, sunny garden sipping iced tea.

The garden was decorated with ball-sized Easter eggs and resin lambs and ducks. A giant blue inflatable bunny was lying like a puddle on the lawn.

Elysia inquired, "Was there any reason to suspect your sister's death was *not* suicide?"

Matt's jaw tightened. "Plenty. Peg was not the kind of person to take her own life. And I never knew her to take a sleeping pill. She was positive, forceful. Does that sound like someone who relied on sleeping pills or would kill herself?"

"Was she in ill health by any chance?"

"Nope. Strong as an ox."

"She didn't leave a note or anything like that?"

"No." Mart added grudgingly, "But even if she did kill herself, she wouldn't have left a note. Peggy had a real thing about her privacy. She wouldn't have wanted any publicity."

"Did you tell the police your suspicions?" asked A.J.

"Sure. They didn't exactly tell me that everyone said the same thing, but I got the impression that a lot of people have trouble accepting a suicide verdict."

Elysia meditatively tapped one polished fingernail on the glass-topped table. "Was your sister involved with anyone? Sometimes when romances end badly a person can experience an emotional low."

"Ha!" At Mart's harsh laugh the birds in the feeder took flight in bright flashes of color. "Not Peg. She wasn't the sentimental kind. Oh, she had her disappointing *affaires de coeur*, but she wasn't the kind of person to sit around brooding and feeling sorry for herself. No, she did her best to get even with the little ba— creep."

A.J. had to admire that skilful look of attentive inquiry from Elysia.

"He was an *artiste*," Mart said. She waved her hands as though playing pat-a-cake. "A sculptor. You know the kind of thing. Nudes that look like Buddhas and sumo wrestlers. My grandkids do a better job with Play-Doh. She should have known better at her age."

"What happened?"

"What you'd expect. She paid a fortune for art classes she didn't need and art supplies she never used. Why not, anyway? They were both consenting adults."

"Why not, indeed," murmured Elysia.

"But Peggy fell in love?" A.J. suggested.

Both Elysia and Mart snickered. "Bless your heart," Mart said. "No, babycakes. Nothing like that. Oh, she was fond of the kid, I guess, but it was just a holiday romance. Except at home. You know the kind of thing."

Elysia sighed and nodded wisely, auditioning for the part of Woman of the World.

"I don't think she gave him another thought once it was over and she was busy with her friends and charity work. But then the letters started."

"What kind of letters?" The penny dropped. "*Blackmail?*"

"Smart girl," Mart said to Elysia. "Yes, blackmail. There were pictures. Graphic pictures—and plenty of them. Well, Peg was furious, but what could she do? She had her name and position to think of. Not that Peg really cared about that kind of thing, but you know how people can be. She was on a lot of committees with a lot of stuffed shirts who would have taken a dim view of any hanky-panky."

"How was she approached? E-mail? Snail mail?"

"Yes. Real mail. The letters were sent from Hamburg and the payments were made to a post office box in Newton."

"Newton," Elysia said quickly.

"It's the county seat," A.J. pointed out. "We can't make too much of that."

"Where did she meet this boy?"

At the same time, A.J. asked, "Did they meet on a cruise by any chance?"

"No." Mart sounded sure. "No, Peggy never went on a cruise. She was deathly afraid of water. To be honest, I can't remember where she said she met him."

"Where did your sister get her hair styled?" Elysia asked.

"Oh that overpriced place in Newton. The Salon or whatever they call it."

A.J. and Elysia exchanged looks.

"Did she approach this boy after the blackmail began?"

"Ohhhh yes," Mart said with grim satisfaction. "Did she ever. And she kept approaching him." She laughed heartily. "He claimed he wasn't blackmailing her. That it was nothing to do with him. He was romancing some other rich widow by then, and Peg did her best to stick a spoke in *that* wheel."

"Did she try approaching the woman directly?"

"No. I asked her about that. She said it wouldn't do any good. The woman wouldn't believe her or was too crazy about the kid to care—and Peg hadn't paid fifty thousand dollars to protect her good name just to reveal it to some stranger who was old enough to know better."

"Fifty thousand dollars," A.J. repeated weakly. "What about those blackmail payments? Did your sister ever try to find who was picking them up from the post office box? Whether it was this boy or not?"

Mart said slowly, "I don't know. She talked about it at one point. I don't know if she ever really did pursue it. If she did, she didn't tell me about it. Peg was private. That's why she let them extort money from her, I guess. Me? I'd have said publish and be damned." She took a defiant swig of iced tea.

"Would Peg have been likely to confront the blackmailer?"

"It's possible. If she could have done it safely—I mean, done it and kept her secret."

"She should have gone to the police," A.J. said. Both Mart and Elysia gave her scornful looks. A.J. insisted, "She's dead because she didn't speak up."

Elysia dismissed this with a graceful flutter of fingers.

A.J. ignored her and asked, "Do you remember what this boy's name was? Was he Egyptian, by any chance?"

"No. Blond and blue-eyed as I recall. His name was something like Cory. I don't remember a last name. I don't think Peg ever mentioned it."

"Would you have an address for him or any idea of how to get in contact with him?"

Mart shook her head.

"What about your sister's papers? Do you think there might be something there that might provide a lead?"

Mart scratched her head, frowning meditatively. "I don't remember seeing anything, but then I wasn't looking for anything. Not to do with the kid, anyway. I tried to find some way to prove she had been blackmailed. But there was nothing." She grimaced. "I'm a pack rat. My sister was the opposite. She never kept anything she didn't have immediate use for. And I've seen banks that didn't have files and paperwork as well organized as she was."

"She wouldn't wish to take a chance on something falling into the wrong hands," Elysia remarked.

"Exactly. That's exactly right. She wasn't someone who left anything to chance. She didn't like to gamble."

"But she took a chance when she had the affair with Cory or whatever his name was," A.J. pointed out.

The other two women stared at her. Then Mart reached over and patted her hand. "You'll understand when you're older, babycakes."

"They killed her," Elysia said with ghoulish satisfaction as they left Mart Crowley's quiet suburban home and started back to Stillbrook. "Either way you look at it, they killed her."

"If she killed herself because she was being black-mailed, I agree that philosophically and ethically the blackmailers are guilty. But I don't know how that would hold up in a court of law. I don't know that could ever be proved since she didn't leave a note."

Elysia shifted into high gear as they reached the open highway. "Immaterial. She didn't kill herself. *They* killed her."

A.J. wasn't so sure. In fact their interview with Mart Crowley had left her less sure. "That wouldn't be so easy to do, Mother. First of all, Peggy didn't typically take sleeping pills, so how would they get her to swallow an overdose?"

"Force-feed her. Slip them in her bedtime warm milk. I don't know. I just know they did."

"But once Mart started claiming foul play the police would surely have checked for signs of violence. There couldn't have been any."

"We don't know that for sure."

"Well, we can find out." Jake would surely do this much for her. A.J. added, "Plus how would the blackmailers have gained access to Peggy's warm milk?"

Elysia said exasperatedly, "I was being facetious."

"I know you were, but the point remains. If she didn't take the pills herself, how would they have been administered? Someone would have to have access to her home and her pills and her food or drink."

"This boy she was having the affair with would have had access. This Cory."

"We don't know that. According to Mart, Cory was just a boy toy. I can't imagine someone as fearful of publicity as Peggy seemed to be giving a casual sexual partner the key to her home."

"Maybe he stole a key."

"Maybe he did, but this is getting totally into the realm of speculation. We don't know that Cory ever had access to Peggy's keys, let alone that she ever brought him home."

"We need to find out."

"We need to be careful," A.J. corrected. "For one thing if there *is* some connection between Maddie's death and Peggy's we don't want anyone to know we're poking around in this. It could prove extremely hazardous to *our* health."

Elysia made a disgusted sound.

"I'm serious, Mother. If Maddie was killed I think there's a very good chance it was because she knew something about Peggy's death. Or someone thought she did. And if that's the case, they acted swiftly and ruthlessly."

Elysia had no response to that.

"Why don't we put together a list of questions and I'll ask Jake—"

"*Jake!*"

"Yes, Jake. I don't have another police contact. Do you? Plus I believe him when he's trying to help you. If we can present him with a viable alternative suspect and motive, he'll take it to the DA. So let's figure out what we need to know. Like did they investigate this Cory at all? Was there any record of where the sleeping pills were purchased? That kind of thing."

"The fact that four people connected to this case are also connected to the same hairdresser is too much of a coincidence for me."

"I agree. But not everyone seems to think it's that amazing a coincidence. And, in fairness, The Salon is *very* popular. Besides, we already knew Peggy went to The

Salon," A.J. reminded her. "Maddie learned about her death at The Salon."

Elysia sighed. "True."

They debated a short list of questions A.J. could present to Jake in hopes that he might follow up where they could not. By the time they had worked out their short list, they were pulling into the long, dirt drive that led to the farmhouse at Deer Hollow.

As A.J. got out of the SUV, Elysia leaned across and said, "Anna?"

A.J. bent, absently reflecting that even a week ago she would have been unable to make so simple a move without pain. "Yes?"

"Thank you."

"Of course!" A.J. said quickly. She wasn't even exactly sure what her mother was thanking her for, but she was a little embarrassed.

"I know you think we should trust the police and leave any further investigating to them. I couldn't do this on my own, so . . . thank you."

A.J. nodded and let the heavy door swing shut.

She was touched, although she wasn't convinced that Elysia wouldn't have forged ahead on her own. She told herself she was acting as a moderating influence, and she hoped that was true. But as much as she wanted to leave the investigation to the police, as much as she wanted to believe that they would find Dicky Massri's real killer without any help from her or Elysia, she knew things didn't always work out the way they should.

She watched the Land Rover bouncing and bumping down the dirt road back to the highway, then she turned and let herself inside the house.

It felt warm and a little stuffy, so she opened the windows and went out on the back patio to call to Monster, who came around the side of the house looking guilty in the way only a dog digging for gophers in the flower beds can look.

"What have you been doing?" A.J. said in the deep, deep voice she always assumed for scolding Monster—on those rare occasions he needed scolding.

Monster promptly flattened his ears and looked cowed, although what he made of the deep, deep voice was anyone's guess. The deep, deep voice was actually as far as A.J.'s punitive measures went. She sort of even secretly hoped that Monster might catch a few of the gophers in a display of natural selection, but she'd never seen any sign of success. Which, on second thought, was perhaps a good thing.

Monster tried to change the subject by indicating it was past his dinnertime, and A.J. fed him, made herself a grilled cheese sandwich, and pulled out Diantha's box of notes and rough manuscript draft.

As always she found it centering, soothing, to read over her aunt's thoughts. Diantha had been a mix of practicality and compassion. Well-educated and informed, she had also been imaginative and fiercely loyal to the causes she believed in and the people she loved. She had not been without her flaws, of course. She had also been stubborn and occasionally judgmental. Once she made up her mind, it was difficult to persuade her to see things another way, which was probably how A.J. and Lily had ended up as co-partners when anyone could see that that was a match made in Hell.

Words have tremendous power. Sometimes in the heat of the moment we forget this. We concentrate on winning the battle at hand and forget that winning a par-

ticular battle may cost us the war. Why do I speak of war and yoga in the same breath? Because our modern lives are full of conflict. Look around you. We all experience tension, conflict, anger. And what are we angry about? We believe that we have been wronged. What happens then? We scream. We scream to be heard. What then can we do for the angry among us? The first and most immediate thing we can do is listen.

A.J. jotted a couple of notes in the margin of the neatly typed page. Through the open window she could hear the sweet song of a bird settling in for the night, and Monster snuffling along the flower bed.

"Monster!" she growled.

The snuffling stopped. But in the silence she heard the approach of a familiar engine. Heart beating with sudden excitement, A.J. rose and looked out the front window.

Headlights were coming down the road.

The familiar four-wheel drive utility vehicle with police insignia pulled into her front yard and Jake got out.

A.J. went out on the porch to greet him. He kissed her hello—not a deep, passionate kiss, true, but not a perfunctory peck either.

"This is a surprise," she said.

"Yeah. Well." He followed her inside the house and down the hall to the kitchen. "I thought since I was in the area I'd come by and tell you what we found out on Dora Beauford."

A.J. studied his stern profile. She knew Jake well enough to know he was about to give her news he didn't want to deliver. Perhaps it was about the case against her mother. Perhaps not. Her nerves tightened.

She made herself guess out loud. "Dora Beauford has an alibi."

He nodded grimly.

"What kind of alibi?"

"She was getting her hair done."

"Where?"

Jake was already shaking his head. "Not at The Salon."

"Did you ask?" She handed him a jar of ground coffee; the lid had a tendency to stick.

He opened it automatically, saying, "Of course I asked. I had to verify her alibi."

"Did you ask her about The Salon?"

He hesitated.

"You didn't. *Why?* What would it have hurt? Couldn't you just this once have—"

"Hold on. Of course I asked," he interrupted. "And, yes, she was a client for a time. But I think you're pinning too much on that connection."

A.J. scooped coffee into the machine. "And to think I believed Mother was jumping to conclusions. Jake, they're running some kind of blackmail scheme out of The Salon."

If she'd imagined she would surprise him with that theory, she was disappointed. Jake said, "I know that's what you think—you might even be right—but nobody tried to blackmail Dora Beauford."

"You questioned her about that? Specifically?"

"Believe it or not, A.J., I do know how to do my job."

She had the grace to blush. "Sorry. It's just . . ."

"I know. This time it's personal."

She grimaced. Personal and painful. Jake's expression was uncompromising; he met her gaze unwaveringly. "I do understand. I promise you I'm following every lead."

"Could Dora be lying?"

He shrugged. "It's always a possibility. I didn't get that feeling, though."

A.J. studied his face. "But still, it's too much to be a coincidence. That all of these women were connected to the same beauty salon?"

"I agree. Up to a point."

"That point being?"

"Motive for murder."

"I'm not following. If all these women are being blackmailed—"

"Honey—A.J. First of all, your mother already admits that she was being blackmailed. So there's nothing new there."

"But it's a blackmail *ring*. It has to be."

"Maybe. We haven't proved that yet. But say you're right. From the perspective of the DA, that doesn't clear Elysia. Just the opposite."

"But it has to throw some doubt. A blackmail ring means that there were other victims. Other women with a motive for wanting Massri out of the way."

"Not necessarily. An argument could be made that all these women were being blackmailed but your mother is the only one who turned violent. You've also yet to prove a connection between Massri and The Salon. Shampoo bottles in the shower aren't going to hold up in court. You said it yourself: the hair care products could belong to one of his lady friends."

"But then Massri himself becomes the connection. The fact that he was involved with all these women and the women all went to the same salon? That has to be significant."

He answered on what appeared to be a tangent. "The other problem I've got, from what you've managed to uncover, it's these other women—the victims—who seem to be at risk." He added quickly, as A.J. opened her mouth, "And from a blackmailer's perspective, that's not good business."

"Maybe it was better business than the alternative. Peggy Graham's sister says Peggy was aggressively pursuing whoever blackmailed her. Maybe someone was afraid of exposure."

"Peggy Graham's sister?" Jake inquired too politely

"Er, yes. Actually, I was going to tell you about that." She said quickly, trying to head him off, "Mother is, as I'm sure you could guess, really upset about Maddie's death and when she remembered that Peggy Graham had a sister—"

Jake interrupted. "She's snooping. Don't bother to gift wrap it. She announced to the entire world she'd solve the damn case herself, and that's exactly what she's set out to do."

The assorted stress and strains of the last two weeks got the better of A.J.'s temper, and she snapped, "Well, do you blame her?"

He stared at her for a long, bleak moment. "No," he said finally. "I don't blame her. I'd probably try to do the same thing, but she's liable to get herself deeper in hot water—and drag you in, too."

This was such an unexpected relenting of Jake's previous attitude that A.J. didn't know what to say. He solved that problem by asking her to fill him in on what she and Elysia had learned from Mart Crowley.

Jake heard her out in mostly silence and sipped his coffee. At the end of A.J.'s recital he said, "Okay, so maybe Peggy Graham's decision to take action against the extortionists made someone nervous and they decided to deal with her. But it wasn't Massri, obviously, since Graham wasn't seeing him."

A.J. bit her lip. "You're saying it's a dead end."

He sighed. "I'm saying . . . that there does seem to be a connection between these women and The Salon, but it's not enough. I don't buy the blackmail angle as sufficient motive for murder. You don't kill the goose that lays the golden egg."

"Then what do you buy? Because if nothing else, it's ridiculous to think my mother would shoot someone in her *front garden*."

"Listen, you don't have to convince me. I don't believe Elysia shot Massri. I admit I initially wondered." He clarified hastily, "It crossed my mind, that's all—but having interviewed her several times since the incident, I agree. She's not our perp. But an argument like that doesn't get us anywhere. People kill other people all the time in stupid and brutal ways. Murder doesn't take a mastermind. It takes someone whose self-interest knows no boundaries, be it a brain surgeon in the Hamptons or a junkie in Harlem."

"Your point being?"

"You're going to have to come up with a better line of defense."

"What about the scandal at the SCA?"

"I'm still working that angle. It appears that Massri accepted bribes not to investigate allegations of illegal excavations and the smuggling of antiquities."

"That sounds promising."

"Maybe. There's no question that illegal trade in antiquities is still big money. Unscrupulous collectors, private and public, are always on the lookout for valuable artifacts. High quality relics are freely available on the international market if you know where to look and so long as the interested parties are prepared to pay enormous sums. And Egyptian antiquities are pretty much as popular as ever."

"Maybe Massri crossed the wrong people?"

"Maybe, but as far as I can tell the people he crossed were the Egyptian government and his colleagues at the SCA. I don't think either of those entities came gunning for him in Elysia's front yard."

"How could Massri get away with that kind of thing?"

"He was in the perfect position to get away with it—he was supposed to be one of the watchdogs."

"That's pretty low. Trading in national treasures."

"It is, but the money being offered for some of these antiquities is mind-boggling. And the people buying aren't always what you'd think. More than one museum curator has been nailed in the illegal trade of antiquities. Sure, sales at reputable auction houses are supposed to be carefully monitored. I guess they are for the most part. Details of the provenance of objects are supposed to be provided."

"Provenance?"

"Documented history of the ownership of an object. They're supposed to get publication details of similar pieces, and a history of the movement of objects through the market. But the system isn't foolproof. To say the least."

A.J. nodded. It was getting late and she was getting tired, although she was doing her best to seem bright and cheerful. The last thing she wanted to do was hurry Jake off. For these few hours she could pretend that everything was still good between them. That they were building toward something that might sustain them through all the years to come. Something more than friendship, although she valued Jake's friendship, too.

He yawned, glanced at his watch.

"Can Dora Beauford's alibi be broken?" she asked quickly, at random.

"I doubt it. Only her hairdresser knows for sure."

"Ouch."

"You asked." He was grinning at her and she grinned back, warmly conscious of the ever present tug of liking and attraction between them. No, that hadn't changed.

Jake seemed to recollect himself. He said more seriously, "I'm double-checking that one. But I wouldn't pin my hopes on it." He hesitated. "I guess . . . I ought to get going."

No you oughtn't. A.J. opened her mouth. She closed it again. She wasn't going to put pressure on him. And she sure wasn't going to beg. Or even ask politely. In case it was misconstrued. This was something Jake had to work out for himself; he knew—could hardly fail to know—how she felt.

"Okay," she said, rising. "Thanks for stopping by."

He stared at her for a funny moment, then rose, too.

They walked out together to the front porch.

He seemed to hesitate. "Night."

"Night," she murmured as he kissed her cheek.

She watched him walk across the yard, boot heels scraping the flagstone walk. The door slammed as he got in the SUV. He backed up slowly, flashed the headlights at her, and drove away into the night.

Eighteen

Morag was making herself right at home. It was not a pretty sight. The contents of Elysia's purse were scattered across the kitchen counter and in the sink. The trash bin had been turned over, the contents of the silverware drawer were scattered over the floor—along with less benign tokens of the ferret's presence.

"Yikes," A.J. said, watching Elysia deal quickly, if grimly, with the mess. The pointy-faced culprit gazed down at them from the recipe books on the shelf above the stove. "Is that—?"

"It is," Elysia said darkly. "We're working on potty training."

"Uh oh."

"Oh, she's not so bad," Elysia said quickly. "A little mischievous, perhaps. In fact I was thinking Monster might like a little sister." As convincing performances went, she'd given better.

"You've got to be joking," A.J. said. "A little *snack* maybe. A little sister, no. He's definitely an only child."

They both studied the ferret peeking out at them.

"She's very cute," A.J. said.

"Yes. I suppose she's missing Maddie."

"Well then she'll probably settle down, don't you think?"

"I think she's a fiend from Hell in cuddly clothing," Elysia stated for the record. "On the bright side, I've been reading up and they don't live that long. Usually six to ten years, and I believe Maddie said something about her being seven years old."

"*Mother.*"

"I'm just being realistic, pumpkin. She's as adorable as a stuffed toy, yes, and if she *were* stuffed, we'd get along beautifully. As it is, she's one hell of a nuisance."

A.J. had to bite her lip to keep a straight face. "Look at that little face. That little pink nose, those little beady eyes."

Elysia sniffed. Morag sniffed back. Or perhaps she hissed. It was uncertain at that height.

"Maybe next time you'll think twice before you nab someone's pet."

Elysia ignored this and went back to restoring order to her ransacked kitchen. A.J. found a sponge under the sink and scrubbed the granite counter as she filled her mother in on everything Jake had told her the evening before.

"Perhaps we should go see Dora Beauford," Elysia said thoughtfully, tossing the soiled sponge in the trash bin.

Her kitchen was once more immaculate. However, if the sounds of tinkling glass from the dining room were anything to go by, Hurricane Morag was striking the west wing of the house.

A.J. thought it might be in Morag's best interests if she were to otherwise occupy Elysia's attention. "I'm not sure there's a point. Jake seemed to think Beauford's alibi was pretty much unshakeable."

Elysia shook her head in the manner of Holmes lamenting Watson's general obliviousness to the significance of tropical flowers. "One doesn't question suspects merely to eliminate or convict them. Suspects often have useful information about *other* suspects. We need to gather as much information as possible to form an accurate picture of what really happened to poor Dicky."

"Dora might not want to talk to us."

"We won't know unless we ask, will we?"

A.J. used her Palm Pre to look up Dora Beauford on the Internet. There were two Dora Beaufords. One was an elderly South Carolina widow who had passed away in 2001 and one was a professor at Warren County Community College.

"Got her!" Elysia's smile would have given Snow White's stepmother pause for thought.

"How do you want to approach her? Drop her an e-mail or call the college?"

"Why shouldn't we call her directly? She's in the phone directory." Still smiling that alarming smile, Elysia held the book up.

Dora Beauford lived in a very old brick apartment building in the small, historic borough of Washington. A.J. had been lucky and caught the archeology professor just before she left the college campus for the day: mention of Dicky Massri had apparently convinced Dora to see them. Within a few minutes of walking into the relaxed but styl-

ish clutter of Dora's apartment it was immediately clear to
A.J. why Dora loved to talk. Especially about herself.

"Coffee, tea, mineral water . . . wine?" Dora inquired
as they seated themselves on the long zebra-striped sofa.
The room's furnishings were modern and eclectic: tailored, upholstered furniture, oriental tables and chests,
lamps of blown glass and bronze, and a quantity of
Egyptian-looking statues and objets d'art.

Replicas?

The long, low, carved table in front of the sofa was
covered with papers, books, folders. Dora appeared to
have been grading papers when they interrupted.

"Tea would be lovely," Elysia said.

A.J. agreed.

"Well, I'm having a glass of wine," Dora stated. She
disappeared in the apartment cubbyhole of a kitchen.

Elysia nodded at the resin cat statue on a low book-
shelf. She raised her eyebrows.

A.J. shrugged. She whispered, "Do you think her voice
sounds anything like the voice we heard in Dicky's apartment when we were searching it?"

Elysia considered. She was still considering as Dora
reappeared with a glass of wine and sat down on a blue
tailored chair across from them. "The kettle's on. Chin
chin." She sipped her wine.

A.J. curiously scrutinized their hostess. Dora was a
trim brunette in her mid-fifties with dark hair and brown
eyes. She was very put together: designer jeans, a short-
sleeved silk blouse, and ethnic jewelry.

"So how did you know Dakarai?" Dora inquired, looking from Elysia to A.J. with her bright, dark eyes.

Elysia said, "We were seeing each other shortly before
his death."

Dora gave an unexpectedly harsh laugh. "Oh yes?" She took another sip of her wine. "Well, if you want to know my opinion, the little twerp got exactly what was coming to him."

It didn't get much blunter than that. A.J. had to wonder at such frankness to strangers. Once again she considered Dora's voice. Had it been the voice of the woman in Dicky's apartment? By now it was difficult to accurately remember those slightly harsh but definitely feminine tones.

"What did he do to you?" Elysia asked the other woman with genuine interest.

Dora said flatly, "He lied to me. He cheated on me. He broke my heart——"

"Did he try to blackmail you?" A.J. questioned.

Dora, mid-tirade, stopped. "Blackmail? No. What could he blackmail me about?"

Now there was a good point. Blackmail was only possible where the victim had something significant to lose by exposure. Dora did not seem like the retiring flower type.

"The papers said something about extortion. Some women are sensitive to—"

"Some women are idiots," Dora retorted. "If that little weasel had ever suggested blackmail, I'd have . . ." She described in lavish and loving detail what she would do to any man foolish enough to, in Elysia's vernacular, "put the squeeze on her."

Two things became immediately clear to A.J. First, Dora had a slight impulse control problem. Secondly, Dora would be a very bad person to try and blackmail. If Dicky had been foolish enough to try, A.J. could believe that Dora might very well have killed him. Unfortunately, there remained the problem of Dora's alibi.

Could it be broken? It seemed unlikely. If there was one person whom it would be all but impossible to fake out, it would be one's hairdresser. She—or he—would be bound to notice one disappearing in the midst of the cut or color.

Besides, Jake was thorough about such things. He understood what was at stake.

Elysia was asking, "Where did you meet?"

"Egypt. I was part of an international professor exchange. My field is archeology. I met Dakarai in Cairo. He told me he was wary of involvement, a poor risk for a relationship; that he was getting over a bad marriage to a rich American actress." She sneered at some memory and took another swallow of wine. "Oh, he did it beautifully, I'll give him that. I realize now none of it was true."

"He was briefly married to a friend of mine," Elysia said. "The actress Medea Sutherland. That was probably what he was referring to."

Dora the Explorer had no comment on that revelation. "Anyway, we had an affair. The sex was *incredible*. Then it was over. Just like that. He dumped me. No warning. I have no idea to this day what went wrong."

Dora was a strange lady, but her pain and bewilderment seemed genuine, and A.J. felt sympathy—even if no one had tried to blackmail Dora, her life had still been disrupted. No one had the right to yank other people around like that.

"How long did you see him for?"

"Five weeks. I was in Egypt for one semester. Frankly, I never expected to see Dakarai again, but one day I was coming out of the dry cleaners, and there he was." Her gaze zeroed on Elysia. "With you."

Elysia's eyes widened like a startled cat, but she said nothing.

Dora smiled. "Oh, yes, I recognized you right away. I followed you that day, you see. And it was obvious that I'd been played. Played from start to finish." She drained her wineglass.

"So you started calling Dakarai," A.J. guessed aloud.

She wondered if they were about to have a Miss Marple in the Drawing Room moment, but Dora scotched that when she said briskly, "That's right. I started calling him. And following him. And, in general, harassing him. I didn't want anyone else to go through what I went through." To Elysia, she added, "Not that you weren't old enough to know better."

Elysia offered an acidic smile.

"In fact I called the DHS to try and get him kicked out of the country. They said they'd look into it, but I don't think anyone ever did anything."

"Did you ever try to talk to him directly?"

"I tried, of course. Oh, I admit when I first saw Dakarai I still had feelings for him. Embarrassing but true. They died fast. I realized he was just on the make. And apparently I wasn't in his target income bracket."

A.J. thought that was one possibility, but more likely Dora's hostility and aggressiveness had made her a bad candidate for blackmail, regardless of her financial standing.

"What did he say when you recognized him?"

Dora laughed that edged laugh. "His first instinct, believe it or not, was to pretend I'd made a mistake."

Not the brightest bloke, Elysia had been right about that. Not even a very developed sense of survival if he'd thought he could possibly get away passing that old line off on Dora. Why hadn't he just told her his puppy ate his homework and been done with it?

Dora said, "Then he tried to suggest that we should . . . relive old times." Her eyes were hard as onyx as they rested on Elysia.

Elysia said mildly, "Well, he would, wouldn't he? That's exactly the sort of thing he'd try if cornered. He was a lover not a fighter."

"He was a user. A liar, a cheat, a—" Dora was on another roll.

A.J. interrupted, "Did you ever hear anything about Massri being involved in the theft or smuggling of Egyptian antiquities?"

Dora didn't answer for a moment, her gaze on her empty glass. "There were rumors. Nothing overt. It was more a suggestion that he was lazy and not doing his job properly. He *was* lazy."

"Apparently it was more than a rumor. He was fired from his position at the SCA."

Dora's eyes narrowed. "How do you know that?"

A.J. lied. "I contacted the SCA directly." She thought it would be better if Dora didn't know that their own relationship with the police was anything beyond adversarial.

"Well, I'm not surprised." The teakettle was whistling in the kitchen. Dora rose to get it.

"She has the wherewithal to commit murder." Elysia kept her voice low.

"The wherewithal?"

"The you-name-it. The gumption, the means, the motive."

"But she's got an alibi. Plus . . ."

"Plus what?"

A.J. opened her mouth, but Dora poked her head out of the kitchen. "Milk? Honey? Lemon?"

"Honey and lemon," A.J. said.

"Milk," Elysia said.

Dora disappeared, but her voice floated back to them. "Were you really going to marry him?"

Elysia's smile was odd. "No," she returned. "My experience was somewhat diffcrent from yours, Dora, but no."

Dora reappeared with two mugs, which she set on the piles of paper on the long table.

"When was the last time you saw Massri?" A.J. asked.

"Months ago." She seemed definite on that point. "After I turned him over to the DHS, I decided it was out of my hands."

"There's a colorful character," Elysia commented as they left Dora's and walked back to where they had parked the SUV.

A.J. snorted. "Boy, if that isn't the pot calling the kettle black—as the Bard would say."

Elysia gave her a cool look. "I do think she was telling the truth, though. At least as far as she understands it."

A.J. agreed. "It seems unlikely that if she had killed Dicky she'd keep talking about how he got what he deserved and how angry she was with him."

"Mmm." Elysia said thoughtfully, "Perhaps. She doesn't strike me as a particularly *wise* woman."

"True." A.J. remembered her impression that Dora might have impulse control issues. "She did seem a little headstrong."

"If someone is running some kind of blackmail scheme

I can't imagine why they'd kill Peggy Graham and leave Dora running loose. I'd kill Dora, given a choice."

A.J. said, hoping to discourage that line of commentary, "First of all, we don't know for sure that Peggy *was* killed. It's still very possible she committed suicide. Secondly, if Dora wasn't being blackmailed, then she didn't have much in the way of ammunition. Thirdly, Dora seems like a woman well able to take care of herself."

"She does. Very true."

"If Peggy really was killed, she must have had possession of damaging information. Dora, well, she knew Dicky was a rat, but there's no law against being a rat, and however much a misery she made his life, she wasn't really threatening the business enterprise because she didn't really know anything."

"Dora was working to have Dicky thrown out of the country. Had she succeeded, that would have been a disruption to the business plan."

"True, I guess. Although there was still Cory. Besides, Dora didn't succeed in having Dicky deported."

"We need to find Cory," Elysia remarked.

A.J. gave her an uneasy glance. "One thing. I thought her expression changed when we mentioned Dicky was fired from the SCA. She sort of hesitated."

"I noticed that," agreed Elysia.

"Maybe it was just surprise, but what if it was something else? After all, her field is archeology. What if all those artifacts and objets d'art in her apartment aren't replicas? What if she was involved in some antiquities smuggling scheme with Dicky and he double-crossed her?"

Elysia looked delighted. "Pumpkin, that's very good. In fact it's brilliant. You're beginning to think like me. Just because Dicky was a blackmailer doesn't mean he was killed because of his blackmailing."

"But we keep coming back to the problem of that alibi of Dora's."

"It is annoying."

"Yes. I don't think it's an easy one to break. You can't really rush out of a salon with those little foils on your head or hair full of glaze and not expect someone to notice."

"Perhaps she has a twin sister. I remember once on an episode of *2*—"

"I really doubt that's the solution. Besides, knowing Jake, he probably checked." A.J. considered their interview with Dora. "Come to think of it, why *wasn't* she able to get Dicky thrown out of the country?"

"Perhaps he was here legally. Some people *do* enter the country legally. I did."

"It would be one of the only honest things he did," A.J. said.

Nineteen

❦

"Mara Allen on line three," Emma said briskly over the intercom.

A.J. blinked at the phone as the call rang through. She picked up on the second trill.

"A.J.," Mara greeted her in that carefully modulated, super-scene voice. "I was wondering if you were free for lunch?"

"Of course." A.J. answered automatically, her gaze sweeping her day planner.

"Wonderful. Why don't I meet you at Butterfly Bistro on Main Street at, say, eleven thirty?"

"I'll see you then," A.J. said cheerfully. In fact she was more curious than cheerful, and her curiosity was tinged with wariness. But at least now she might finally hear exactly what was behind these weird rumors of buyouts and takeovers.

The morning flew by. A.J. taught her Itsy Bitsy Yoga

class, her Yoga for Kids, put together an ad for hiring a masseuse, and before she knew it, it was time to leave for her lunch meeting with Mara.

She opened her office door and found Suze and Emma Rice hovering.

"What's up?"

"What did Mara Allen want?" Suze demanded in a stage whisper Lily could probably hear through the hallway walls.

A.J. threw a meaningful look at Lily's closed office door and Emma said, "She's upstairs teaching Attila the Hun Yoga."

A.J. bit her lip. It would be highly inappropriate to laugh at such disrespect. It wasn't easy to keep a straight face, though. She said truthfully, "I don't know what Mara wants. I guess I'll find out at lunch."

"I know exactly what she wants," Suze said. "She wants Sacred Balance."

"You can't sell to her," Emma said. "I've seen those commercials of hers on late night TV. She's like . . . like . . ."

"She's like one of those energy vampires!" Suze exclaimed. "Like a succubus."

Emma and A.J. said at the same time, "A *what*?"

Suze blushed. "Maybe that's not the right word, but she's . . ."

"She's wrong for Sacred Balance," Emma said firmly.

"That's okay because I have no intention of selling to her or anyone else." A.J. slipped past them. "But I have to hear her out. I *want* to hear her out. I want to know what exactly is going on around here. Don't worry. I'll fill you in when I get back."

Their worried expressions did not alter as she hurried out the glass doors.

* * *

Butterfly Bistro was the newest restaurant to try its luck in the troubled economy of Stillbrook. It was a small European-style café with an emphasis on trendy rather than good food.

Mara was already waiting at an outside table when A.J. arrived. She was signing an autograph for a teenaged girl.

"She's not even one of my students," Mara said, amusedly as the girl departed. "Perhaps she's a Sacred Balance student?"

"I've never seen her before."

Mara raised her pale eyebrows. "A yoga aspirant on your own front doorstep and you didn't know. It's a world of endless surprises."

That was one of Mara's catch phrases on her infomercials. *It's a world of endless surprises.*

They ordered their meals. Vegetarian and decaf for Mara, and a chicken and walnut salad for A.J.

"How is business?" Mara seemed very sincere.

"It's good."

"Is it? I'll be honest. I've heard rumors that you're struggling a little."

"I'm quite sure where you heard those rumors," A.J. said dryly. "But as much as Lily would love to believe I'm ready to throw in the towel, I feel very happy and satisfied with everything we're achieving at Sacred Balance."

"And what is that?" Mara was smiling, there didn't seem to be any bite to the question, and yet A.J. couldn't help feeling as though a pop quiz had just been sprung on her.

"Teaching our students the integration of mind, body, and spirit through the practice of yoga."

"But there's so much more to yoga than health and self-awareness."

"I realize that. But—"

"When you stop to consider that Maharishi Patanjali's Yoga Sutras are the oldest known writings available to us. Just imagine. Those sutras date back to two thousand BC . . ."

Mara was off and running, and A.J. listened politely, nodding noncommittally and wondering when Mara was going to get to the real point of this meeting. If her intention was to reiterate how much more she knew than A.J. about yoga and running a studio, she could have saved herself the cost of an overpriced lunch. A.J. knew only too well how much she had yet to learn.

"So you see, A.J., there are other considerations here."

A.J. realized that Mara was looking at her expectantly. It was the same expression she used so effectively in her infomercials as she was asking viewers to reach for the phone, credit cards in hand. A.J. racked her brains trying to remember the last things Mara had said. A.J. had been thinking about Jake and the funny pause before he'd left her house on Tuesday night, about Dora and whether hers could have been the voice in Dicky Massri's apartment, and about whether she had time to squeeze in a quick visit to Mr. Meagher's when she and Mara finished up.

Apparently they were closer to finishing than she'd realized.

"Sorry?" she said. "I missed that."

"I'd like to make you an offer for Sacred Balance."

"Sacred Balance is not for sale."

"A.J." Mara's serenity nearly slipped. She must have

been offering her best sales pitch while A.J.'s mind was wandering. No wonder she was exasperated. "I have to say that your attitude is not in keeping with the true yoga spirit."

A.J. took a moment to consider the best way to say what she needed to say; she didn't want to be aggressive because Mara might not realize how insulting she was. "I know I still have a great deal to learn. I know that I make mistakes. I know that I might not even be the right person to manage Sacred Balance, but the studio was left in trust to me."

Mara opened her mouth, but A.J. kept speaking politely, but firmly. "I know some people think that the only reason I'm hanging on is out of the desire to honor my aunt's wishes, but that's not true. Well, it's partly true. I do want to honor her wishes, but even more important to me is what the studio, what rediscovering yoga, has brought to my life. And that journey is something that we're all sharing at Sacred Balance."

Lily's scowling face appeared in A.J.'s mind's eye. "Well, maybe not all of us, but most of us. We're all learning together, we're all growing together, we're all harvesting Aunt Di's legacy together. So while my decision may not be the best decision from a business standpoint, I do think it is in keeping with the yoga spirit."

Mara smiled without warmth. "You can't say I didn't try."

"I would never say that."

"It's unfortunate that we find ourselves in the position of business competitors rather than sisters in yoga."

"I don't see why we can't be both." A.J. picked up her purse. "Thank you for lunch."

* * *

After lunch A.J. stopped by Mr. Meagher's office for an update.

"A.J., me wee girl," Mr. Meagher said with every evidence of pleasure, although she couldn't help but notice that he did look briefly past her to see if Elysia was in the vicinity.

"I just dropped by to see how things are going. Mother is getting pretty frustrated with the lack of information she's getting from her lawyer."

"We're still weeks away from going to trial," Mr. Meagher pointed out.

"I know. But . . ."

Mr. Meagher sighed. "Aye, aye. Your mither was never known for her patience. The truth is, there's little news to share. Right now it's a matter of evaluating the police investigation and evidence against her. Her defense team is searching for some reason to have the case dismissed."

"Is that likely?"

"I don't think so. I've looked at the arrest report and the evidence. The police have been meticulous. If anything, Jake erred in not arresting Elysia faster."

A.J. knew that had been a favor to both her and her mother. She nodded.

"So defense counsel is investigating the facts, questioning prosecution witnesses, and seeking their own witnesses and forensic experts who may be able to supply a different perspective than the prosecution's. Not the kind of thing Elysia wants to hear, I know."

The only thing her mother wanted to hear was that all charges had been dropped and the real murderer was in custody. A.J. knew that as well as Mr. Meagher.

"Did you have any luck tracking down Massri's gambling connections?"

Mr. Meagher had moved to the cockatoo's cage to feed the bird a cracker through the bars. The white cockatoo watched him with its bright eyes, then took the cracker delicately in its razor-sharp beak. Mr. Meagher was saying, "I did. I've explored that avenue, and it's a dead end. Oh, Massri liked to play the ponies, true enough, but he never failed to honor his gambling debts. No, if his bookie were to send enforcers after anyone it would be whoever killed young Massri."

Watching him, A.J. once again had that uneasy feeling that perhaps Mr. Meagher was not being completely honest. She was annoyed with herself for entertaining such suspicions, yet they persisted.

"Why do *you* think Massri was shot in Mother's yard?" she asked.

Mr. Meagher glanced at her quickly and then away. "Perhaps it was a matter of expediency."

"But for all the killer knew he was shooting Massri in front of a house full of people. It was Easter morning. Well, late Easter morning—all the more reason to fear a house full of people."

Mr. Meagher seemed to mull this over as he moved away from the birdcage to his sofa. He scraped the usual pile of newspapers off the cushions to the floor. "Perhaps there was some time factor we're unaware of. Some reason Massri had to be eliminated right then."

"The police found an engagement ring in a hollowed chocolate egg."

Mr. Meagher's expression was hard to decipher. "I was thinking more in the nature of some vital information he might have revealed."

"Like what?"

Mr. Meagher shook his head.

"What could Massri have known that would be time-sensitive enough to risk killing him in front of witnesses?"

Unless the killer had known the house would be empty? Was the killer someone who knew what time Elysia's guests were arriving? Could the killer have possibly known that Elysia had left the house to try and find evaporated milk?

Mr. Meagher seemed to have no answer. He said, "Revenge perhaps?"

"Revenge against Mother?"

"I was thinking Massri, but I suppose the other is possible. I suppose someone might have wanted your mither blamed for the crime."

That tied all too well into A.J.'s only half-considered theory that Mr. Meagher might have killed Dakarai in such a way as to put Elysia in a situation where she needed his help. It was so . . . so Machiavellian. But beneath his slightly foolish-seeming demeanor Mr. Meagher was a shrewd and intelligent man.

A.J. said awkwardly, "You've known Mother a long time."

Mr. Meagher's face softened. "Aye. Since she was sweet seventeen."

"Do you think—?" She stopped. How on earth could she ask someone like Mr. Meagher if he was a) in love with her mother, b) jealous enough to kill a romantic rival, and c) crazy enough to frame the object of his romantic interest?

"Our theory is that it was another one of his blackmail victims," she said instead. "Maybe the person just snatched the first opportunity." Except where did Maddie's death fit into all that? "Or if Massri was part of a blackmail ring . . ."

She was thinking aloud now. "Suppose he was sincere about marrying Mother?"

"I can't see why he wouldn't be," Mr. Meagher said gruffly.

"Perhaps someone wanted to punish him for trying to leave the blackmail operation."

"A ring, is it? Couldn't Massri have been working on his own?"

"We don't think so. It seems to be larger scale than that."

"It's a wee bit of a severe punishment," Mr. Meagher pointed out. "And it wouldn't change the fact that this person or persons would be left shorthanded."

She thought of the sculptor named Cory who Peggy Graham had been involved with.

"Maybe the killer knew there were plenty more Dakarai Massris where he came from," she said.

A.J. was reading through her aunt's manuscript and trying to decide whether she should bother cooking something for dinner or if that evening might be the special night for which she was saving that tub of Oreo ice cream, when a voice echoed from down the hallway.

"Oi!"

A.J. peeled herself off the ceiling. "Mother, what are you doing skulking around here?"

"Skulking? I am not *skulking*. I come bearing gifts." Elysia held up a bag of KFC.

A.J. moaned. "I'm not supposed to eat stuff like that."

"I don't know why not. You spend your day working out. If anyone deserves to eat like this it's you."

Elysia led the way into the kitchen. A.J.—and Monster—followed hopefully.

Before long chicken, mashed potatoes, corn on the cob, and biscuits and honey had been dished up, mouth-watering aroma filling the air.

"Not that I don't appreciate this, but why are you here?" A.J. asked, biting into a honey-slathered biscuit.

"I thought it was time to reflect and review." Elysia shoved a purple legal pad, curling pages covered in scribbles, across the table. "I've made a few notes."

"A few notes? It looks like you're planning on writing your memoirs."

"It's interesting you mention that. I've had two offers this week for my life story."

"Please tell me you're not . . ."

"I hardly have the time," Elysia said. "Perhaps if I wind up nicked, I'll reconsider."

A.J. picked up the legal pad, glancing through it. "Unfortunately we have a distinct shortage of suspects."

"I like Dora for it," Elysia said promptly. "She has a vengeful nature and makes no bones about wanting poor Dicky punished. She stalked him. Some of those phone messages she left were more than a little scary. She's not afraid to take risks *and* they may have been partnered in illegal activities with antiquities."

"She has an alibi."

"I don't believe in that alibi. Alibis can be broken, as we both know."

"No one seems to think this one is breakable. Also I think we can scratch the theory of the homicidal bookie. Mr. Meagher says that's a dead end."

"Did you speak to Bradley today?" Elysia's attention

seemed focused on eating corn on the cob without dropping a single kernel.

"I did. I had a lunch meeting with Mara Allen and I stopped by his office."

Elysia said nothing.

"So," A.J. continued into that silence, "He says that line of inquiry can safely be closed. Dicky did gamble but he paid his debts promptly and he didn't win more than he lost. A good customer, in other words, and they're apparently sorry to lose him."

Elysia seemed to be brooding.

"Which leads us to the next theory. Angry ex-lovers. Yours and Dicky's."

"Mine?" Elysia did look startled at that.

"Yes."

"I don't have any angry ex-lovers." Elysia's expression altered. "You can't be serious."

"According to what Maddie said, Mr. Meagher has had a thing about dating you back to about one million years BC."

"Thank you for reminding me, pumpkin. I'd nearly forgotten those happy days when he used to take me out for pterodactyl rides."

"Come on, Mother. Even I've noticed Mr. Meagher is crazy about you."

"He'd have to be crazy indeed to shoot someone as foolish and as harmless as poor Dicky. Bradley had no idea I was seeing Dicky, and if he had known it, he'd have quickly seen how utterly unimportant that relationship was." Elysia's cheeks were pink and her tone sharp. Apparently, unexpectedly, this line of inquiry was hitting a little too close to home.

"Mr. Meagher knew what time we were having Easter dinner."

"Of course he did. So did you."

A.J. said reluctantly, "Did he know you were leaving the house to go buy milk?"

"Of course n—" Elysia's face froze.

Seeing her startled expression, A.J.'s heart sank. "*Did* he know?"

Elysia whispered, "He called to verify at what time we were eating just as I was leaving for the shop. I told him I was running out to buy a tin of milk."

A.J. wasn't sure what to say.

Elysia straightened. "This is bloody ludicrous," she snapped. "Bradley Meagher is no more a murderer than I am. The case against him is utterly and ridiculously circumstantial. I refuse to discuss this line of reasoning any further." Her eyes were very bright.

"Okay," A.J. said mildly. She turned the page of the legal pad.

"Bradley is not a murderer."

"Got it." A.J. glanced over the scrawled notes on the next page. "That leaves Dicky's vengeful ex-lovers."

"Dora."

"Besides Dora."

"We don't know any of his ex-lovers except for Maddie. Which reminds me. Maddie's death is somehow connected to Dicky's, and Bradley Meagher wouldn't have harmed a hair on Maddie's head."

A.J. said thoughtfully, "That's a good point. What if Dicky and Maddie's deaths have nothing to do with blackmail at all?"

"What do you mean?" Elysia looked wary, still on guard against further attempts to implicate Bradley

Meagher. "They were divorced. What other connection could there be?"

"I'm not sure. I'm just brainstorming here. They were divorced, but what if there was still some financial connection? Some property or business interest they jointly owned?"

Elysia brightened. "That's very good. Perhaps Maddie never changed her will? She was quite wealthy; although I think she spent a small fortune on that money pit she called a renovation."

"But Dicky died first," A.J. pointed out. "So I don't see how that helps even if Maddie didn't change her will. Dicky died first so anything he might have inherited from Maddie would surely be null and void." A.J. propped her chin on her hand, thinking it over. "And where does Peggy Graham tie into this? Assuming she was murdered."

"She had to have been murdered."

"Maybe. But if Peggy's tied into it, then we can probably eliminate the antiquities theft line of investigation."

"Not so fast," Elysia said. "Don't forget that Mart Crowley said her sister was on a number of boards for charities and the arts. Perhaps she was on the board of some museum? Perhaps her death does tie in with the illegal sale of antiquities."

"Not bad." A.J. made a note to follow up on that. "There aren't any bones in that, are there?" she added as Elysia tossed Monster a piece of chicken skin.

Monster caught it in one snap, like a hungry shark.

"Of course not."

"There is one other theory we haven't really even considered."

"What's that?"

"Maybe Dicky was telling the truth all along."

"About what?"

"About you. Maybe he was serious about giving up his life of crime for you."

To her surprise, Elysia flushed. "That's sweet, lovie. But you needn't worry about sparing my feelings. There were no illusions on my side."

"But hear me out. Suppose Dicky *did* want out of this hypothetical blackmail ring. Suppose he wanted you to make an honest man of him. We've already established— well, theorized at least—that there are potentially ruthless people running some kind of extortion racket targeting single, middle-aged women. If we're right about all that, and if it's true that these people silenced Peggy Graham, then what wouldn't they be willing to do to stop Dicky from bailing out?"

"Why wouldn't they just let him go? He was hardly the type to incriminate himself by going to the police."

"Maybe your reputation preceded you. Or maybe mine did."

"Your what?"

"I know it's a stretch, but hear me out. There was a write-up on us in the *Stillbrook Streamer* last summer after we solved Nicole's murder. Maybe the amateur sleuth thing factored in for Dicky's partners in crime." A.J. added with triumph, "And maybe *that's* why he was killed in your front yard. Maybe it wasn't someone taking a big chance, maybe it wasn't by chance after all. Maybe it was a deliberate attempt to throw suspicion on *you*!"

Twenty

❧

Lily called in sick on Friday morning and A.J.'s sleuthing had to take a backseat to the scramble of trying to cover the Number One Instructor's classes.

"She's flexing her muscles," Emma remarked as A.J. glanced over Lily's calendar. "She really doesn't think this place could survive without her. Do you know she hasn't taken a vacation of more than two days in a row in over five years?"

"I know she hasn't taken one in the last year."

"Five years," Emma said doggedly. "This studio is her life."

"She probably heard from Mara Allen yesterday that I'm not going to sell Sacred Balance."

Emma looked relieved. "I can see that might make her feel a mite queasy."

A.J. studied Lily's schedule and decided they could manage without trying to call Denise Farber in from her day off. "If Suze can take Lily's Teens class and Simon can take the Teacher Training class and her Yin Yoga we can do this. It's my heavy day, but I can take her Vinyasa and still catch my Restorative evening class."

"Don't go throwing your back out after you've just got on your feet again."

"I won't. I think these months of yoga are to thank for my being back on my feet so quickly. The last time my back went out I was out of action for six weeks."

"Just don't overdo it."

A.J. looked up, smiling. "I think this might work pretty well, actually. I'm going to hold a mini staff meeting before the evening sessions start. I want to put to bed the rumor that I'm selling once and for all."

"I think that's a wise move," Emma said.

A.J. went back to her office and ordered pizzas to be delivered for lunch. It was clearly going to be one of those days.

From that moment on it felt like she never stopped moving. When she had finally had a free moment late in the morning, she phoned Jake.

He didn't pick up. The most likely explanation was that he was busy and it wasn't convenient, but with their changed relationship, A.J. was finding an unexpected streak of paranoia within herself.

"Hey there, it's me," she said pleasantly as she left a message for him. "I have a . . . well, maybe not a lead, but Dora Beauford mentioned that she'd sicced the Department of Homeland Security on Massri. She wanted him thrown out of the country. Since that never happened, she assumed the DHS never acted on her call. I'm wondering if that's true. She believed he'd entered the country illegally. If he didn't enter illegally, that *could* be a lead. Immigrants still have to be sponsored or married to a US citizen, as far as I know."

She hung up and waited for a few minutes but she didn't really expect him to call back this quickly. It wasn't an emergency after all. She left her office and went to cover the Yoga for Teens class.

The pizza delivery was a big success and the rest of the afternoon passed relatively quickly despite numerous complaints about having eaten way too much to possibly do yoga.

At the end of the afternoon during the two-hour break between the day and evening sessions, A.J. held a quick and informal staff meeting.

"It's come to my attention that there are some rumors flying around. Rumors about my personal plans and my plans for Sacred Balance. Some of you may even have heard that I met with Mara Allen of Yoga Meridian yesterday for lunch."

No one said anything, but judging by the shifting in chairs, clearing of throats, and shifting of gazes, she'd hit the nail right on its head.

"This isn't going to be a very long meeting because the fact is my plans for Sacred Balance remain absolutely unchanged. I did meet with Mara yesterday; she did indicate she and her investors would be interested in acquiring Sacred Balance. I told her exactly what I'm now telling you. It's true that I took on the responsibility of Sacred Balance because that was the wish of my aunt, but this place—and all of you—have come to mean so much more to me. Rediscovering yoga has changed my life, given it focus and balance. As far as I'm concerned that journey has just begun, and I have no intention of leaving this path for another."

Simon Crider, one of the senior instructors and one of Diantha's original staff asked, "I know I'm speaking for most of us when I say that's excellent news. But what about the rumors we keep hearing that financially we're barely keeping our head above water?"

"It's not true. I can tell you why I think that rumor began circulating in the first place and who I believe is behind it, but that's not productive. We're doing very well. We currently generate a pretax profit margin of twenty-five percent. Sacred Balance is not only supporting itself, it's making a profit."

There was a round of applause.

"And because you're all a part of that success, it's only right that you should share in the rewards. Lily and I have talked about paying annual bonuses based on meeting the goals we set together as a team. We'd discussed implementing that for next year, but I think we've got a tough few months ahead of us. Yoga Meridian definitely has us in their sights. We need everyone on board and focused, and as an incentive, we're going to start looking at performance bonuses for everything from increasing student enrollment to broadening your own training and expertise. I'll have more details on that later. Right now I just want to thank you for all you've done to make Sacred Balance everything it is. We're taking this journey together. I promise you that I will be with you every step of the way."

A.J. was surprised at the applause she got for that one, but perhaps it was as Suze said when she dropped by her office afterward. "Nobody wants to leave. But if the studio is folding, then no one wants to be the last one out the door either."

"We're not folding. We're doing fine."

"I believe you. I think everyone in that meeting believed you." Suze rolled her big blue eyes. "But I don't think Lily's going to be happy when she hears the news."

"It shouldn't be news to Lily. She sees the financial reports. She knows we're doing fine."

"Just don't be surprised if she needs another sick day."

"She can have all the sick days she wants," A.J. said. "I'm planning on figuring a way to make her take a full-blown vacation."

"I hear Nepal is nice this time of year."

Of course the fact was that if Lily really did take off for a month they would be stretched perilously thin, but A.J. was tempted to believe the positives would outweigh the negatives. She felt that she and Lily were fast reaching their own personal China Syndrome and that the continuing conflict between them was creating an increasingly toxic environment for staff and students alike.

Per the terms of her aunt's will the only way to end their odd-couple partnership would be if one of them relinquished her position as co-manager. Or died.

Now there was a gruesome thought, but given how much of A.J.'s attention these days seemed to be on crime and murder investigations, maybe it wasn't surprising. It was definitely a challenge trying to feel her way along the spiritual eightfold path while a murder investigation proceeded around her.

By the time A.J. completed the final Restorative course of the day and bade her students good night, she was genuinely exhausted. Her back was pain free and holding up to the challenge of teaching again, but she was looking forward to lying down and putting her feet up—seeing that her other options for Friday evening entertainment were severely limited.

Jake had not returned her call and, although she tried to stay optimistic and not read anything into that unusual silence, she was disheartened.

Her cell phone rang as she was pulling in the drive. A glance informed her that it was Elysia, and her spirits dropped more.

"Hi!" she said as cheerfully as she could.

"Why don't you come by for dinner and we'll review the case again."

A.J. groaned inwardly. "Mother, I was thinking maybe a hot bath and an early night."

"We can't afford to let any grass grow under our feet. I've been on the phone to my contacts—"

"Your *contacts*?"

"Yes, and I'm putting together a profile of our suspects. I think you'll be very interested in what I've discovered."

"Maybe tomorrow? I'm really beat tonight."

"The clock is ticking on me, pumpkin. Right now that bloody swine of a district attorney is weaving the rope to put around my neck—"

"All *right*! I'm on my way." A.J. clicked off. Her phone immediately rang and she answered automatically. "Twenty minutes, Mother. I have to pick Monster up."

"It's me," Jake said gruffly.

"Oh." A.J.'s heart skipped a beat. "Hi."

"Hi. Sorry I couldn't get back to you earlier. I was tracking down a robbery suspect in Phillipsburgh."

"A robbery suspect? Aren't you still investigating Massri's death?'

"It's been forcibly pointed out to me that the DA's already brought charges against your mother. I'm not going to be part of any further investigation involving Elysia."

"What happened?"

"Pretty much what you'd expect. Someone noticed I appeared to be playing for the wrong team. Anyway I'm looking into a rash of Texaco Fast Fares robberies."

"Gas prices *are* pretty high."

"Funny."

A.J. said guiltily. "I'm sorry if—"

"Nah. Don't sweat it. It's nothing I can't handle. Look, I did some checking into this complaint Dora Beauford filed against Massri with the DHS."

Could there be anything more heartwarming than one's possibly ex-boyfriend utilizing all the resources at his command on one's behalf?

"Why didn't they prosecute? Or did they?"

"They didn't prosecute because Massri was in this country legally. He had a sponsor. A Mabel G. Chalthoum."

"Who's Mabel G. Chalthoum?"

"I have no idea. But she guaranteed that Massri would have a place to live and be gainfully employed. He got his visa and his green card."

"If he was supposed to be guaranteed employment, what was he employed *as*?"

"Sales rep."

"For what?"

"I don't know. There seemed to be some confusion on that point. Hey, I've got to go, A.J. I'll talk to you later."

"Wait! Just one thing. Two things."

He didn't speak.

"Did you have a chance to look into whether Peggy Graham's death was suicide or not?"

"No, I didn't."

That was blunt enough. A.J. didn't dare push it.

"Did you—could you—did you check into Mr. Meagher's movements the morning Massri was killed?"

"Bradley Meagher?"

Jake sounded astonished. Not a usual state for him.

"Yes."

"No," he said slowly. "We had no reason to consider him a suspect. Is there reason?"

"I . . . don't know." A.J. felt horrible for even making the suggestion. But if it came down to a choice between her mother and Mr. Meagher, then as fond as she was of Mr. Meagher, there *was* no choice. Not if he had committed murder. "I think it might be worth looking into."

"Like I said, I've been removed from the case, but I'll pass the word along."

"Thanks, Jake."

He grunted and disconnected.

A.J. drove to the farmhouse, changed into jeans and a T-shirt, collected Monster, and headed back to Starlight Farm.

"**So.** To recap."

A.J. groaned and reached for another piece of toasted bread, scooping bruschetta onto it. "Haven't we recapped enough for one night?"

They had been at it most of the evening, eating bruschetta and black olive tapenade on toasted French bread while they went over and over their suspects and theories.

"The problem with our recapping," Elysia retorted, "is that we seem to be closing off avenues of investigation. At this rate, *I'm* going to believe I'm guilty."

"Jake is still looking into whether Peggy Graham killed herself or was murdered."

At least A.J. hoped he was.

"I don't believe there's any doubt that she was murdered."

"Well, there we disagree because I think there's a lot of doubt. The fact that Peggy didn't seem like someone who would commit suicide isn't indicative of anything more than she was a private person who didn't share her thoughts and feelings—and we already know that from how she reacted to being blackmailed."

Elysia scowled at her purple sheaf of notes. "Can we at least agree that The Salon seems to be at the center of everything?"

"Yes. The Salon does seem to be the common denominator for every line of query except two: Dora Beauford and this Mabel Chalthoum, whoever she is."

"And yet I find it very, very coincidental that Dora Beauford's alibi is that she was at a hair salon at the time of Dicky's death. A hair salon on Easter morning?"

"I hadn't thought about that," A.J. admitted. "That does seem odd. But Jake had to have checked. That's not something he would miss."

Elysia looked unconvinced.

"We could check ourselves," A.J. pointed out. "Mr. Meagher would be able to get the name of the salon for us. Your criminal lawyer has access to all the information uncovered in the police investigation."

"I'll follow up on Dora's alibi," Elysia said grimly.

"Just stay clear of Dora herself. I get an odd feeling from her."

Elysia brushed this aside. "We also need to follow up on this Mabel Chalthoum, whoever she might be."

"Yes, but we need to proceed cautiously there, too,"
A.J. warned. "Mabel could very well be our Madame X.
Dicky's unknown jealous lover. She sponsored him
so she's probably someone who stayed involved in his
life. He never mentioned her or you never saw any signs
of her?"

"Signs? What did you have in mind, pet? Rhino spore
in the bedroom? Perhaps the hair products in the bathroom were Mabel's. Which, again, leads us back to The
Salon."

"He never mentioned her and you never thought to ask
about the details of his coming to this country?"

Elysia sighed. "We talked a great deal, but . . . none of
it was really of a practical nature. He did speak of his family and home in Egypt. He was a little homesick, you
know. I think we avoided specifics because they would
have inevitably reminded us of unpleasant reality."

"Like the fact he was blackmailing you?"

"Exactly."

A.J. shook her head. "Okay, well we need to investigate this Mabel. I suppose the easiest thing might be to
start at The Salon. If she was a customer there, that sim-
plifies things. What actually do you know about The
Salon? The website says they opened in 1990 and that
Gloria was a former model and Stewie worked for the
studios."

"She was a catalog model," Elysia said dismissively.
"Discount clothing and farm equipment."

"Well, what does that matter? She was a model. What
about Stewie?"

"Supposedly he did work for Paramount or something
like that. My understanding is that they were friends for

years before their careers stalled out and they decided to take their investments and go into business together."

"How successful is The Salon?"

"Very."

"Are either of them married?"

"Stewie's gay."

"Do the words *my ex-husband Andy* mean anything to you?"

"As far as I know, Stewie is still playing the field. Gloria . . . might be married. She's always been close-mouthed about her private life."

"Two thoughts occur to me—"

"It's the quality not the quantity, pumpkin."

"Ha. The first is that the male and female voices we heard at Dicky's apartment could have belonged to Gloria and Stewie."

Elysia's eyes narrowed as she sought to remember. "Did the voices sound like Gloria or Stewie?"

"I can't remember. It's been too long. But so far they're the only mixed pair we've come across. Everyone else we've talked to has been pretty much a solo act. But Gloria and Stewie are both connected to The Salon and The Salon does seem to figure in here somewhere."

"True. What would they have been looking for?"

"I have no idea, but that brings me to my second point, which is if there *is* some kind of blackmail ring being run out of The Salon, Gloria and Stewie would probably have to be involved in it. They might even be the masterminds."

"Ah." Elysia sat back on the sofa, fingers pressed together prayer-style as she seemed to channel her inner master detective. "Yes. I think that's an excellent point."

"So if Dicky was working for them as a part of their blackmail scheme, they'd have to scramble to try and find any incriminating evidence—anything that might lead the police back to them. That would be true whether they had anything to do with his death or not."

"Do you think—?"

"I don't know. Not necessarily. If Dicky was threatening to quit the operation and go straight, so what? So they would have to replace him. Killing him wouldn't solve that problem. It would actually make it worse because surely a full-scale homicide investigation would be the last thing they'd want."

Elysia nodded. "Agreed."

"And, I might be wrong about this, but I don't get the impression that Dicky was the kind of person who would consider it necessary to go to the police and make a clean break of everything as part of his going straight process."

"No." Elysia smiled faintly. "That would be the last thing he would do. He would be terrified of being chucked out of the country."

"So I really don't see that Dicky's plans to marry you would be a threat to any nefarious business going on at The Salon. I think it's more likely that one of Dicky's clients flipped out when she learned she was being blackmailed or used."

"Madame X," Elysia said with dark satisfaction.

"Yes. We've heard about how Peggy Graham reacted to the threat of blackmail, and we've seen how Dora reacted even when she wasn't being blackmailed, so what if this Mabel Chalthoum, for example, sponsored Dicky into this country and then discovered that she was being used—maybe even blackmailed?"

Elysia's expression brightened. "Yes. Yes, I see . . . As the Bard said, hell hath no fury—"

"The Bard didn't say that," A.J. interrupted. "I just read that on my box of muesli. It was William Congreve in *The Mourning Bride*."

"The point," Elysia said patiently, "is that a woman scorned is a dangerous and unpredictable creature."

"Yes. And if Madame X knew about you—as Dora seems to have—that might have made everything worse. That might be the reason Dicky was shot in your front yard and suspicion thrown on you. Not because of your reputation as a sleuth, but because you were a romantic rival."

Elysia nodded slowly.

A.J. said, "This Mabel may or may not be connected to The Salon, but I think The Salon remains the obvious starting point for us. But we have to proceed carefully. We can't just barge in there and start asking a bunch of questions. For one thing, if Dicky was killed by a jealous lover, I'm not sure how that connects with Maddie's death or Peggy Graham's. For another, we're both known—you especially—by Stewie and Gloria."

Elysia's face took on the grim expression it had worn in many a thrilling episode of *221B Baker Street*. "If your theory is correct," she said darkly, "those blighters are going to pay."

A.J. murmured noncommittally. She agreed with the sentiment, but they were still a long way from being able to prove any of this.

Elysia sat up. "Why, it's so simple. I should have thought of it sooner. We'll set up a sting operation!"

"Mother—"

A.J. might as well have saved her breath.

"What we have to do is get them to blackmail one of us."

"Uh, they're *already* blackmailing you. Or were. And even if Dicky was running his own extortion sideline, that's still not going to work for the reasons I've just said. They already know both of us."

Elysia subsided, scowling into some bleak distance. Then her face lit up. "*Andy.*"

"No," A.J. said firmly. "Absolutely not. Nick will have both our heads if we drag Andy into another murder investigation. Besides, Andy's not blackmailable. He's out. And even if he wasn't, this ring targets women. Women of a certain age and income bracket. Whoever is behind it, the focus is fine-tuned to the clientele of The Salon. I don't think *that's* a coincidence."

Elysia subsided, frowning. She sipped her tea. "Who else do we know?"

A.J. shook her head. "It needs to be someone—"

"Expendable."

"What? No, not expendable! It needs to be someone under the radar, but also of the right age and income bracket."

Elysia said nothing, continuing to stare off bleakly into space.

"I don't know anyone like that. She'd have to be willing to go along with us, for one thing. . . ." Her voice trailed as she uneasily absorbed Elysia's expression.

Elysia was smiling, but it was the kind of smile that generally had the minions of evil overlords quivering in their pointy-toed boots.

"Mother," warned A.J.

"I have just the person in mind." Elysia practically

purred the words. "Yes. Yes, she'll do perfectly. In fact it couldn't happen to a nicer person."

"Mother . . . ?"

"Let's ask Stella Borin." Elysia's eyes were glinting like a hunting cat's in the night. "I believe she owes me one."

Twenty-one

⚬

"I don't know about this," Stella said.

They stood in the front parlor of Little Peavy Farm, Stella's home. The room was a bewildering visual galli-maufry of patterns and colors: green and red flowered chintzes vied with black and yellow checks and blue and pink stripes for air space. The only consistent motif was cats. Live ones—four full-sized and very friendly cats were closely investigating the visitors—and representa-tional ones. A cat-faced wall clock offered a Cheshire grin, cat-shaped throw pillows littered the sofas and chairs, and there were paintings of cats, cat-shaped candles, and numerous cat statues.

"You're beginning to sound like a broken record. It's quite simple," Elysia was apparently working from the hypothesis that if she kept playing her own broken record long enough someone would be bound to believe her. "You'll get in and establish your cover, that you are filthy rich, have a big fat mouth, and are lonely and desperate. Then you'll bugger off. With a new hairdo. What is there to object to in any of that?"

Stella stared at her long and steadily. "They're not just going to instantly start trying to blackmail me. It'll take time to find me the right man."

"A lifetime. But they're not actually going to *try* to find you the right man," Elysia said. "You do realize, I hope, that all this is not in aid of improving your social life?"

A.J. put in hurriedly, "Don't worry, we're not going to try to crack the blackmailing operation ourselves." She ignored Elysia's obvious displeasure; they had argued this point at length. "We're not expecting you to do any real investigating. All we're trying to do is show the police that there are sufficient grounds here for their own in-depth investigation—and that Mother is not the only viable suspect."

Elysia smiled sweetly when Stella glanced at her.

A.J. said, "So all we really need is for the blackmailer or blackmailers to approach you, to make the first move in setting up a scenario that would obviously leave you vulnerable to blackmail. We can take that to Jake who can then take it to his superiors."

"Like what kind of scenario?"

"Well, for example, if a young, handsome man suddenly asks you out."

"We all know how unlikely that is," Elysia drawled. A.J. shot her a look, which Elysia blandly ignored.

Stella still looked doubtful.

A.J. said, "I promise you don't have to go through with anything you don't want to."

"I just don't think I'd be any good at this kind of thing." Stella said.

"It doesn't matter," Elysia replied. "We're going to sweeten the deal and make you all but irresistible. We have a theory that they'll be looking for one quick, easy score. They have to know time is running out on their operation."

That was Elysia's theory; A.J. wasn't convinced.

"But what if these people running The Salon *are* the murderers? If they've killed three people to protect this blackmail operation, I can't imagine they'll abandon ship now," Stella said.

"We think Stewie and Gloria are probably in cahoots in a blackmail operation, but we don't think they're killers. Of course, we don't *know* that for a fact, it just doesn't seem like very good business."

"*There's* an assumption," Stella commented.

"There's no danger. They have no reason to connect you with us or with any investigation. As far as they know you're just another lonely, frumpy dowager."

"Dowager!" Stella gave a hoot of laughter.

A.J. shot her mother a repressive look. "We don't think there's any danger, but you would have to be careful, obviously. These murders may not be connected. We don't even know for sure that Peggy Graham *was* murdered. But if someone was frightened or desperate enough to kill once, there's no telling what they might do if she or he thought you were snooping."

"I'm betting our friends Gloria and Stewie know that once they've been brought to the attention of the police, they'll never be fully forgotten again. Greed will make them want to go for one last score, but they wouldn't take any foolish chances."

"But once again," A.J. reminded them both firmly, "We don't know how deeply Gloria and Stewie are involved. We don't know who Madame X is. It could be Gloria."

"It could be Stewie," Elysia put in. And at the look A.J. gave her, she made a little moue. "Probably not. Dicky was fairly conservative in his tastes."

A.J. continued, "We think she's a customer at The Salon, but she might not be. She might have no connection with The Salon at all. You have to be on guard. Remember, she's not your target. We're strictly interested in proving there's a blackmail ring so that the police will investigate further."

Stella considered this grimly. "What if this Stewie and Gloria don't take the bait?"

"You'll have had a complete makeover. That alone is a service to mankind," Elysia stated.

Stella gave her a withering look. "I can't afford that kind of thing."

"I'll pay. It's my neck on the block, after all."

Stella opened her mouth, but A.J. said quickly, "It's worth it to us, Stella. We have to do something to show the police that there's more than one motive for Dicky being killed. We don't have anything to lose by trying—so long as you're careful and don't take any foolish chances."

"But how long would I have to keep this charade up for?"

"We don't know," admitted A.J. uncomfortably. "Hopefully not too long. If we can't get them to move within two weeks, we'll have to try something else."

"*Two weeks*! You want me to go somewhere and pretend to be someone else for two weeks?"

"We have to establish a cover for you. You can't be living here as Stella Borin and going to The Salon as someone else because they're bound to check up on you."

"But where am I going?"

"Oh, we'll figure that out. We're going to devise a legend for you," Elysia said.

"A what?"

"Your cover story." Elysia apparently saw herself in the film adaptation of a le Carré novel. "Now I think the best thing will be to introduce you as my long-lost great aunt."

"*Great aunt!*" Stella objected. "You're as old as I am, Elysia Alexander!"

"No," A.J. interrupted. "Stella can't be associated with us in any way. Three people have died already. We have to make sure there's no obvious connection between Stella and us."

Elysia said reluctantly, "I suppose you're right. Although I think it's worth the risk."

"I've been thinking about this part. Andy will help us. Stella can pretend to be *his* widowed aunt. She can stay at his parents' vacation home in Byram. It keeps her safely away from Stillbrook, but it's close enough to Newton that it's not unreasonable she might go to The Salon."

Stella had been listening to this with a deepening dismay. "But what about my critters?"

"A good shampoo will take care of that," Elysia said blandly. "You'll see."

Stella gave her a stony look.

"I'll take care of your animals," A.J. promised. "You can just tell me what to do."

"Not with your back," Stella said. She turned a considering eye on Elysia. "But if Elysia gives me her word she'll take care of my farm while I'm away, then I suppose I could do her this favor."

The gazes of the two older women locked. After an

apparent inward struggle, Elysia summoned a gracious smile. "Of course. It will be my pleasure."

"Then I guess I agree."

Elysia said smoothly, "And I'll stay with Stella to monitor the operation."

Stella said, "I'd rather take my chances with the murderers."

"I'll stay with her," A.J. intervened. "You just promised to take care of the animals."

"I can drive back and forth."

"No you can't. That's ridiculous. We've already said there can't be a connection to us. Me staying with her is bad enough."

"Then I'll pay someone to take care of the animals. You have a business to run."

"Oh no," Stella said flatly. "I'm not trusting my critters to paid strangers. You gave your word."

"But—"

"But me no buts," Stella said. "Either you take care of the critters or I stay to take care of them."

"Oh, for—!"

A wide smile broke across Stella's face. "Don't you worry. I'll leave you detailed directions on exactly what to do, Elysia."

Lily was in her office when A.J. arrived at Sacred Balance. A.J. went into her own office and called Andy, explaining what she and Elysia were planning with Stella's help. As she had surmised, he was enthusiastic about the idea.

In fact his only regret was that he would be unable to take a more active role as he and Nick were going out of town.

"You're going on vacation? Where?"

"Paris." He sounded a little smug, and she wasn't surprised.

"Oh, you lucky dog."

He chuckled. "Yeah. But not to worry, I can lay the groundwork for the sting."

A.J. sighed. "You and Mother are a pair. I swear we were switched at birth and you're her real child."

She could hear the smile in his voice as he said, "I'll call The Salon and set up the appointment for my widowed auntie, and I'll be sure to drop a few tantalizing tidbits about how rich and reckless she is."

"Perfect. Don't overdo it, of course, but make her sound like the perfect mark."

"Don't worry. She'll be chum to the sharks."

A.J. inwardly shivered at that description, but there was no use pretending that they were not trying to turn Stella into irresistible bait for some very unscrupulous people.

She and Andy chatted a little longer. He promised to call her back as soon as he'd finished working out the details, and she rang off.

Turning on her laptop, she began to go through the day's e-mail. She was tempted to call Jake and tell him what she, her mother, and Stella were planning, but she fought back the urge. As Elysia had often pointed out, it was easier to ask forgiveness than permission.

There was a soft knock on her half-open door.

A.J. glanced up to see Chess Cox standing in the doorway to her office.

Startled, she rose and pulled open the door. "Hello!"

"Hi. Do you have a minute?"

"Of course. Come in." A.J. was surprised at this impromptu visit, but Chess seemed perfectly nice and there was no reason they shouldn't be at least cordial. Right?

So why did A.J. feel suddenly on the defense?

Chess entered the office and sat down. A.J. sat, too. Chess was smiling, her light eyes studying A.J. with friendly curiosity. "I probably should have called first, but since I was here anyway, I just thought we should get to know each other a little."

Why? A.J. wondered. But she didn't say that. "Of course. What do you think of the studio? Did you enjoy your class?"

"Oh, it's wonderful. You've got a terrific operation here."

"Thank you." There was a pause and A.J. offered Chess tea, which she declined.

"I won't stay long. It's just . . . it's such a strange situation." Chess was smiling. "I guess there's no way to prepare for something like this."

"I guess not."

Chess seemed open, even unnervingly candid. Generally A.J. appreciated the direct approach so she couldn't understand her own resistance to the other woman's friendly overture, unless it was something as simple as good old-fashioned jealousy. She'd have liked to think she was a little more sophisticated than that, but maybe not.

Chess said, "I'm going to be honest here. I'm just feeling very much on the outside. Everyone speaks so highly of you. And Jake is obviously very fond of you."

"Oh."

"I'm not criticizing anyone, but I do get the feeling that some people see me as an interloper. Not Jake, obviously. Jake couldn't be more—"

No. She couldn't do this.

"I don't mean to be unkind," A.J. interrupted. "But I can't sit here talking to you about my relationship with Jake—or listen to you talk about it."

Chess looked instantly serious. "I understand. I just thought if we knew something about each other, it might make it easier."

Make what *easier*? A.J. wondered. How was knowing each other going to make anything easier? Did Chess honestly think they were going to be friends? Did she think there was some way to share Jake? What *was* she thinking? A.J. couldn't figure her out at all.

"I've known Jake for a long time," Chess said. "Leaving him was the hardest thing I ever did in my life, but I had to do it to protect him."

A.J. stared at her earnest lovely face, and something clicked into place. Chess was playing on her sympathies, on her guilt. Chess wanted her to back off—why? A.J. had already backed off. If Chess didn't know, it was because Jake wasn't sharing that information, and A.J. felt immeasurably better. Whatever was between her and Jake was still between her and Jake.

"I can't judge," A.J. said. "I wasn't there."

Chess said wryly, "People say that when they're judging you."

A.J. stood up. "Chess, I can't begin to understand your situation, so I'm not judging you. But I know Jake—maybe not as well as you did—but I know him well enough to know what he would think about us sitting here talking about him."

"I thought we were talking about us," Chess said coolly.

A.J. smiled. "I don't think we are. Not really. And I think it would be difficult for us to be anything more than polite acquaintances at this stage." She added, "But I appreciate the gesture. You're very gracious."

Chess rose, too. Her smile was terse. "Well, that's clear enough."

"I appreciate the gesture," A.J. repeated.

"Nice chatting with you."

"Good-bye," A.J. said firmly.

She closed the door softly, carefully, after Chess walked away.

Twenty-two

❧

Stella was still laughing heartily as they drove away from Little Peavy Farm on Tuesday morning. They had left Elysia scowling over the long list of detailed chores Stella had handed over, which included things like *slop pigs*.

"I can't wait till she and Big Oscar come face-to-face."

"Who's Big Oscar?" A.J. asked nervously, glancing back in the rearview mirror half expecting to see a mushroom cloud over the farm.

"My four-hundred-pound, prize-winning hog."

"Oh," A.J. said faintly.

Stella shot her a sideways look. "Don't worry. Elysia isn't about to risk putting *her* back out slopping hogs or feeding calves. She'll hire someone to come out and take care of the heavy lifting." She was still chortling at some evil thought. "I knew that. But she'll have to supervise them, and the day starts at four in the morning. That alone is worth this."

A.J. was tempted to ask Stella her side of the story regarding A.J.'s father and the supposed affair, but the idea made her stomach churn nervously. Was it really her business?

Instead she and Stella chatted about a recent séance Stella had held and some of the things happening at Sacred Balance.

They stopped for lunch and reached Andy's parents' house in Byram around one o'clock to find Andy waiting for them.

A.J. and Andy kissed lightly and she looked him over with affectionate concern. Her ex-husband and former business partner was tall and lanky with chestnut hair and blue eyes. In fact they had occasionally been mistaken for brother and sister when they were married. He had been diagnosed with MS the previous summer but, although he was a little thinner than usual, he looked healthy and happy to A.J.'s critical gaze.

"How are you?" she asked.

"I'm fine," he told her. And then at her expression, he said, "I really am feeling pretty good right now, which is why we're taking this trip to France. Everything seems to be in a holding pattern. I think happiness is good for my health."

There was certainly truth to that.

A.J. reintroduced Stella to Andy. She could see from Andy's carefully neutral expression that he remembered attending a séance at Stella's house; Andy had about as much patience for the supernatural as Jake did, although he was a little more polite about it.

"Did you want a quick tour?" he asked.

A.J. had stayed at the house several times over the years with Andy and his parents, but she nodded and Andy led the way inside, showing them such refresher essentials as how to work the security system and where to find the TV remotes.

The house was comfortable and secluded, surrounded by rose bushes and tall hedges. The long trimmed lawns stretched down to the small lake in the rear. Inside, it was elegant and immaculate if slightly impersonal.

"Stella's all set for her appointment tomorrow. For the record, I think you're onto something with this hair salon," Andy said as they trekked through the gleaming kitchen with its view of the lake and small pier.

"Who did you talk to?" A.J. inquired.

"I started out with some kid, but I asked for the manager and got a guy named Stewart Cabot. I said I wanted to make sure my sweet old auntie received the deluxe treatment. That she was widowed last year and was only now getting back into the swing of things after her breakdown."

"Breakdown!" Stella looked offended at the idea that she would ever have something as feeble as a breakdown.

"You didn't make this too complicated, did you?" A.J. said. "Stella's got to remember her cover story."

Andy grinned unrepentantly. "It'll be fine. I just told them how Stella had nursed her beloved husband through his long, lingering illness—I never did say what illness, so you can pick whatever you like—and then cracked up herself. But now Auntie is ready to start her new life and I wanted her to have the full, deluxe treatment. Head-to-toe total makeover."

Stella gave a gruff laugh. "Elysia is going to have a fit."

"So what makes you think we're onto something as far as The Salon goes?" A.J. inquired.

"Stewart was way too interested in all the gory details. People aren't, you know. Even kind people aren't that interested in all the details. Plus it was the kind of things he asked. He didn't flat out ask about her bank balance or her net worth, but in his own diplomatic way, he pried out the information he wanted. And he was definitely interested in three points: how wealthy she is, how emotionally vulnerable, how involved is her family."

"What did you tell him?" A.J. asked.

"Very wealthy, very hard up for male companionship, and other than her self-absorbed workaholic freelance consultant daughter, I was her only relation and was going to be in France for several weeks."

"Nice. You pretty much put her out there on a cake plate."

"Yep." Andy sounded pleased with himself. "I would be very surprised if they didn't bite—and fast."

"You think Stewie bought it?"

"Hook, line, and sinker."

A.J. smiled and kissed him. "I knew there was some reason I wanted to keep you in my life. I just never dreamed it would be your pathological aptitude for lying."

"For those who are called according to His purpose. As the Bard would say."

"Funny."

Andy grew serious then. "Be careful, A.J. Beneath all that warmth and charm—and Stewart is a very charming guy—I got the sense that this is cold, hard business. They're not fooling around there. I think you should wear a wig anytime you go outdoors."

"Huh?"

"In case they send someone to check out the house. You said you'd been to this salon, right? Well, they're liable to recognize you. I'd wear a wig when you go out in case they do a little reconnaissance."

"Are you serious?"

"I am, yeah. That's why I cooked up the workaholic consultant daughter. Talking to Stewart I got a definite sense that he's a guy who dots his *I*s and crosses his *T*s."

She thought this over as they walked out to his car.

"Does Jake know what you're up to?" Andy asked suddenly.

She was surprised at the pain that flashed through her. "Jake and I are sort of on hiatus right now."

"*Why?*" Andy was staring at her in disbelief.

"Believe it or not, it's not my choice. In fact it's nothing to do with me at all. It's a long story so unless you're staying for dinner—"

He shook his head. "I want to get back. Nick will be worrying."

"Are you okay to drive?"

Andy made a face. "Yes. Power steering, power brakes, and I know my limitations."

They hugged and Andy got in the car.

She watched him reverse in a slow, careful arc and then start down the long, paved driveway.

When the car was lost to sight she turned and went inside.

A.J. and Stella spent the remainder of the afternoon quietly. A.J. caught up on her mail and industry reading and finished reading through her aunt's book. They had a quiet supper and settled down to watch TV, something neither of them generally had time for.

A.J.'s phone rang and her heart sped up as she recognized the number as Jake's.

She went into the dining room to take it, staring through the bay windows at the lake glittering in the moonlight.

She opened her mouth to greet him, but Jake beat her to the punch.

"Where are you?"

This was something she hadn't taken into account. She had been the one contacting Jake over the past few days; she hadn't been thinking about him initiating contact. "I-I'm taking a few days off."

"I know. I called the studio and they said you're going to be out for the rest of the week."

"Yes. Just a couple of days." She lied. "I can't do much at the studio with my back the way it is."

There was silence, then he said, "I thought your back was better."

"It was. It is. I just . . . need a little time away."

"What does that mean?"

"Just that. I'm taking a few days off. I haven't had an actual vacation since I took over the studio, and I thought this might be a good time."

"Now?"

"Er, yes."

There was an entirely different note in his voice as he asked, "Is Elysia going on this getaway?"

"No." She remembered that Jake was the one who had spoken up on behalf of Elysia, had defended her when the DA and others deemed her too great a flight risk, had looked into each of her requests for information. He had a vested interest in Elysia not fleeing from justice. "Just me. And just for a couple of days."

Silence.

Racking her brains for something to say, A.J. came up with, "I was thinking about you. I had a visit from Chess yesterday."

"Yeah?" He sounded wary.

A.J. chuckled. "Not to worry. No fur flew and all fingernails remain intact."

He made a sound that was supposed to pass for amusement, but clearly took effort.

There was another pause and Jake said, "The reason I called was I did some looking into Peggy Graham's death. I talked to the Andover police, looked at the ME's report. It's a definite suicide."

Despite the fact that A.J. had been arguing this all along, she was startled. "Are you sure?"

"Yep. Zero doubt. She'd picked the pills up herself that afternoon. The drugstore clerk remembered her. There were no signs of violence on the body, no signs of forced entry, or that the bottle had been tampered with. Furthermore, she suffered from depression."

"But her sister said she didn't."

"All I can tell you is Graham had been seeing a doctor for over a year and she'd been treated for depression. Families don't always know everything."

That was certainly true. A.J. was silent thinking all this over. She considered the implications of this news. Peggy's death was not part of some larger conspiracy; she had not been silenced to protect a blackmail ring. Granted, if she was suffering from depression, the blackmail could well have figured into whatever pushed her over the edge.

But it didn't change the fact that she had not, technically, been murdered.

Which, considering their plans for Stella, was kind of a relief. Briefly A.J. considered whether to tell Jake about their undercover assignment for Stella, but she decided discretion was the better part of valor.

Into her prolonged silence, Jake said suddenly, awkwardly, "Listen, A.J. . . . your leaving doesn't have anything to do with something Chess said to you, does it?"

"No. Why?" A.J.'s heart dropped. "What is it you think she might have said?" Had she interrupted Chess's announcement that Chess and Jake were resuming their former engagement? Maybe she should have shut up and let Chess talk.

"Nothing. It just seems sudden, this trip of yours."

"No." A.J. said, relaxing. "Word of honor. This trip has absolutely nothing to do with you or Chess."

"All right. Well . . ." He was clearly at a loss and so was A.J. It was difficult to casually chat given how much she was keeping from him.

"Thanks for checking up on the Graham case for me," she said.

"Sure."

"I'll . . . talk to you soon."

"Yeah. Okay." He sounded uncertain about that.

"Bye," A.J. said.

"Bye," Jake answered.

In the morning Stella bade A.J. good-bye and drove the rental car into Newton to The Salon.

Even though A.J. knew it was highly unlikely that anything could possibly happen to Stella on her first visit to

The Salon—and in broad daylight no less—she found herself too nervous to concentrate on anything for long.

She did her morning yoga, then, bearing Andy's warnings in mind, she borrowed a headscarf from her ex-mother-in-law's drawers and took Monster for a long walk down by the lake.

When she got back she read through her e-mail, answering the numerous inquiries from Sacred Balance about what her employees should do on all kinds of matters that they would never have bothered bringing to her attention were she actually *in* the office, charted out fun new workouts for her Itsy Bitsy, Doga, and Yoga for Kids courses, and fixed herself an omelet for lunch. Now she remembered why she didn't do vacations anymore. What fun were vacations if you didn't have someone to vacation with? And meanwhile, while you were not having fun, the work at the office was piling up.

Shortly after lunch A.J. heard the sound of a car in the driveway and went to the front window. The silver rental car was parked out front. A plump, silver-haired woman in Stella's polyester pantsuit was walking up the front door.

A.J. threw the door open.

"Oh my gosh, Stella!"

Stella grinned. "Not too shabby, is it?"

"You look gorgeous." The transformation was truly remarkable. Stella's hair was cut and styled in short, silver layers. Her skin looked smooth and glowing, and the makeup was skillful and subtle.

"You should see my feet," Stella said. "I never had a pedicure before." She went straight to the oval mirror in the hallway and gazed at her reflection, shaking her head.

"They can't be all bad," A.J. murmured. "They do get some wonderful results."

Stella turned away from the mirror.

"They're sending me out with a personal buyer tomorrow."

"Oh?" A.J. blinked. "How did that come about?"

Stella shrugged. "Stewart said that my nephew suggested the works. Total makeover from the ground up. I wasn't sure if that was true or not, but I figured you wanted me to make myself available to the blackmailer."

Knowing Andy's sense of humor, A.J. could easily imagine it was true. But it did make sense. The more contact Stella had with The Salon, the better their chances of luring the blackmailer into approaching her.

"How did it go today? How did they treat you?"

"Everyone was as nice as could be. Gloria arranged weekly facial treatments for me. I agreed, but I hope no one is expecting me to spend more than two weeks out here."

"Er, no, no."

"A very nice young man named Alessandro cut my hair. He asked a heap of questions."

"I've had the Alessandro treatment. Did he . . . do anything to suggest he might want to make advances toward you?"

"Toward me?" Stella was laughing at the idea. "No. He's a kid!"

The problem—one of the problems—was that they had no idea how all this worked, and they had a timetable that did not give them much leeway. They had to hope that Stella would be recognized as a pigeon perfect for plucking and that someone would begin to lay enough of a foundation that they could show it to the police as grounds for further investigation.

The truth was they were trying to rush something that probably would take weeks, maybe months. It was a crazy plan and if they weren't so desperate—and trading on the blackmailers feeling the same—they wouldn't have contemplated it.

Stella, kicking off her ugly square pumps, said suddenly, "Stewart is accompanying me tomorrow. So maybe that will be the start of something."

"Stewart's going with you to meet the personal buyer?"

Stella nodded.

"We should call Mother. She'll be wondering what's happened, whether we've made any progress."

Stella raised her brows but said nothing.

A.J. phoned Elysia. It was obvious that Elysia, having spent the morning trying to get Stella's livestock fed and watered and taken care of, was not in the best of moods, but she heard the unexciting report of Stella's day in silence and then said, "She needs to be wired."

"*Wired*?"

"Of course. We did it all the time on *221B Baker Street*. It never failed. We need proof in case anything is said or suggested to her that might help us build our case."

A.J. said, "I think it's a little early for *wiring* her."

"I don't agree. What if we miss something crucial tomorrow?"

"Mother, we have no idea how to wire someone."

"It can't be very complicated."

"It *can't*? To start with, what equipment do we buy? Where do we buy it? And then, assuming we can figure out how to wire Stella properly, do not forget that the person wearing the wire will be Stella."

Silence.

"I suppose you have a point," Elysia conceded.

"I'll just loan her my cell phone. It has just about every app in the world."

Elysia sniffed in disapproval.

A.J. remembered Jake's call and informed Elysia that Peggy Graham had not been murdered.

Elysia heard this out in grim and unconvinced silence.

At last A.J. said, "I'll talk to you tomorrow, Mother. Try not to worry. We knew we wouldn't have all the answers we needed in one day. I think it went very well today. From what Stella says everyone at The Salon was asking questions of her. I think they're bound to have picked up all the information we wanted them to."

Elysia sighed.

Twenty-three

When A.J. returned to the living room where Stella was watching TV, Stella glanced at her and said, "Not happy is she?"

"No."

Stella shrugged.

"It's the strain of waiting," A.J. said. "The DA is building his case against her and there's not much she has in the way of defense. Except that she's innocent. And that doesn't seem to count for much. This is such a long shot, but it's all we've got."

Stella turned back to the TV. "I don't mind helping her," she stated.

"It is *really* generous of you," A.J. admitted. "Given that Mother has never been . . ."

Stella snorted.

They watched the TV for a time, some thriller where the good guy turned out to be the bad guy despite the fact that the bad guy had never given any indication of bad guyness. All the time A.J. was trying to summon the nerve to ask Stella about the supposed affair with her father.

On the one hand she was uncomfortably aware that her parents had a right to their private lives. On the other hand it really bothered her to think that her father had had an affair. She couldn't help but remember Andy's affair— and the subsequent destruction of her marriage. She hated thinking these terrible, harsh things about her beloved father.

But perhaps there was no affair?

Elysia seemed convinced that there was. And Elysia should know, right? And would hearing Stella confirm that A.J.'s father had cheated on her mother really help her come to terms with the situation?

Back and forth A.J. went. If there was ever going to be a time to ask, this was it. She and Stella were alone, no one would ever know they had discussed this.

The thriller ended. The news came on. Stella didn't move and neither did A.J., but A.J. had the sense that Stella wasn't watching the television any more than she was.

"Stella," A.J. said suddenly, surprising herself.

She was more startled when Stella made a sound one of her pigs might have recognized. "I know what you're going to ask, A.J. I've been waiting for you to ask for nearly a year now."

A.J. met Stella's dark, round eyes, bracing herself for the truth.

Stella said "There wasn't any affair. Not the way Elysia means it. Your daddy just liked to come and have a quiet drink and talk and think. This was when your ma wasn't . . . herself."

"She was herself," A.J. said. "She just happened to be a drunk."

Stella smothered a cough. "Well, they were separated and your daddy was pretty miserable. He never cared about anyone like he cared about your mama."

That was certainly true. As much as A.J.'s father had loved her, Elysia had come first. Elysia had also come first for Elysia at that time in her life, but how long did you continue to blame someone for hurting you once you understood that they were truly sorry and would undo the past if they could?

At some point you had to let go of the old pain and anger.

Stella was still talking. "You have to understand. I'd known your daddy since we were kids. Yes, we were sort of sweet on each other at one time, but that was far in the past. Once he saw Elysia, well that was it. I don't think he ever looked at another woman. But he liked to come to my place and he liked to talk. And I liked that, too."

Had Stella loved A.J.'s father? A.J. had no idea and didn't think she should pry; that truly was not her business. Stella had never married. But that could mean a lot of things, including the fact that no one wanted to live with four cats.

"Did Mother—"

"I tried to tell Elysia the truth a long time ago. She wouldn't believe me. Didn't want to hear it. If you want my opinion, I think the betrayal for Elysia was that your daddy was talking to me about private and personal things that Elysia wanted to believe no one else knew about. I don't think she ever really believed your father and I were having a *romance*."

There was probably a lot of truth to that.

"Thank you for telling me," A.J. said.

Stella nodded, rising and tying her thick, plaid bathrobe more tightly around her burly frame. "Busy day tomorrow," she said.

A.J. nodded.

Stella hesitated. "I don't like your mother, I won't pretend I do, but I respect Elysia. I admire the way she pulled herself out of that gutter. It wasn't easy for her, but she got herself dried out and she made your daddy very happy those last years."

A.J. blinked back the unexpected sting in her eyes. "I know. Thank you."

"Sweet dreams," Stella said.

Shortly after breakfast the next morning, Stella waved good-bye to A.J. and set off in her rental car to meet Stewie at The Salon.

A.J. spent the morning surfing the Internet trying to find an agent to handle Diantha's memoirs. She was trying to figure out what was involved in putting together a cover letter when the phone on the desk she was working at began to ring.

A.J. jumped and stared at it trying to remember who, besides Andy, had the number to this house.

Stella.

A.J. glanced at the clock.

Shouldn't Stella have been back by now? How long did this personal shopping thing take? They weren't driving to New York for heaven's sake. *Were* they?

The phone rang again.

Elysia, of course. Elysia had the house number, but Elysia would try A.J.'s cell phone. Except Elysia knew that A.J. had loaned Stella her cell phone for the day. So . . . Elysia?

A.J. picked the phone up and said cautiously, "Hello?"

"What the hell is going on?" Jake demanded.

"Sorry?"

"What exactly do you think you're doing?" He bit out each word.

A.J. was still trying to assimilate the fact that it was Jake and not Elysia calling. "How did you get this number?"

"From Emma Rice. She said this was the number to call in case of emergency."

"Is there an emergency?"

"I would say so. *Where* is your mother?"

"At home, isn't she?"

"No. And she's not answering her cell phone either. Did the two of you cook up some idiotic scheme like sending her undercover at the damned hair salon?"

"No, of course not," A.J. said guiltily, thinking of the idiotic scheme they *had* cooked up. "Why?"

"Because I did a little background checking and Mabel G. Chalthoum is the name of one of the owners of The Salon."

A.J. swallowed so hard she knew Jake could hear it on the end of the line. "Gloria—?"

"Gloria Sunday is the professional name, the stage name, of Mabel G. Chalthoum. Gloria Sunday was Massri's sponsor into this country."

Gloria was Madame X.

"Oh my God," A.J. said. "Jake, Mother is probably at Stella Borin's farm. She's been taking care of Stella's ani-

mals while Stella"— she gave another of those little
gulps— "tries to gather information at The Salon."

The silence was deafening.

Then, so tersely she pictured him having to chip the
words out, Jake said, "I'll try the farm," and hung up.

A.J. dialed Elysia's cell phone. It rang and went to
message.

She tried again. Same result.

But after all, Elysia often left her cell phone at home.
This really meant nothing.

Would Elysia leave her cell phone behind when she believed they were in the middle of a big sting operation?

A.J. grabbed her purse, dug out Stella's phone number,
and tried the farm. The circuits were busy. She realized
she and Jake were probably calling at the same time. She
hung up and counted to ten, then dialed again. The phone
rang and rang and then an answering machine came on
with Stella's brusque invitation to leave a message.

"Mother, pick up," A.J. commanded. "Are you there?
Pick up!"

Why did people always say things like that? Obviously
if Elysia was there she would pick up. If she wasn't there,
what was the point of asking whether she was there?

A.J. hung up and put her face in her hands.

Next to her elbow the phone rang again and A.J.
snatched it up. "Yes?"

"It's me," Jake said. "You better explain to me exactly
what's going on. Start at the top."

"You know most of it already." A.J. began to explain
into the vast and intimidating silence on the other end. She
had reached the part about Stella going off with Stewie for
a day of shopping when she heard a car outside.

"Hang on," she said and hurried to the front door,

nearly falling over Monster in her haste. She threw open the door in time to see Stella and the tall, elegant form of Stewie Cabot getting out of the rental car.

"Have you talked to Elysia this morning?" Stella called.

A.J. shook her head. "I can't reach her."

"Come on," Stella said. "We've got to find her. Stewie thinks she's in danger."

Stewie did look pretty worried. His silver hair was standing on end as though he'd been running his fingers through it.

"I'm on the phone to Jake," A.J. said.

"Tell him to get over to my place," Stella told her.

"Don't move." A.J. flew back to the phone. "Jake, I don't have all the details yet, but Stella is back and she says Mother may be in danger. She said you should head for Little Peavy Farm. I'm on my way and I'll call you as soon as I have the details."

"You stay right where you are," Jake said. "Call me when you've talked to Stella. I'm leaving now."

He disconnected.

A.J. grabbed her purse and keys, called to Monster, and ran to join Stella and Stewie.

"I was burned," Stella said and the rental car, driven by Stewie, tore back down the highway toward Warren County and Stillbrook.

"You were . . . what?" A.J. pushed Monster's head away as he leaned across her to get to her window. What was wrong with his own window? Only Monster had the answer to that one.

"Burned. My cover was blown yesterday," Stella, who

had clearly been hanging around Elysia too long, explained.

"I'm not following."

Stella looked at Stewie. Stewie, his gaze on the road ahead, said wearily, "Go on. Tell her everything."

"I was 'made' at The Salon yesterday," Stella said. "It turns out one of the stylists working there was a kid who'd bought his calf from me a couple of years back when he was in 4-H Club. He didn't know what was at stake, naturally, but he happened to mention it today in front of Gloria."

"Oh no," A.J. said.

"When I got to The Salon this morning, Gloria was acting a little weird, but Stewie got me out of there before I had time to make much out of it."

Stella looked at Stewie again, but he volunteered nothing.

"Well, it didn't take me long to see from the way Stewie was acting that something was wrong."

This time the look Stella gave Stewie was softer. More astonishing was the look Stewie threw Stella. Observing this, A.J. said, "I thought . . ."

"Oh, Stewie's not gay," Stella said. "That's just something he says to keep the ladies at bay."

"Oh. Oh?" Apparently Stella was not a lady Stewie wanted to keep at bay, even now that he knew the truth about her. "What did Stewie tell you?" A.J. was looking at Stewie but asking Stella.

"He confessed everything."

"*Everything*?"

The car swerved, and Stella said calmly, "About the blackmail scheme. Stewie and Gloria have been running a blackmail business out of The Salon for the last five years. They got into financial trouble, you see."

"I know how it looks," Stewie said. "But you have to understand. Once I got into it, there wasn't any getting out. Gloria doesn't take rejection well."

"I think I see," A.J. said. "How did it start? Let me take a wild guess: Gloria went on a vacation cruise to Egypt five years ago?"

Stewie's eyes met hers in the rearview. He nodded glumly. "That's exactly how it happened. Gloria went on vacation and came back with an idea of how we could get The Salon out of the red. The way she looked at it is we were sort of providing a public service to lonely women, and it was as reasonable to be paid for that as a haircut or a paraffin bath."

Stella snorted.

Stewie said defensively, "Most of our ladies could easily afford the amount we charged. We weren't greedy. They enjoyed the attention and the wining and dining and the . . ."

"Sex," Stella said.

"Yes. And the sex. Most of them thought the social fees were a small price to pay. It's not like we continued to charge them forever. We always let them off the hook after a couple of years."

"After a couple of *years*," A.J. repeated. "You blackmailed them. Social fees? Those were penalty fees for being lonely. What a horrible thing to do to people. And, no, they weren't all okay with the social fees. Peggy Graham wasn't okay with the social fees."

"We didn't have anything to do with Peggy Graham's death," Stewie said quickly.

"You may not have doctored her sleeping pills, but you sure did have something to do with her death. She was suffering from depression and you blackmailed her. I'd say that was a contributing factor to her death." A.J. steadied her voice. "What about Medea? She knew something. She called you after she learned that Peggy had killed herself and you came to her house and shot her."

"No!" Stewie said, and the car swerved again. Monster sat down in A.J.'s lap.

"Whoa," Stella cried. "Let's slow down and take this one thing at a time or we're going to end up in a ditch and then what'll happen to Elysia?"

"What *will* happen to Mother?" A.J. demanded.

Stella looked at Stewie who shook his head. She said to A.J., "You have to understand that Stewie doesn't know anything for sure—"

"I'm afraid of Gloria," Stewie said. "I think she's gone off the rails. I tried to talk her out of doing anything rash, but she was in love with young Massri, and she blames your mother for his death."

"She blames *my* mother?" As though someone else's mother were a possibility?

Stewie said heavily, "She accused your mother of persecuting her and sending her undercover operative into The Salon. That's why I got Stella out of there first thing. I wasn't sure what Gloria might do."

"Yes, you were sure," A.J. said fiercely. "You know exactly what she might do because she's done it twice already. She killed Massri and deliberately framed my mother. And she killed Maddie because Peggy must have told Maddie enough that Maddie suspected or knew you and Gloria were involved."

"I didn't know for sure! I still don't."

"If you don't, it's because you don't want to see the truth of your own part in all this."

Stella said, "Stewie's afraid that Gloria might go to my

farm to see what she can find out about me or she might go gunning for Elysia."

A.J.'s heart pounded in dread. "I need my cell phone, Stella." To Stewie, she said, "Either way, if Gloria goes to your farm she'll find my mother."

"That's what I told him when I finally got the story out of him. It took a while." Stella handed A.J. her Palm Pre and A.J. began dialing Jake's number.

"If something happens to my mother . . ." A.J. couldn't finish it.

"Stewie feels pretty bad about everything that's happened," Stella volunteered.

Jake's phone was busy. A.J. groaned and tried Elysia's number again. "Pick up. Pick *up*."

"You don't know Gloria," Stewie said. "You don't cross her and think there won't be repercussions."

The first sign that something might be seriously amiss was as they started down the road to Little Peavy Farm and spotted one of Stella's milk cows grazing contentedly by the side of the road.

"Someone's left the barn open," Stella exclaimed.

It was clear from her expression that if Elysia hadn't been in danger before, she would be now.

Reaching the farmhouse itself they found Jake's police SUV parked in the front yard. Aside from the police vehicle, it looked like one of those rustic scenes from a pastoral painting. Chickens, goats, a donkey wandered about the porch and grass. The front door to the farmhouse stood wide open.

"Oh, no," Stella cried.

A.J. barely waited for the car to stop moving before

she was out and running up the steps. She ran straight into Jake coming out the front door.

He caught her by the arms. "*A.J.* What are you doing here?"

"Where's Mother?"

"I don't know. I'm looking for her now. She's not inside."

They both froze at the sound of gunshots.

A.J. turned to start back down the steps, but Jake grabbed her. "*No.*"

She tried to yank free, and he gave her a hard shake, saying, "Listen to me. I need you to get on the radio in my car and call for backup."

Without waiting to see if she would comply, he jumped down to the ground and sprinted off around the corner of the house. After a fraught moment, A.J. ran over to Jake's SUV, passing Stella and Stewie who were standing beside the rental car looking bewildered.

"What's happening?" Stella asked.

A.J. scrambled into Jake's SUV, grabbed the radio mike, and pressed the button.

"I have an emergency!"

There was static and the police operator came on the line asking who she was and what was the emergency.

"Officer needs assistance," A.J. said.

"Ma'am, can you—"

Tersely, A.J. spelled out the situation and then handed the radio over to Stella who was hovering in the car doorway.

"Stay on the line with him."

"A.J.," Stella protested. "Stay here!"

A.J. was already racing toward the back of the house, Monster galloping behind, under the impression they were playing some new game.

She reached the back of the house and stopped, peering around the corner. There was no sign of anyone. Not Jake, not Gloria, not her mother.

Monster sat down and licked his chops, waiting for their next move.

"Stay," A.J. instructed in a whisper as she started to cross from the corner of the house to the nearest little outlying shed. Monster rose, tail wagging, and followed.

The distinctly unmellow smell of pigs reached her as A.J. ran to the back of the barn. She reached it safely, glanced around the corner, and nearly jumped out of her skin. Jake leaned against the wall of the barn, his pistol in both hands, braced to fire.

He lowered the pistol and was softly, fiercely uncomplimentary, finishing with, "I *relied* on you to make that damned call."

"I *did* make that call!"

He relaxed infinitesimally. "All right then I want y—" He broke off, his expression changing at the sound of voices. "Stay here."

He turned, edging down the side of the barn. A.J. followed at a discreet distance, listening tensely. She could hear the excited snufflings and snorts of pigs. They must be very near the pens.

Elysia's cool voice carried clearly although she sounded like she was speaking from inside the barn perhaps. "Maddie was uncomfortable with Peggy's obsession, and she let the friendship lapse. But when she heard about Peggy's supposed suicide, she *knew* it was all true. She rang you up and told you she knew you'd murdered Peggy."

Gloria's sharp voice sounded closer. *She must be on this side of the pens*, guessed A.J.

"We didn't have a thing to do with Peggy Graham's death. That's the ridiculous part of it. She killed herself. It had nothing to do with us. But that pigheaded fool Maddie insisted that we'd murdered her. She said she was going to the police. I told her she was making a mistake, that the situation wasn't what she imagined. I asked to meet her at her house at six. I arrived an hour early and went around the back. There was a little gate there. It was perfect. I went into the yard and she was right there, gardening. I shot her."

"You used a silencer, which is why I didn't hear you."

"That's right. You can buy them right on the Internet. I lost mine in the garden. Now climb out of that pigpen or I'll shoot you *and* the pig."

In other circumstances A.J. would have found Jake's expression priceless.

He moved away from the safety of the barn wall, bringing his pistol up. A.J. darted forward to see. Two things happened. Jake yelled, "Hold it right there." And an enormous pig suddenly burst out of its pen nearly knocking Gloria over.

Jake leaped for Gloria, who fired her pistol as she staggered. The pig, which was as big as a comfortable chair, panicked, squealing, and careened into Jake, throwing him off balance. Gloria slipped in the mud outside the pen. Elysia darted out of the pigpen, and wrestled her for the pistol she had dropped and was scrabbling to retrieve.

Elysia grabbed Gloria's arm, yanked it back, and flipped Gloria right over in a move straight out of *221B Baker Street*.

"Freeze!" Elysia cried.

Oddly enough everyone did. Jake slowly lowered his

weapon, taking in the picture of Elysia triumphantly holding Gloria's gun and Gloria on her back in the mud blinking up at all of them.

Even Oscar the pig seemed to pause and reflect, before sticking his pink snout out and snuffling Gloria's face. She shrieked as the big, spotted pig, gave her a wet, wheezing kiss.

In the far away distance floated the sound of sirens. More immediately came the pound of footsteps as Stella and Stewie raced up to the tableau around the pigpen.

"Bloody Hell," Elysia said, as Jake prudently stepped forward to remove the pistol from her hand. "I finally caught my own villain!"

Twenty-four

Funny how you could solve a murder on Tuesday and still need to be back at work on Wednesday morning.

When A.J. arrived at work—admittedly late—following Gloria's arrest the afternoon before for the murders of Dicky Massri and Medea Sutherland, she had to make her way through a gauntlet of concerned and curious employees and students.

"Your mom was great yesterday!" Suze exclaimed and A.J. winced.

The minute Elysia had completed her part of the police investigation into the events at Little Peavy Farm, she had driven into Stillbrook and held an impromptu press conference on the steps of the police station. Reporters had already gathered as the news of Gloria's arrest had spread. Elysia had taken advantage of that to announce that she had in fact cracked the case—as she had said she would.

She then demanded a full apology from everyone from the police to the courts.

"She's something else," agreed Emma Rice.

"Isn't she?" A.J. said weakly.

"So why did Gloria Sunday kill Elysia's boyfriend?" Suze asked as A.J. tried to edge down the hallway to her office.

"It turns out that Gloria was actually in love with Dicky. When she learned that he was going to marry Elysia, something must have snapped. Plus it sounds to me like she didn't trust him not to give away their black-mailing scheme."

"Did you hear about Yoga Meridian?" Simon asked quietly, following A.J. to her office door.

"No. What?"

"Apparently it's been bought out by Tussle and Rossiter."

"Who?"

"The two business entrepreneurs who've been buying out some of the nation's oldest, most prestigious yoga studios. The word on the street is they're planning to create a national chain of yoga studios."

"Corporate yoga?"

"Maybe. But they're promoting the idea that their studios will feature highly-trained teachers, high-quality classes, and still preserve that authentic, community feel of a neighborhood studio."

"And they're buying up established studios?"

Simon nodded and named two well-known California studios. "And get this. Mara Allen was let go."

"They *fired* Mara Allen?"

"I don't know about that. She may have left of her own free choice, but . . . either way she's gone."

Her mind reeling, A.J. let herself into her office. A branded national chain could mark the beginning of the end for yoga as they currently knew it. With corporate resources and money behind them, Tussle and Rossiter could quickly drive a lot of small studios out of business. Much of the individual charm and creativity of these individually owned enterprises would be lost as commercialism took over what was at heart intensely spiritual.

A.J. let herself into her office and sank down in the chair behind her desk.

There was a white envelope propped against the phone. Her name was typed on the envelope face. A.J. picked it up and ripped it open.

It was dated the previous afternoon.

Dear A.J.,

This is to formally notify you that I am resigning from my position as co-manager of Sacred Balance Studio, effective immediately. Had you been in the office at any time during the past three days, I would have discussed my reasoning in person with you, although my decision would have remained the same.

I appreciate the opportunities both to learn and to teach given to me by your late aunt and my dear friend, Diantha Mason. However a new opportunity has come my way, which I feel it is my duty to pursue.

I wish you luck in your future endeavors.

Yours sincerely,
Lily Martin

What the . . . ?

The phone rang and A.J. picked it up automatically, still staring at the letter in her hand.

"Bonjour!" said Andy cheerfully. His voice sounded so clear he could have been in the next room.

"Hey! How are you?"

"*Très bon* as we say in Gay Paree." His voice faded and came back on the line. "Nick says hi."

"Hi to Nick," A.J. returned politely.

"We just saw on the news that Ellie was cleared of all criminal charges. They're saying she solved the murder—although something may have been lost in translation."

"No, that's pretty much the story. Mother cleared her name. With a little help from me and Stella Borin."

"That's great! What happened?"

A.J. filled Andy in on everything that had happened since he had left them at his parents' vacation home on the weekend. She finished, "So Mother is demanding a full apology from everyone up to and possibly including the governor and Stella has sworn to stick by her man. Although she may have to stick for a long time given the charges of extortion and accessory to murder."

"And what about you and Jake?"

"He was great. He probably saved Mother's life although she's sure she did it all herself."

"No, I mean what about *you* and Jake?"

"Oh. Well, there's nothing to tell there. We're still—"

She could hear his sigh all the way across the Atlantic. "Can I give you some advice?"

"No. I do not want romantic advice from my ex-husband. My gay ex-husband."

"You're going to get it anyway. Stop being so freaking chivalrous about this Witness Protection broad and go talk to the guy."

"He knows where to find me, Andy. If he wanted to—"

The door to A.J.'s office burst open and Suze, her blue eyes nearly bugging from her excited face, gasped, "Oh my God! Lily has been hired as the new manager of Yoga Meridian."

Somewhere in the background A.J. could hear Andy saying, "He probably feels like a jackass. Give the guy a—" She absently replaced the receiver, still staring at Suze.

"Say that again."

"You heard me. Lily has been hired as the new manager of Yoga Meridian. She's replacing Mara Allen."

"I don't believe it."

"It's *true*." Suze was gleeful.

The phone rang. A.J. picked it up. "Sorry, Andy. I just had some unexpected—"

"It's me, pumpkin," Elysia chirped. "I'm at the airport."

"What? Which airport? What are you doing at the airport?"

"I'm flying to Los Angeles for a meeting with Brad Schuster."

"Who's Brad Schuster?"

"He's a Hollywood producer. He called last night to tell me about a TV series he's putting together featuring a team of 'mature' female sleuths. I'm flying into LAX for lunch with him tomorrow."

"Wait a minute. Are you sure this guy is legitimate?"

"Oh yes. He's produced all kinds of shows. He describes this as a cross between *The Golden Girls* meets *Charlie's Angels*. He saw me on the news last night and was so impressed that he tracked me down then and there."

"How long are you going to be gone?"

"Oh, just a day or two," Elysia said cheerfully. "Unless I get the part. Then I suppose I'll move to California for at least part of the year."

"What? *Mother!*"

"Must run, lovie. They're calling my flight. I'll ring later. Cheerio!"

There was a dial tone in A.J.'s ear. Slowly she replaced the receiver.

Jake's sports car was parked out in front of his house. There did not appear to be any other car on the street, which was a relief. No way was A.J. marching up to that house to have a dreaded Talk with Jake if Chess was anywhere in the vicinity.

The fact that Chess was *not* in the vicinity seemed like a positive sign. A.J. knew it was Jake's day off because he had casually mentioned it in passing when he'd called the night before to let her know that Stewie had been booked and was already spilling his guts in the hope of a plea bargain.

She went up the tidy walk and knocked. She could smell something good cooking and hear music through the door—The Boss, she thought.

She was just reflecting that this impromptu visit might be a really bad idea when the door swung open.

Jake stared at her through the black mesh. After a long moment, he reached forward and unlocked the security gate. "This is a surprise."

"Pleasant or unpleasant?"

He flicked her a quick look. If it had been anyone else, she'd have thought he was uncertain. "I guess that depends."

She followed him inside, looking around. She'd been to his house a few times and everything looked unchanged. What was she expecting? Telltale signs of gingham curtains and antimacassars on the chair arms?

"So how's Chess?" she asked as Jake led the way to the kitchen. He was apparently having his supper. A newspaper lay folded beside a half-finished plate of frozen pizza. He didn't take his seat at the table, however. He leaned against the sink.

Jake wasn't looking at her as he answered. "She's requested the WPP to move her again. She told them she's been recognized, which is true."

A.J.'s stomach was churning as she asked, "Are you going with her?"

Jake shook his head. "My life is here."

She had to get the nerve up before she could ask, "But is there anything here that you couldn't find somewhere else?"

In the silence between them she could hear the rattle and hum of his aged refrigerator. "You," he said at last.

Relief washed through her. "Then if you feel that way," A.J. said, "*why* haven't you called or been to see me?"

Jake winced, shaking his head. "I wasn't sure what to say to you. I feel like a complete jackass. I couldn't imagine you being anything but totally finished with me."

"Me either." His expression told her now was not the time to joke—not about this. "But, well, at least you had a really good excuse for being a . . . a . . ."

"Jackass."

She bit her lip. "You were honest with me. That helped. It still hurt, but it helped. It is—was—kind of an unusual situation, you have to admit."

"Yeah, I freely admit that."

"So," A.J. said tentatively, "it's over between you?"

Jake nodded. "I admit I was confused when Chess showed up. I thought I'd never see her again and you know how you build something up when you don't have a say in losing it—even if it's something you weren't sure you really wanted."

"You weren't sure you really wanted Chess?"

"The engagement was broken off twice before that last time. I loved her, but I don't think it would have lasted with us. In fact I know for sure it wouldn't have lasted. We don't actually have anything in common. To tell you the truth—" He stopped.

"What?"

"I don't like her all that much."

A.J. relaxed. She couldn't have stopped herself from smiling if her life had depended on it. "Oh? Do you like me?"

His mouth quirked reluctantly. "Yeah. You make me laugh. You make me think."

"I make you mad."

"Sometimes. Yep." He was grinning. "Somehow it doesn't matter. You make me happy."

A.J.'s throat closed with unexpected emotion. "You make me happy, too."

"Yeah?" He stretched his hand out and A.J. placed hers in it. His fingers closed warmly, gently around hers. "Where do we go from here, A.J. Alexander?" His smile was uncharacteristically tender.

"I don't know yet," A.J. admitted. "But one thing I've learned. It's as much about the journey as the destination."

Exercises

These two exercises are good for back trouble—however, always consult your physician before beginning any new exercise routine, especially if you do have health issues.

Happy Baby Pose (nighttime)

Step One: Lie on your back. Breathe deeply and evenly. Relax.

Step Two: Exhale, bend your knees into your chest.

Step Three: Inhale, grip the outsides of your feet with your hands, widen your knees and draw them toward your armpits.

Step Four: Your shins should be perpendicular to the floor as you balance your ankles over your knees. Flex through the heels. Gently push your feet up into your hands as you pull down to create resistance.

Step Five: Ease your thighs in toward your torso and then tug your knees gently toward the floor to lengthen your spine and release your tailbone toward the floor.

Step Six: Don't stop breathing as you hold the pose for the count of thirty.

Step Seven: Exhale and release your feet back to the floor.

Cat Stretch (morning)

Step One: Begin by sitting on your heels, relaxed and focused, breathing evenly.

Step Two: Move onto your hands and knees. Knees comfortably apart, hands with palms on floor (don't bend elbows).

Step Three: Mouth closed, look straight forward.

Step Four: Inhale, lift head and neck, curving spine (back becomes concave).

Step Five: Hold for count of five.

Step Six: Exhale and lower head.

Step Seven: Arch your back like a frightened cat, tucking head to collarbone.

Step Eight: Hold for count of five.

Step Nine: Exhale and relax.

Recipes

~

Barley Soup
with Porcini Mushrooms

(Serves 6)

2 ounces dried porcini mushrooms (2 cups)

2 cups warm milk

2 tablespoons extra-virgin olive oil, plus more for
serving

2 tablespoons butter

1 medium onion or 2 shallots finely chopped

1 celery rib, finely chopped

1½ quarts chicken stock or canned low-sodium
chicken or mushroom broth

1 bay leaf and/or 1 teaspoon minced sage (both
are optional)

½ pound pearl barley (1¼ cups), soaked
overnight and drained

    ¾ pound Yukon Gold potatoes, peeled and cut
       into ½-inch dice
    Salt and freshly ground pepper
    Freshly grated Parmesan cheese, for serving

Cover the porcini in a bowl with the warm milk and let stand until softened (20 minutes). Rub the porcini in the milk to rinse off any grit, then coarsely chop them. Reserve the milk.

In a large saucepan, heat the olive oil and butter. Add the onion and celery, cook over moderate heat until browned (15 minutes). Add the porcini and cook for 1 minute, stirring. Add the stock, bay leaf, sage, and barley and bring to a boil. Cover and simmer over low heat for 30 minutes, stirring occasionally. Add the potatoes, cover and simmer until the barley and potatoes are tender (30 minutes). Stir in the reserved milk, stopping when you reach the grit at the bottom. Simmer for 5 minutes. Discard the bay leaf and season with salt and pepper. Ladle the soup into bowls and serve, passing olive oil and Parmesan cheese at the table.

Chicken Walnut Salad

(Serves 6)

3 pound roasted chicken
1½ teaspoons salt
1½ teaspoons freshly ground black pepper
4 garlic cloves sliced thin lengthwise
½ cup chicken stock

Walnut Salad
¾ cup walnuts coarsely chopped
3 tablespoons walnut oil
1½ teaspoons champagne vinegar
1 shallot minced
¼ teaspoon salt
¼ teaspoon freshly ground black pepper
5 cups green leaf, red leaf, or other leaf lettuce or
    a mixture

Much of the success of this recipe depends on how you choose to roast the chicken. I prefer an herb-roasted or garlic-roasted chicken, but a light lemon roast can be lovely as well.

After the chicken is roasted, transfer to a carving board.

Toast chopped walnuts in a small fry pan over low heat for approximately 10 minutes. Shake often. Transfer walnuts to a plate and set aside.

In a large bowl whisk together the walnut oil, vinegar, shallot, salt, and pepper.

Tear the lettuce leaves into bite-size pieces (please!) and add them to the bowl with the dressing. Toss lettuce to liberally coat with dressing. Sprinkle with half of the toasted walnuts.

Carve the chicken breast, cut into bite-size pieces (a major part of the success of salad is being able to eat it without embarrassment!) and add to salad mixture. Toss again.

Sprinkle with the remainder walnuts and serve warm.